Cathy walke[d]  crib and sta[red] child regar[ded her with] those calm eyes that seemed ancient beyond the infant's years.

"She's beautiful," she whispered to Matt. She brought the baby over to the changing table so that she would have more room to examine her.

"What's the verdict?" Grazer asked.

She didn't reply, her attention still riveted to the baby. She was pulling a double-bellied Newcomer stethoscope out of her bag.

Sikes watched carefully. This part should have been routine. Clearly, though, it wasn't. There was bewilderment on Cathy's face as she moved the stethoscope around the baby's chest. After a moment, pure shock crawled across her face.

"She . . ." Cathy looked as if she were trying to remember the words. "She has only one cardiovascular system."

Grazer, who fancied himself an expert on the affairs of all things Tenctonese, said firmly, "That's impossible. She's a Newcomer."

"Maybe she isn't, not entirely," said Cathy, clearly trying to sort it out as she spoke. "One heart . . . no spots. And the motor skills . . . they're more consistent with the development of a human infant."

She paused as if about to leap off a high dive into a pool drained of water. "I think she might be a hybrid. . . ."

Published by POCKET BOOKS

For orders other than by individual consumers, Pocket Books grants a discount on the purchase of **10 or more** copies of single titles for special markets or premium use. For further details, please write to the Vice-President of Special Markets, Pocket Books, 1230 Avenue of the Americas, New York, NY 10020.

For information on how individual consumers can place orders, please write to Mail Order Department, Paramount Publishing, 200 Old Tappan Road, Old Tappan, NJ 07675.

#3 ALIEN NATION™

BODY AND SOUL

A NOVEL BY PETER DAVID
BASED ON THE TELEPLAY BY DIANE FROLOV & ANDREW SCHNEIDER

POCKET BOOKS

New York   London   Toronto   Sydney   Tokyo   Singapore

An *Original* Publication of POCKET BOOKS

POCKET BOOKS, a division of Simon & Schuster Inc.
1230 Avenue of the Americas, New York, NY 10020.

Copyright © 1993 by Twentieth Century Fox Film Corp.

ALIEN NATION is a trademark of Twentieth Century Fox Film
Corporation

ISBN: 0-671-73601-9

First Pocket Books printing December 1993

10 9 8 7 6 5 4 3 2

POCKET and colophon are registered trademarks of
Simon & Schuster Inc.

Printed in the U.S.A.

To Kenneth Johnson,
who pulled off the rare feat of producing a
TV show that surpassed the movie.

BODY AND SOUL

CHAPTER 1

THE BUILDING SAT upon a desert that was as arid and flat as any alien world . . . which, to the inhabitants of the building, it was.

The full moon had risen, hanging there like a great, pupilless eye gazing down upon the silence. Far beyond the moon the stars twinkled through the cloudless heavens. One of those stars, so very far off, beckoned to the inhabitants of the building. But that summons would remain forever unanswered. As it was, it was simply a . . . a sort of tease. Frustrating, irritating, and ultimately unsatisfying.

Then the silence of the desert was disrupted by the slow, steady grinding of a vehicle with an improperly fitted muffler. Its wide tires crunched across the road and then made a wide right turn into the little-used driveway.

There a guard was waiting for them. His gaze darted around nervously, as if apprehensive that somehow, in some insane fashion, someone would suddenly manage to pop out of hiding and surprise him.

When the truck pulled up, the headlights catching him square as if he were about to be roadkill, he squinted against it and gestured frantically for the lights to be shut off. Likewise, he made a throat-cutting motion with his other hand to indicate the motor should be cut.

The occupants' heads were unadorned by hair . . . or, for that matter, earlobes. The passenger resembled the driver rather closely. Indeed, the main manner in which they could be distinguished one from another was that the passenger's chin was slightly more outthrust, and their heads were splattered with large brown and black splotches in patterns that differed.

The driver opened the door and hopped out of the van. The passenger followed suit. They approached the guard slowly, their hands at their sides. Humans were jumpy enough around them, even under the most casual of circumstances. A situation like this, where a human with a guilty conscience was jumping at shadows, could suddenly become very difficult if not handled just right.

The guard looked from one to the other, squinting. "You River?" he asked the driver after a moment.

The driver shook his head. "Penn," he said. He inclined his bald head toward the passenger. "That's River."

"Sorry," murmured the guard.

"I know," said Penn. "We all look alike." He made no attempt to hide his sarcasm. All of his people were clearly such individuals to him, that it was an utter mystery how humans could be so brainless that they could not tell various members of his race—collectively known as the Tenctonese, although informally they were called Newcomers—apart.

"What are you doing here?" asked the one called River in annoyance. "There's no reason for you to be here. You were paid."

"I was . . . I was just saying good-bye to them."

River and Penn looked at each other incredulously, and then back at the guard. "What difference does it make to you?" said Penn after a moment. "Don't tell me you're getting sentimental about those . . . things."

"No," replied the guard quickly. "But . . . well, look. Humans sometimes form attachments to stuff they become familiar with, just from the sheer repetition of it."

"I thought familiarity bred contempt in your culture," River pointed out, with just enough of a sneer to make his own disdain noticeable.

The guard's lips thinned. "Depends how contemptible the thing we're becoming familiar with is," he said tightly.

"You didn't tell them where they're going," Penn said abruptly.

"I don't *know* where they're going," the guard pointed out. "I just told them they were leaving. That they were being moved. That they'd be happier because they were going to be going with some of their own people."

River's eyes narrowed. "You told him he was going with his own people?"

There was something about River's tone that the guard didn't like. "Yeah. What? Is there a problem with that?"

River started to say something, but Penn held up a long, bony finger. "No," said Penn sharply. "No problem at all. So you've said your good-byes. Is there any reason for you to be hanging around here?"

"Uh . . . no," admitted the guard. "Not really."

"In that case . . . good-bye."

The guard slowly bobbed his head. He took a couple of steps back, his gaze not leaving the two Newcomers.

Was he a loose end that they were now going to tie off? Would there be a sudden, silenced gunshot penetrating his forehead? Or, if he turned his back, would one of the Newcomers move with that incredible speed and strength that they commanded, and break his neck before he even knew what happened?

As casually as he could, he turned on his heel and walked with measured strides to his car. He felt the muscles around his neck bunching involuntarily, as if preparing for a sharp blow to be delivered.

There was a loud, sharp noise that sent him jumping into the air. He whirled, grabbing his car's rear fender to stop him from falling.

River, who had not moved an inch, had coughed.

The guard tried to slow down his racing heart. River, utterly nonchalant, brought the edge of one hand under his nose and waved cheerily with the other one.

The guard waved back, and then stared at his own hand as if surprised that it existed. He reached around without looking to the door handle of his car, swung it open, and jumped in. Moments later, the car peeled out, tires screeching. He checked his rearview mirror half a dozen times, and the Newcomers were already heading for the building, giving him no thought whatsoever.

They approached the building silently, and then the back doors of the van opened. The occupant hopped out, and he did not look especially pleased. He was eminently human, with short-cropped black hair and an impatient air. "Are you guys going to screw around all night here?" he demanded.

[*"Suck a lemur"*] River said.

"What?" snapped the human. "What the hell did you just say?"

"I said, 'We're getting right on it.' Don't worry, Mr. Perkins. We'll be out of here in five minutes."

The one he'd called Perkins regarded him suspiciously for a moment. "Well, get a move on," he said, finally.

River inclined his head slightly, and the two of them entered the building.

[*"You're getting the hang of dealing with humans?"*] asked Penn. [*"Why bother getting into fights with them? They're not worth it."*]

[*"True enough"*] acknowledged River. [*"They're worthwhile for grunt work. That's about it. Did you see the way that idiot tripped over his own feet getting to his car? He thought we were going to kill him."*]

[*"He overrates his own importance"*] Penn said with a chuckle. [*"As a living man who was bribed, he must keep silent. His presence as a corpse could speak volumes."*]

[*"I wish he'd kept silent about telling the subject of Tenctonese involvement"*] River grumbled. [*"Why give a hint?"*]

[*"Why worry?"*] Penn said. From his sport jacket pocket, he removed a small, narrow case. He flipped it open to reveal a syringe, carefully seated in a felt outline. [*"There's one of him against the two of us. How difficult can this be?"*]

River nodded in agreement, and then he pulled out a pack of cigarettes, palming a lighter with his other hand. He started to remove a cigarette from the pack, and Penn abruptly reached over and batted the cigarettes from his hand.

[*"What are you getting involved with that human garbage for?"*] he demanded.

[*"What's your problem? These are specially made. Rates highest in tar and nicotine."*]

5

[*"We dress like them. Talk like them. The more time we spend acquiring their habits, the less time we'll have for maintaining our own. Whatever happened to racial purity?"*]

River made a scoffing noise, but elected not to press the point. He dropped his lighter back into his jacket pocket and said nothing more about it.

They made their way through the building, moving softly and silently.

A musty smell hung as heavily as the silence. River and Penn ignored the monstrosities that lined the walls of the building.

The target lay upon the huge, metal frame bed. Next to it was a large pitcher with water and a carton of unrefrigerated milk. The target was curled up, his back to them, his chest rising and falling slowly indicating that he was clearly asleep. Situated directly next to the bed was a crib, the small form within obscured by a pink blanket.

There was a single window above, and moonlight streamed through, illuminating the sleeping pair.

River and Penn approached carefully, trying to be as smooth and unnoticeable as possible. As they passed the crib, Penn cast a glance into it . . .

And gasped.

River shot him a fierce look, for the sound was like a thunderclap in the stillness. But the figure on the bed hadn't stirred. River now took a glance, as well, and immediately understood what it was that had prompted the sound from Penn.

He turned to Penn and mouthed a very human word, *"Wow."*

Penn nodded in agreement, and then turned his attention to the larger figure on the bed. He had the syringe out, and started to lean forward to make the injection. Then his eyes caught something on the wall. Something had been scribbled there in the unmistakable alphabet of the Tenctonese.

Three simple words that spoke volumes to the two Newcomers.

Penn turned to River, his expression one of utter mystification.

[*"How did he—?"*] he started to ask.

But he didn't get the entire question out.

The occupant of the large metal bed had turned with a speed that seemed completely at odds with his bulk. Still on his back, but with his eyes open and blazing, he reached out with one large hand that clamped firmly around Penn's throat.

River took a step back, alarmed, and as the bed's occupant rose from his faked slumber, so did Penn rise with him as well; his legs pinwheeled helplessly. The syringe slipped from his fingers and crashed to the floor.

River had been informed, of course, of what they would be facing. But hearing about it and encountering it firsthand were two entirely different things.

Penn was being suspended in the air by a creature that looked, for all intents and purposes, like a Newcomer. But he was a Newcomer the likes of which had never been seen before. He was fully seven feet tall, wearing what appeared to be some sort of green jumpsuit, which was clearly too small on him.

His expression was a mixture of fury and fear.

[*"Do something!"*] shouted Penn frantically, pummeling the massive forearm that held him.

The giant shook Penn in the way that a cat might shake a bird that it has just captured. Penn emitted a high-pitched shriek, the world spinning around him. And then the giant turned and flung Penn with, frighteningly enough, only a small measure of the strength he truly possessed.

7

Penn hurtled across the warehouse and crashed into some crates. There was the sound of splintering wood and Penn lay there, a low moan being the only indication that he was still alive.

The giant turned and faced River. The huge Newcomer's mouth was drawn back in a grimace. Fear was vanishing from his face with every passing moment, leaving behind only the anger.

River took a quick step to try and angle toward an exit, but the giant matched his motion. This caused River to halt in his tracks, because no matter which way he moved, the giant would manage to head him off.

He glanced in the direction of the crib. Newspapers, rags, and an old soiled sheet were scattered nearby.

The giant followed his gaze, his obvious concern for the occupant of the crib momentarily overwhelming everything else.

It was at that moment that a sudden inspiration hit River. And with the inspiration, just as quickly, came the action.

With the giant's gaze momentarily averted, River stabbed a hand into his jacket pocket and came up with the cigarette lighter that Penn had so cavalierly dismissed. He offered up a very quick prayer to a Tenctonese god and flicked the lighter.

The flame came up on the very first try.

The giant's scrutiny swung back to River, attracted by the flickering of the lighter. He frowned, puzzled and uncomprehending.

River made a quick sideways throw, and the lighter skidded across the floor and nestled comfortably amidst the newspapers and rags directly under the crib. Immediately the trash went up.

The giant screamed, a roar of inarticulate, horrified rage. River chose that moment to try and bolt.

He had not reckoned with the giant's fearsome single-mindedness. Moreover, he had not properly taken into account the giant's reach. River had taken three steps when the giant's knuckles crashed squarely into his nose.

There was the sound of shattering bone and suddenly River was airborne. He crashed to the ground, dazed, the world whirling. As it happened, he was only a few feet away from Penn.

The sounds of the giant's hysterical screams now mingled with the crackling of the fire.

He grabbed at the crib, momentarily beaten back by the rapidly rising flames, and then—heedless of his own safety—one of his massive hands clamped around the crib railing, and he yanked as hard as he could.

Truthfully, it didn't require all that much strength. The crib wasn't especially heavy. It skidded across the floor at the first pull, shooting safely away from the flame and ricocheting off the large bed that the giant had been lying on.

The giant scooped the occupant of the crib into his arms. For the briefest of moments, an expression that transcended human concepts of devotion passed across the creature's face. Then he clutched his precious cargo to his massive chest and, with a last howl of defiance, charged toward an exit.

Perkins was getting impatient.

He also had to take a leak—badly. He'd swilled down several beers during the long, boring drive from the city.

"Screw it," he muttered. If the two slags felt like they had all the time in the world, why should he have to suffer?

He moved away from the truck to a corner of the building, discreetly blocking himself from view, and relieved himself. He gave the deep, relaxed kind of sigh that one can give only when one's bladder is being alleviated from tremendous stress.

And then, as he started to zip himself up, he smelled something.

Something burning.

At that moment, the door several feet away from him exploded outward.

His mouth dropped open in surprise as a giant Newcomer burst out, almost knocking the door off its hinges. The creature was cradling something in his arms, and his huge head was swiveling back and forth like a conning tower.

Then he spotted the truck.

The giant charged across the driveway, and that was when the immensity of a situation gone wrong fully occurred to Perkins. Some major mishap had occurred in the building, and what was supposed to be a simple pickup operation had become a debacle.

If the giant got away, Perkins was going to have to return to his employer, explain precisely what had gone wrong, and take responsibility for it.

It was not so much bravery, or even dedication to duty, so much as just plain fear of what would happen if he didn't take every possible step to salvage this mess, that prompted Perkins's next actions.

The giant had already leaped into the cab of the truck. For one moment Perkins thought that maybe his life was going to be simple. That the giant would sit there in utter futility, unaware of how to pilot the vehicle, until the other two slags showed up and did what they were supposed to do—namely, overpower the damned giant and get him safely under wraps.

Perkins's hope was dashed when he heard the clicking of the engine. One of the most annoying things about most slags is how quickly the damned things learned, and the giant was apparently no exception.

Perkins was unarmed, but not undetermined. He scampered toward the van and, just as he got within reach, heard the engine roar to life.

He leaped desperately, snagging the back of the van just as the vehicle lurched forward. The giant was a fast learner, but Grand Prix material he was not. The van started, stopped, and then pitched forward again. The motion of the van accomplished for Perkins what he had been trying to do in the first place—specifically, get inside.

He tumbled into the interior of the van's cargo bay. Inside were a couple of bolted-down gurneys that had been prepared for the giant to lie on once he was inside.

The giant wasn't going to need it. He was in the front, driving. But Perkins latched onto it, holding on desperately so that he wouldn't be thrown back out of the van. As he did so, the rear doors of the van swung back around on their well-oiled hinges and slammed shut, closing him in. When this happened, he breathed a sigh of relief. At least he didn't have to be concerned about being thrown out the back of a moving vehicle.

The van was picking up speed. Perkins thudded and thumped around inside, tossed around like a poker chip as the van skidded out onto the main road and roared toward . . .

Where?

Sealed in the back, Perkins had absolutely no clue as to where they were going. But at least, whenever they got there, he would be able to inform his boss that, yes, things had not gone quite according to plan. But he, Perkins, was still on top of things.

At least for the moment.

* * *

River felt an earthquake, and it was shouting his name.

Then his mind focused in, and he stared dazedly up at Penn. [*"What's . . . ?"*]

[*"Will you come on?!"*] shouted Penn angrily.

And then Penn actually managed to catch a break.

His despairing gaze noticed a literal godsend. On the wall to his right, a fire extinguisher was serenely perched. If the damned thing could have spoken, it would undoubtedly have said something along the lines of, "It took you long enough to notice me."

Penn stood up quickly, momentarily forgetting about River. The result was that the semiconscious Newcomer's head thudded to the floor with an impressive *crack.* Penn paid it no heed, for he had other things on his mind. He crossed quickly to the fire extinguisher, grabbed it off the wall, and prayed that the idiot guard had seen to it that the thing was maintained. Otherwise the fire was going to blaze out of control, and River might very well be toast.

But Penn caught his second break in as many minutes. He flipped the fire extinguisher over, aimed, and fired. Moments later the roaring fire had been smothered. All that was left was a thick, acrid smell and a faint hissing and popping noise.

Quickly he turned back to River and knelt down beside him. He winced at the blood that was pouring from the Newcomer's nose. It was out of joint as well. Clearly the giant had broken it.

There was no time to carp over it, however. [*"Come on"*] he clicked, and hauled the groggy River to his feet. River stumbled momentarily and then righted himself.

Seconds later, they were out on the road, just in time to see the van heading in the direction of Los Angeles.

[*"Let's go! They're getting away!"*] shouted Penn.

12

Spurred on by the anger in his partner's voice, River started off, and the two of them pounded down the road after the speeding van.

Their Newcomer physiology made them stronger and faster than any human, but all the alien musculature in the world wasn't going to do a thing when it came to keeping pace with a speeding armored van. Eventually, after several miles, the two Newcomers slowed and then came to a stop, chests heaving and their double hearts pounding.

They bent over, their hands resting on their knees, as the van vanished into the distance. Penn looked woefully at River.

[*"He's not going to be happy about this, you know."*]

[*"I know"*] said River, unenthused. He touched his damaged nose tentatively and winced. Then he looked around, a thought occurring to him. [*"Where's the human?"*]

Penn looked behind them, and realized that he hadn't spotted Perkins when they came out of the building. [*"You know . . . maybe . . ."*]

[*"He's in the rear of the van?"*]

Penn nodded. [*"I'll bet that's it. And since it's separate from the cabin, then the giant won't spot him."*]

[*"Perfect."*] River paused. [*"You know . . . I'll bet the giant heads to Little Tencton. He'd be drawn to it."*]

[*"The highest concentration of our people"*] Penn nodded. [*"It makes sense. All we have to do is get to the city as quickly as possible and maybe we can salvage this."*]

It didn't take them all that long to find the one service station in the area . . . which was closed. Parked to one side was an older car with a sign on it that read For Sale—$500.

The Newcomers looked at each other.

[*"Sold"*] said Penn.

Moments later, the car successfully hot-wired, the two Newcomers sped off down the deserted highway. Far in the distance, the lights of Los Angeles, twinkling like the stars, beckoned to them . . .

CHAPTER 2

MATT SIKES STARED at himself in the steamed-up mirror, trying to decide whether or not to shave.

He was somewhat scruffy at the moment, having come off a particularly grueling case that had occupied several months, on and off. And during the final week, when everything had come to a head, he had really let himself go as he fixated on bringing down a drug dealer that he'd been pursuing for ages.

With matters at a satisfactory conclusion, Sikes had come home and promptly crashed for twelve straight hours of shut-eye. He had taken the time off at the urging of his partner, George Francisco. George, the only Newcomer to have reached the rank of detective in the LAPD (not to mention detective sergeant, a promotion that had caused no end of grief between them), had stridently encouraged Matt to take a day off after the grind they'd been through.

"Matthew," George had said in that faintly

15

schoolteacher manner of his that sometimes drove Sikes to complete distraction, "you will be doing no one any good—neither myself, with whom you're partnered, nor the public which we are supposed to be serving and protecting—if you are out on the streets in a diminished capacity."

"I am not diminished, George!" Sikes had said angrily, dropping down in front of the desk that faced directly across from Francisco. It had taken him months to get accustomed to staring into the face of a slag every single day . . . and indeed, he had only gotten used to it when he'd finally started to think of Francisco as a person rather than a racial epithet.

"Yes, you are," George had replied. "And you do not have to shout, Matthew."

"I'm not shouting!" Sikes had shouted. He slid open his top desk drawer and shoved his gun in. "And I'm not diminished. How come you're not 'diminished'?"

"I have greater durability than you," George had said, with no trace of smugness. As far as he was concerned, it wasn't a boast. It was simple fact. "I do not become as fatigued, nor do I—"

"All right, George," Sikes had said sharply. He had been in no mood for a litany of Tenctonese points of superiority. "You're too good for words. We should just dress you up in a blue body stocking with a red *S* on it, okay?"

George had stared at him. "Why?" he had asked incredulously.

"Never mind." Sikes had waved him off. "I'm telling you, I don't need time off. Okay? I'm as sharp and on top of things as I ever am . . ."

And as he slammed the desk drawer, the gun went off.

Immediately every cop in the squad room had dropped, yanking out their weapons and aiming at the source of the explosion.

Every cop except George, who had sat there, staring impassively at the stunned Matt Sikes.

Sikes had stared at the sea of drawn guns and then said slowly, "Maybe a few hours wouldn't kill me."

"It will go a long way towards not killing anyone else," George had said reasonably.

Sikes fell asleep the moment his head hit the pillow.

He had not bothered to set his alarm clock because he hadn't really believed that he'd fall asleep . . . overestimating, as always, his own durability. So it was fortunate that he awoke when he did, because when he saw what time it was he realized, with a start, that he had a date with Cathy that night that he had already put off twice. If he put it off a third time, she might put him off permanently.

Cathy Frankel was the attractive Newcomer doctor who lived across the hallway from him. She had been occupying his thoughts a great deal lately, and for someone as resolutely single-minded as Sikes, this was something of an accomplishment.

Now he stared into the mirror, rubbing his hand across his beard stubble. He had trouble believing that he was giving this much thought and second-guessing to what Cathy might think of his appearance.

To shave or not to shave, that was the question.

"Think this out," he said to no one in particular. "Newcomer males are hairless . . . so it might be that if I'm clean shaved, I'll remind her more of what turns her on. Yeah. That's it."

He started to lather up, but then paused.

17

"But . . ." he continued, "perhaps the thing she likes about me is that I'm hairier. That could be it," he told the mirror. "She likes the hair. It's unusual. It's a turn-on. That's what she goes for."

He washed off the lather . . . and then paused again.

"But if that's it . . . and she knows that I figured out that that's it . . . then coming in with all this beard will seem like I'm coming on to her too much . . . which might be a turnoff."

He regarded himself a while longer.

"You're an idiot," he told the mirror image. His reflection nodded in agreement.

He lathered up and shaved, and as he did so he muttered to himself. "No point to this anyway," he said. "If something was gonna happen between us, then it would have happened by now. You can't force these things. Either they happen or they don't. Gotta face it . . . Cathy isn't turned on by me, hairless or hairy. And frankly, well . . . she doesn't really do it for me, either. I mean . . . those spots and everything. And the way she looks at me sometimes, like I'm . . . I'm so odd-looking to her."

He took a long, hard look at himself in the mirror.

Usually he liked to think of himself as "ruggedly handsome."

But now he really studied himself. His brown hair, slicked down from the shower, hung raggedly around his ears. And he could see that it was just starting to thin on top. His chin was particularly strong, he decided, and his lips were just way too thick. His face looked like . . . like an assemblage of random parts, rather than something that formed one cohesive whole.

Mentally he called to mind Cathy's image. Everything about her was aquiline and graceful. Her face, her head, her movements that were as fluid as a dancer's, and she wasn't even trying.

His going after her was like a mutt sniffing around a golden retriever.

"Okay," he said finally. "Okay. The physical thing . . . it's not going to happen. Ever. That's fine. So there's no reason that we can't just be friends. None. I mean . . . how often have I heard the 'let's be friends' speech. So . . . it'll be nice. Get the female perspective of things without the tension of the sex stuff. That's it. That's good. It's a good thing." He continued to shave and said once more, "It's a good thing."

He finished shaving and dressed. As he did so, he told himself how nice it was going to be having a female who was just a friend and nothing more. Indeed, it would probably be a good experience for him. Give him the hang of thinking of females as something beyond sex objects. Not that he'd ever had that much personal use for females *beyond* their being sex objects but, well . . . he'd heard that it was possible to have relationships with a woman where sex didn't enter into it.

And . . . let's face it, he reasoned . . . Cathy wasn't really a woman. She wasn't even human. She was, as they liked to say in science fiction tomes, humanoid. Humanoid with the general appearance of a female, but a biology and society that was totally divorced from anything in human experience.

If there was any living being who was a candidate to have a simple platonic relationship with, it was definitely Cathy.

Friends. Buddies. Compadres. Someone to unload on. Someone who was . . . best of all . . . not a cop.

He buttoned his blue flannel shirt. Not that he had anything against cops, lord knew. But everyone in his workplace was a cop. All his friends were cops. Everyone he socialized with was a cop. Every major social function he attended involved cops . . .

"Oh, Jesus," he said, and thudded himself in the head with the base of his palm. "The dinner."

He ran out into the living room, his shirt buttoned askew, and grabbed at the pile of bills, notices, and letters stacked up in the fashion that passed for a filing system. He sorted through them at light speed and finally found the one he was looking for. A light gray envelope with, of course, a police return address. Specifically, the Office of Police Affairs.

He pulled out the letter and checked for the RSVP date, and moaned. It was that day. He glanced at his watch and saw that it was already past six. There was a pretty good chance that no one was going to be there, but he had to take a shot at it.

He grabbed up the phone, dialed quickly, and breathed a silent prayer as he listened to the phone ring. After five rings Sikes was giving up hope, but on the seventh ring, someone picked up.

"OPA," said a brisk voice.

"Yeah, hi," said Sikes. "I'm calling to RSVP the Perelli dinner."

There was a pause, and then a low chuckle. "I was already out the door when I heard the phone ringing. And I thought to myself, 'Should I bother?' And then I figured, 'Yeah, I better. It's probably that sorry Sikes cutting it wafer thin, like always.'"

Sikes frowned in confusion, but then the voice clicked. "Kristofal?"

"Yeah, who else?"

"Aw man, Kris, I owe you one. I really do."

"What the hell kept you, man? You musta got the letter over a week ago."

"Yeah, well," said Sikes, tapping a pencil absently

on the table. "I was out a lot, keeping all kinda crazy hours. And it just snuck up on me."

"When the replies were comin' in, I couldn't believe I wasn't seeing your name there. Testimonial to Perelli, man. You, of all people . . ."

"Tell me about it," said Sikes. "Look, tell me I'm still in time."

"Just. Tomorrow morning, nine A.M., the list is on my supervisor's desk. Lucky you, I've saved your sorry ass. Hear that sound? That's my pencil scratching your name in on the guest list."

Sikes sighed in relief. "I owe you, Kris. Big time."

"Bet your ass you do. What's your date's name? I'll list her on here, too."

"Uhm . . ." Sikes paused. "I, uh . . . don't know yet."

"Can't find a girl who's not embarrassed to be seen with you, huh?"

"Screw you," said Sikes good-naturedly. "Just have to figure out which one is going to be the lucky girl."

"The one who doesn't have to go with you," Kristofal told him.

"Y'know what we used to call you behind your back?" said Sikes. "Christ-awful. And I'm starting to remember why."

"I never called you anything behind your back."

"Yeah. Everything was to my face."

"Hey, man, it wasn't easy looking into that hangdog thing to insult it, I can tell you."

Sikes grinned. "Thanks for answering the phone, Kris."

"No problem. Be sure to call me back with your date's name when you can. Make sure she has a name tag and everything."

"Sure. You bet."

21

He hung up and sat there for a moment.

"Name tag and everything," he repeated.

As Cathy and Sikes finished the dinner she had made, it was nothing short of amazing to Sikes that she had adapted as well as she had to the notion of cooking Earth food. When he had first started seeing her, he had been trying to think of ways that he could politely beg off from sampling such delicacies as Shake-and-Bake Squirrel. He had been pleasantly surprised, then, when Cathy had proven herself capable of producing perfectly acceptable dishes that were more in line with human tastes.

It was clear, though, when they ate together, that such "delicacies" as hamburgers and hot dogs were not exactly her food of choice. Matt had gamely endeavored to be as adventurous as Cathy, taking a stab at eating Newcomer cuisine with as much enthusiasm as he could muster. As it turned out, Cathy was far more successful in the enthusiasm-mustering department than he was.

"So . . . how was the macaroni and cheese?" she asked him eagerly.

He smiled gamely. In truth . . . it hadn't been *bad*. "It was . . . different," he said.

Her face fell. "You didn't like it."

"No, I did! Really! It was just different, that's all. Different doesn't mean bad. I mean . . . look at you. You're different. You're not bad. In fact . . . you're pretty good." And he grinned broadly.

His smile was infectious. She looked down, charmingly embarrassed. "Well . . . I'm glad you liked it, Matt."

"What was—if you don't mind my asking—what did you mix in there? There was some ingredient in there I couldn't quite place."

Her hairless brow wrinkled for a moment, and

then brightened. "Oh. That would probably be the sour cream."

In a masterpiece of poker face, Sikes didn't flinch. "Sour cream."

"Yes." She started to gather up the dishes. "The recipe seemed a little bland, so I decided to add something that would give it some kick."

A swift kick, he thought bleakly.

"Oh," she said, as she placed the dishes in the sink. "Can you keep Saturday the fourteenth open?"

"The fourteenth." He frowned. "What's the fourteenth?"

She walked back to him, her delicate hands waving excitedly. "A grateful patient," she said, "actually managed to get me two tickets to the most sold-out show in town, *Phantom of the Opera.*"

"No kidding."

She sighed. "I hear that Foghorn Leghorn is supposed to be magnificent in it."

He raised an eyebrow. "It's a cartoon?"

She looked at him, confused. "Of course not." She leaned against the video cabinet and said incredulously, "Don't tell me you haven't heard of Foghorn Leghorn? The single greatest musical performer in Tenctonese theater?"

The light began to dawn. "This is a Tenctonese version of *Phantom.*"

"Of course. Didn't I mention that?"

"No." He laughed. "No, you didn't. Sorry. I thought you were talking about the other Foghorn Leghorn."

"There's another Foghorn Leghorn?"

He paused. "Uhm . . . this may sound like a silly question . . . but Yosemite Sam isn't costarring with him, by any chance?"

"Of course not!"

"Oh. Okay."

"Yosemite Sam is in the other national touring company."

"Ah."

Sikes sighed and leaned back in the chair. Every so often he was still caught off guard by the prank that had been perpetrated upon the 300,000 Tenctonese who had landed in Los Angeles several years ago. When they'd been processed through immigration, the agents had to come up with names for them, since their natural names were by and large unpronounceable for humans.

The first Newcomers, like Cathy, had gotten fairly normal names. Names that were neutral, or even vague transliterated approximations of their own names. But as hours had turned into days, and wave upon wave of Newcomers had passed through the processing offices, the folks in immigration either started to get (a) punchy or (b) resentful, depending upon whose version of the story you believed.

And the names of the Newcomers had started getting . . . exotic. Even downright weird.

Sikes had run into all kinds. Eleanor Roosevelt. Rudyard Kipling. Art Deco. Johnny B. Good. And even his own partner, George Francisco, had originally been tagged Sam Francisco. Francisco, like most of the Newcomers, had been unaware of the derivation of the names and that humans were sharing a collective joke at Newcomer expense. Refusing to join in the joke, Sikes had arbitrarily rechristened him George Francisco, naming him in honor of Sikes's personal favorite space man, George Jetson.

Rather than dwell on it, he shifted his focus to the date under discussion. "The fourteenth . . . that's familiar. Oh! Can't do it." He shook his head. "Got a dinner."

"A dinner date?" She arched one of her nonexistent eyebrows.

"Huh?" Was it his imagination or did she sound, just for a moment, a bit jealous. "Oh. No. It's a . . . whattaya call it . . . testimonial dinner, for this guy, Jack Perelli. He's retiring next month and, well . . . he was kind of a mentor of mine."

"Really?" The idea seemed to amuse her, and he frowned slightly.

"What's so funny?"

"Oh, nothing, Matt. Really. It's just that . . . well, you're always so . . . don't take this wrong, but you're always so sure of yourself and so singularly positive that you know the answer to everything, that it's hard for me to picture you just . . . just *learning* from someone. I mean, that you would hold anyone in enough esteem that way."

He tried to take offense at the observation, but he couldn't. He had to admit there was a lot of truth in what she said. He smiled gamely. "What can I say? I was young. It was back before I learned everything there was to learn. I was partnered with him for a while, and the stuff he taught me . . . I mean, what can I say? It was . . . well, actually, it was a pretty rough time for me. My marriage was falling apart. My work habits had gotten sloppy. And he pulled me through a lot of that, and helped focus me. And there's this dinner now to honor him, and naturally I should be there."

"Oh. All right." She paused. "Well, maybe I'll just sell the tickets. Better yet . . . I know someone I can give them to . . ."

"Whoa, wait! Why don't you just go alone? Or . . . or take somebody else?"

She shrugged—a human gesture that she'd picked up from Sikes. "It wouldn't be the same, that's all."

25

He tried to hide his astonishment. That single comment from Cathy had just gone a long way toward completely blowing all of his earlier conceptions out the window. Maybe she actually . . .

But no. There was nothing in that remark that implied any sort of sexual attraction. She just meant . . . well, she could have meant a lot of things. She . . .

She seemed to be staring at him expectantly. And he abruptly realized that the whole dinner question was still open. Because, of course, he could bring a date.

He stared at her. Stared at the Newcomer woman who was smiling at him.

And he thought about Perelli.

"Uhm . . . y'know . . . I wish I could bring you along," he said slowly. "But it's, uh . . . it's pretty tight seating. Spouses are okay, but otherwise they're asking that you don't bring dates . . ."

She knew. She must have known that he was lying. Sikes felt as if he were the world's worst liar. As if the moment a blatant untruth passed his lips, his hair changed color or fireworks went off, or maybe, in the best tradition, his nose grew. But Cathy didn't react in the slightest, other than to say simply, "That's quite all right, Matt. I still doubt I'll go to *Phantom.* It'll be playing for a while."

"Well . . . whatever . . ."

Cathy seemed to shift uncomfortably, and then abruptly, as if anxious to get on to a new topic, she suddenly turned toward the videotapes that were stacked up on the cabinet. "Are you interested in watching something?"

"Uh . . . yeah. Sure." Watching TV was a convenient out. It helped to put a tape into the machine when conversation was moving in a direction that made either Sikes or Cathy uncomfortable. He was beginning to sense that there was a lot that made them uncomfortable, because there was a lot that each wanted to say or do, and neither was ready for those things to be said or done.

She took down a tape that was in a blue and white plastic case. "That nice Mr. Chafin, the manager over at Blockbuster, said that this was a good one. I told him I wanted something about football."

"Football?" He tried not to laugh. "Since when are you interested in football?"

"Well, it seems to preoccupy you a great deal. And I thought that . . . well, I thought maybe that I should try and see what you find so interesting about it."

"Baby, you're the greatest."

She pointed in recognition. "'The Honeymooners,' right?"

"There's hope for you, Cathy. There's real hope."

She smiled gratefully and bobbed her head slightly in appreciation as she popped the tape into the player. She pressed the Play button, and then dropped down next to Matt on the couch. Matt took notice of the sleeveless blue dress she was wearing and the sleek curve of her shoulders.

This business about thinking of her only as a friend didn't seem to be working out, especially as he became more acutely aware of her presence as a female. Not an alien. Not a nonhuman. But a female, with the allure that just seemed to come with the territory.

He forced his attention back to the screen.

The title came on, and his jaw dropped.

"The Cheeky Cheerleader?"

"Yes," she said. "The description on the box made it sound like a great deal of fun. Romping and excitement and such. There weren't all those technical terms that you're always tossing around."

27

"Yeah, but Cathy . . ."

But Cathy was no longer paying attention to him. She was staring at the screen.

And staring.

And staring.

The intrepid cheerleader on the screen had crawled between the legs of the small circle of football players on the field and was in the process of performing some acts that were causing the players to shake in their cleats.

Sikes cleared his throat. "Uh, Cath . . ."

She looked at Matt. "Is this what normally goes on in the huddle?"

"No. No, not really. I mean . . . y'know, if it did, I doubt they'd do anything *but* huddle. It'd be a . . . well, a very different game."

"I should say." She looked back at the screen. "No wonder so many people like the sport better than baseball."

Sikes held his face in his hands, embarrassed on behalf of his entire species.

When he dared to look up, the scene had shifted to a bedroom. The intrepid cheerleader was now on a bed with a single football player, which was the closest thing to restraint the film had, apparently. The lights were low, much like the lighting in Cathy's living room, Sikes realized.

He watched her carefully, waiting for some indication that she was repelled by what she was seeing on the screen. Repelled, or maybe amused.

But no. She was staring at the film, apparently fascinated by what she was seeing. Sikes couldn't believe it. As he had learned the details of various Tenctonese mating and reproduction patterns (particularly during the conception and birth of George Francisco's youngest child) he had had to fight down his initial shock and/or repulsion in every instance.

Cathy, on the other hand, seemed eminently fascinated. Maybe it was because she was a doctor.

The cheerleader was kissing the football player passionately, having worked his shirt up and over his head. Her hands played across the well-formed pectorals.

Cathy was enthralled.

And it was at that point that all of Sikes's meticulously formed rationale over how they were going to be just friends went completely out the window.

He tried to be as nonchalant as he could. Just in case Cathy reacted in a negative fashion, he wanted to be able to quickly chalk it up to only the most casual of misunderstandings. He draped an arm around her, allowing his hand to rest on her far shoulder. He was amazed at the warmth of her. Also, holding her this close, he was aware of a faint natural, musky scent that arose from her. Nothing unpleasant. Quite the contrary. He found it enticing.

Cathy snuggled closer to him, but her attention was still fully on the television. He wasn't sure whether she was getting closer to him reflexively, or was actually fully aware of his proximity . . . and perhaps even his thoughts.

The cheerleader and football player were locked in a passionate embrace. Cathy's eyes widened in what could only be described as awe.

"They kiss so well," she said.

Sikes wasn't sure if it was his imagination or not, but her voice sounded slightly hoarse to him. It was as if she were having trouble getting the words out.

"Yeah," he said. He pulled her a bit closer and, emboldened by the moment, said, "All it takes is practice."

He waited to see her reaction, wondering if she would pick up on the unspoken message.

She turned and looked right at him. Her face was

29

close to his, so close. Her eyes seemed to sparkle in the dimness of the room, where the primary illumination was the flickering of the TV screen.

He leaned forward and kissed her.

Her eyes went wide for a moment in surprise, and then, all at once, she seemed to relax against him. Her eyes closed to narrow slits. Sikes, who had kept his eyes open since he desperately wanted to see her reaction, felt the tension starting to drain out of him only to be replaced by another sort of tension. Now his eyes fluttered closed as he relished the touch of her, the feel of her. Her lips were slightly drier than a human woman's, but the taste was not unpleasant.

Cathy, for her part, opened her eyes again, and stared at the TV screen.

Aware that she was on very uncertain ground, she became slightly panicked and suddenly felt the need to acquire pointers wherever she could. And the cheerleader seemed to be quite the expert in these matters.

The cheerleader was running her fingers through the man's hair.

This seemed a little strange to Cathy. Having no experience with hair, she wasn't sure whether this was a particularly sensual, or sensitive, part of the human male anatomy. But she was game for anything at this point, feeling herself swept along in the rush of emotion, and not wanting to risk dampening it through her inexperience.

She slid her fingers through Matt's hair. She liked the shape and texture of it. There was something exciting, even slightly forbidden, about it. She nuzzled it, and the motion brought her throat up against Sikes's mouth.

Sikes started to nibble at her neck, his tongue playing along her throat just under her chin. It was a move that other women had reacted to rather well, but Sikes quickly became aware that he might as well be licking a block of wood. Cathy wasn't responding to it at all.

Don't be a macho jerk a voice inside him warned. *Ask for help or you're going to lose the momentum.* It was the same voice that earlier had been telling him that there was nothing physical between him and Cathy. Nice to know that inner voice was willing to change its tune at a moment's notice.

He murmured low, "What do you like?"

Cathy paused, and for a moment Sikes was certain that he had blown it. That by asking such an overt question, he had reminded her of just what was going on and what they were getting involved in.

But Cathy's breath was coming in short, steady gasps. It was quickly apparent that she was becoming as caught up in the heat of the moment as he. She hesitated only a moment, and then she offered him the crook of her arm.

Once upon a time, Sikes would have been brought to a screeching halt by this apparent non sequitur. But he had long since become accustomed to the concept that the Newcomers were structured radically different from humans. That their points of sensitivity did not always match up.

And so, unfazed, Sikes took Cathy gently by the arm and lightly ran his lips across the inside of her elbow.

He wasn't precisely sure what he expected, but what he got completely surpassed whatever might have occurred to him. Cathy gasped, and her back arched, lifting her buttocks off the couch. Sikes thought, *Wow. When these people are sensitive, they're really sensitive.*

It was incredible. With the other women Sikes had known, it had always been something of a guessing game. Rarely did any of them know so precisely what it was that turned them on. But Cathy not only knew, she was completely wired in to her entire system. And Sikes was about to be an electrician.

His kisses moved slowly up her arm. He was moving into uncertain territory, so just to play it safe, he kept massaging the crook of her arm with his thumb. It had the desired effect. Sikes didn't know whether Cathy was aware of what his mouth was doing or not. Ultimately it didn't matter, because he knew that he was savoring the taste of her, and she was certainly enjoying herself.

All because of the crook of her arm.

Boy, one case of tennis elbow for these women and it's good-bye, sex life, he thought, as his mouth moved over the smoothness of her shoulder.

He saw the spots that trailed down over the nape of her neck. For a long while, he had secretly wondered about the texture of the Newcomer spots. Whether they felt different from the nonspotted portions of the skin, whether they were in any way distinguishable.

His lips moved over the uppermost spots on her neck.

He wasn't at all prepared for what happened. If he'd thought that Cathy had reacted strongly to his kissing her elbow, that was nothing compared to what happened when his lips brushed her spots.

She let out a shriek of ecstasy so loud that it nearly deafened him. Her body twitched and writhed spasmodically, and from the way her eyes rolled up in her head, he thought she was going to pass out.

He drew back, a bit intimidated by the intensity of the reaction. My God, that had been just a light kiss. He had a feeling that if he'd sucked on the things, it might have blown the top of her skull off.

It was as if what she felt, in addition to filling her

32

with euphoria, had also been the equivalent of a bucket of cold water. Her eyes cleared momentarily, and she placed a hand against his chest. "We . . . we can't . . ."

He couldn't believe it. He was so pumped up he was ready to chew the furniture. He had been woefully wrong earlier—clearly she was hot for him. He knew that he was for her. All of his repressed desire, his fascination, his (admit it now) curiosity, were bubbling over. He had been responsive to what she wanted. So responsive that he thought this creature from the stars was liable to go nova any moment. He wanted to say, *What the hell do you want from me?* but he got as far as "Wha—?"

She placed a hand lightly over his mouth. He wasn't sure whether it was to stop him from talking, or to stop him from kissing her, or just to keep his face at a distance. The passion in her eyes indicated that if his face got close enough to hers, she might tear it off with her teeth. "We're going too far," she said.

She spoke with the air of a guide in those adventure movies where the hero has ventured into the sacred stronghold of some ancient race, and all sorts of booby traps were about to spring if another step was taken. Indiana Sikes, daredevil explorer. Part of him wanted to laugh, and say, *Quick! You throw me the idol, I'll throw you the whip!*

But another part of him was taking matters very seriously and demanded immediate attention. "Cathy, we're consenting adults," he said, trying as much as he could to sound reasonable.

She looked at him with incredulity, as if he had missed a point so obvious that a child would have picked up on it. "It's not that. It's . . . it's dangerous. Physically dangerous."

33

Now it really was all he could do not to laugh. She was worried that he was going to hurt her! He refrained from saying the clichéd "I'll be gentle," and instead rested a hand on her shoulder. "Cathy . . ." he began, trying to sound as considerate as possible.

She slid across the couch, away from him and up. She sat balanced against the arm of the sofa, placing her hand flutteringly against her breast and trying to send her breathing rate back to a normal level. "A Tenctonese woman," she managed to say, "if she's not in sync with her mate . . . she could cause him serious injury."

That took Sikes aback. She was trying to tell him that *she* was afraid of hurting *him?*

It was nonsense, of course. He went to the gym three days a week. He jogged. He lifted weights. He wasn't exactly Hercules, but he wasn't any ninety-pound weakling. He wondered if she was really concerned about hurting him, which seemed ridiculous, or whether she was, in fact, simply nervous about the thought of doing it with a human male.

Yeah. That was probably it. He rubbed his chin thoughtfully as he tried to think of how to proceed, and was thankful that he'd shaved. It had been the right move. The sheer masculinity of the facial hair might have been too much for her.

Go for the easy answer, he reasoned. She just wants reassurance.

"So we'll get in sync," he said easily.

He started towards her. She didn't move away, but she clearly wasn't encouraging him. "There are stages," she said, starting to adopt that same slightly pedantic tone that George sometimes used. "You need to learn how to approach me. How to hum. You need training . . ."

"Training?" He couldn't believe it. This was going too far. Now both of his male prides, the one above his belt and below, were swelling. "Hey, Cathy, if there's one thing I don't need, it's training. What're they going to do, give me a condom with little wheels on it? Trust me. I know what I'm doing."

Cathy turned away from him, clearly ready to get up. But Sikes was too quick, darting across the couch and nuzzling the back of her neck.

Cathy practically melted. Not literally, but damned close. Her verbal protests had been a desperate gambit because her body had been screaming for release. And now, with Matthew right there again, with his tongue gently stroking her spots, she had absolutely no resistance left. She gave in to him, her body going limp against his, supple and pliable. Her breath was coming faster and faster.

He eased her back down onto the couch. She didn't even seem completely aware that he was there anymore, so caught up in the sensations of her body was she. He grabbed the remote off the coffee table, aimed it, and turned off the television. The cheerleader and the football player vanished.

"Matthew . . ." she murmured, but whether it was from desire or from warning, he couldn't tell. He also didn't care, fully confident that he would be able to handle whatever happened.

She lay back, her hands grasping at him. She pulled at his flannel shirt, and he started to unbutton it. She, however, didn't wait, and ripped it open. There was the sound of several little plastic buttons flying off their threads and landing at various points throughout her apartment.

"I never liked this shirt anyway," he gasped.

She ran her hands over his chest, pulling on the chest hair with such force that he wanted to cry out.

35

But he bit down on his lower lip, determined not to let her think for a moment that she was hurting him. Hell, he'd been hurt before. He had the scratches on his back to prove it. But it had been a delicious kind of hurt, the kind that gives you pleasure when you think about it.

Her dress had ridden up to her waist. Her legs, incredibly muscular, were working their way up his arms, towards his neck. She was groaning, whispering his name amidst other words that had no meaning to him.

Her buttocks slid across the couch, bringing her back up against the arm of the sofa, pushing her to a half-raised position. Both the crook of her arm and the spots on her back were within range of him. As her toes tickled his earlobes, Sikes wet the tips of his fingers for heightened sensation, and rubbed one hand into the inside of her elbow while, at the same time, stroking her spots with the other.

Cathy shrieked.

So did Sikes, although not for the same reason.

For Cathy, it was because every nerve ending in her body was erupting simultaneously.

For Sikes, it was because Cathy's legs had clamped around his neck with the power and pressure of a vise. His head snapped forward and to the side, and something inside wrenched.

His shriek was truncated, however, as Cathy, writhing in spasms of delight, twisted at her waist. Like a wrestler, she sent Sikes hurtling off the couch and crashing into the floor.

Sikes, moaning, tried to get up to his knees, which was his latest, and last, mistake. Cathy, still in the throes of passion, snapped a foot around and tagged Sikes solidly in the jaw.

Police brutality flashed through his mind as he fell

backwards. He lay there in the darkness, stiff and unmoving—partly because he was unable to move, but mostly because he was afraid to.

He moaned in quiet pain as Cathy's far louder and enthusiastic whimperings trailed off. It took about five minutes.

Then, from what seemed a very great distance, he heard her say, "Maaatt?"

"Yeah."

"Matt, are you . . ." And then she realized where he was speaking from, and also recognized the agony in his voice. He heard her sit up. "My God . . . you're hurt."

"I'm fine. Just . . . gotta stand up."

The lamp quickly snapped on and there was Cathy, kneeling on the couch, having just lit the lamp. Her dress was in complete disarray. Under ordinary circumstances, Matt would have considered it singularly attractive. Instead, at the moment his main concern was trying to restore feeling to the rest of his body.

"Oh, Matt, I—"

"S'okay. Really." He smiled through gritted teeth as he pulled himself to sitting. He tried to keep his upper body turned away from her, because he had a feeling that there was going to be a beauty of a bruise coming in fairly shortly. Also, he realized very quickly that he couldn't turn his head. "I knew the job was dangerous when I took it."

"Matt, let me—"

"No!" he shouted. "I think I . . . maybe it'd be better if I . . ."

"Matt, please, I'm a doctor."

"Bill me, then." He stood on uncertain legs, trying not to stagger. He didn't succeed. He lurched toward the door as if he were on the deck of a ship.

"Ohhhh, Matt." Cathy sighed mournfully. "Please . . . I know we can be good together. If we could just . . ."

"Cathy, I hear my mother calling. Okay?"

And with that, he was out the door, leaving a perplexed Cathy sitting on the couch. She pulled her dress back into place around herself and frowned.

"His mother?"

CHAPTER 3

LITTLE TENCTON WAS a ghetto, of course. All the cute names in the world couldn't hide that simple fact.

It was a section of Los Angeles that had been taken over by the Newcomers. All it had taken was some government subsidized housing, moving in a few thousand Newcomers into apartment complexes that most humans didn't want to go near. And presto: instant plummeting real estate values. Humans had taken off from the area so fast that they'd left skid marks.

Undaunted, the Newcomers had displayed that incredible capability for work, learning, and initiative that would become their hallmark and, in time, would also become the thing that humans resented the most. Some found human backers. There were landlords, stuck with property that had been going nowhere, who decided to ignore the axiom against throwing good money after bad and fronted some of the more business-wise Newcomers in their various enterprises.

It seemed the sleazier the businesses, the better they did. Strip joints, sex palaces, and the like turned an extremely tidy profit. The appeal was interracial. When the Tenctonese had traveled through space, cooped up and enslaved on the ship that eventually crashed on earth, they had lived a very rigid and insulated existence. The freedom to follow their impulses once they had arrived on earth had triggered in some the baser instincts. Sexual freedom, and the privilege of ogling Tenctonese females openly displaying their wares, was like a narcotic to many. They worked that much harder to be able to afford frequenting such places.

And there were plenty of humans turning up at such places, too. The alienness was an irresistible lure to many an Earth male. How were they like Earth females? Where were the differences? It was an enticing guessing game, and anyone could play.

As the sexual tension bubbled through Little Tencton, other businesses began opening to support it. Food stores. Laundries. Housing that ranged from being rented yearly to being rented hourly.

As time passed, Little Tencton developed an almost schizophrenic personality. During the day, it was somewhat run-down, although no more so than other parts of Los Angeles. Newcomers eked out a living where they could, some holding genuine jobs while others settled for begging in the streets. Unlike other ghettos, though, Little Tencton actually attracted a fair share of tourists. It wasn't exactly the safest part of town, but that hint of danger just added to the appeal.

But night was when Little Tencton really came alive.

It was not a healthy sort of life. Indeed, it was the
sort of thriving life that one sees when one lifts a
rock.

But it was life.

It was a little after 1:00 A.M. The streets were fairly
quiet, with the silence punctured every time someone opened the entrance to a bar or strip joint.
During those moments you could hear shouting and
music and the sounds of raucous laughter before it
was cut off by the slamming door.

A car was cruising down the street. In it was a
plumbing supply salesman from out of town. It was
his first time in Los Angeles, and he was curious to
see Little Tencton.

On the one hand, he was disappointed. It looked
about as unappealing as any other lower scale part of
town in any city he'd been to.

On the other hand, he noticed the little things. The
graffiti, in particular, all written in that bizarre alien
language that looked like one of those lines that
tracks someone's heartbeat. And there were the store
signs as well, written in both English and Tenctonese.

Over on the corner was one place in particular
with a sign across it that made the salesman chuckle.
It read CLANCY'S MILK BAR. He'd heard that the
Newcomers were unaffected by alcohol, but could get
really tanked up on sour milk. Go figure.

By seeing these subtle hints of the alien culture
that existed in little Tencton, it all became that much
more real to the salesman. Hell, if the whole area had
been redone to look like the surface of some alien
planet, then it would have seemed hokey. Unbeliev-
able, like something out of that television show
about the bald captain and the android . . .

The door to the milk bar opened, and the salesman

41

saw his first Little Tencton residents. A man and a woman, looking down on their luck and shabbily dressed, were being ushered out of the milk bar. They didn't look especially happy about it, and they shook their fists and cursed loudly in Tenctonese.

The salesman had slowed for a light, and as he watched the minor drama, the door of the bar was slammed in the face of the indigent Newcomers. They continued to hurl profanities at the uncaring door. The salesman chuckled. It was fascinating to see how some forms of behavior seemed to cross all lines.

He was so caught up in the plight of the two indigents that he didn't hear the shouting and sounds of running feet that were coming from his left.

The light changed and he eased the car forward . . .

And plowed directly into a Newcomer.

And as if hitting a living being wasn't horrific enough, he caught a quick glimpse of a small bundle, wrapped in a blanket and being cradled in the Newcomer's arms.

A baby. Dear God, he'd hit a father and his baby.

The salesman took no time to wonder why a father and infant child were walking the streets of Little Tencton after midnight. Instead he slammed on his brakes.

The Newcomer bounced off the hood and fell to the right of the car. For a moment the salesman—a confirmed atheist—found himself desperately praying.

He started to open the door and called out, "Are you okay?"

The Newcomer stood up.

The salesman gasped and leaped back into the driver's seat. The Newcomer had to be six . . . no, seven feet tall. The baby was still safely cradled in his arms. The salesman had heard that Newcomers were tough, but even so . . .

The giant Newcomer staggered slightly, but otherwise appeared unhurt. The salesman couldn't quite make out the child in the alien's arms, but it, too, looked all right. Apparently the Newcomer had protected the infant child and taken the full force of the impact himself.

The giant shouted something incomprehensible.

It sounded like a record being played backward, with some sort of clicking sound tossed in. He shook his head signaling that he did not understand.

An air of desperation surrounded the giant, and panic lit his eyes. He started to speak again and then appeared to see something. Whatever it was, it sent him dashing off in the direction of the milk bar.

The salesman turned toward where the giant had been looking and spotted two men who were clearly in pursuit. One was a Newcomer, the other human.

They dashed around the car, barely affording the salesman a glance. For the next five minutes he sat and watched with stupefication. Every moment of it was permanently embedded in his memory, which was fortunate; because an hour later the salesman would be relating to the police every incredible moment of what he had witnessed.

The giant shoved past the two Newcomer transients the moment he became aware that they were of no use to him. He could smell the aroma of sour milk on their breath, and see the giddy blankness of their expressions.

It was an indication of his state of mind that he didn't turn and stand his ground. But the giant was a primal creature. Since he was being pursued, the only course of action that he could find it within him to take was to run. He had allowed a certain blind panic to overwhelm him—particularly when the vehicle he had been driving ran out of gasoline on the outskirts of Little Tencton.

When that had first occurred, he had thought himself safe. His ebbing fear had given way to exhaustion, and he had sunk down in a small, ramshackle shell of a burned-out building and rested there. The giant had clutched his precious cargo close to him, and every so often would peer down at her, his expression a mixture of love and awe.

He had no idea who he could trust, and no concept of where to go. He had stayed there, drifting in and out of slumber, for who knew how long.

He did not realize that Perkins had taken the opportunity to slip out of the back of the van and call in to his boss to relate all that had happened.

Over two hours later, Perkins, River, and Penn had finally connected up, and stealthily approached their target.

It had been the giant's light sleeping that saved him. As he had sat there, only half dozing, he had suddenly felt a warning deep within him. What the source of that warning had been, he could not say. All he knew was that he had suddenly snapped to full wakefulness, just in time to see River, Penn, and Perkins ten yards away and closing fast.

Immediately the giant was on his feet. With a quick sideways movement, he had slammed into a piece of wall. The wall didn't need much incentive to fall over, and what the giant provided was more than enough. The bricks and mortar fell, cascading in a pile of rubble and dust, driving the three pursuers back for the instant that the giant needed to get a head start.

The chase was on.

The giant had been developing a significant lead, his huge strides eating up distance. But he had made

the mistake of glancing over his shoulder to see just
how far ahead he had gotten, and that was when he
slammed into the car. He had only enough time to
see the shocked expression of the human behind the
wheel and then he'd gone down, clutching the infant
to his chest and absorbing the impact with his elbow
and shoulders.

It had taken him only a moment to catch his
breath, and then he'd been back up on his feet. He
had barely glanced at the human before running
toward the milk bar, seeking the help of the transients.

[*"Help me!"*] he had shouted. [*"Help me!"*]

Quickly he had moved on, and now the giant
began pounding on doors all down the street. Over
and over he called out [*"Help me! Help me!"*]

The thing that the giant, in his drive for survival,
did not realize was that in Little Tencton no one
helped anyone. It was never wise to stick one's spots
into someone else's affairs. The chances were that it
would just get you into more trouble than you
bargained for.

This was particularly the case when the supplicant
was as massive as the giant. Up and down the worst
street of Little Tencton, Diller Avenue, windows
were flying open and angered Newcomers were sticking their heads out. Many of them gaped at the size
of the being who was shouting for aid. Here was
obviously someone who was more than capable of
taking care of himself. Why in hell was he bothering
the neighborhood?

They shouted angrily at this clear breach of Little
Tencton etiquette.

[*"Get away from here!"*]

[*"Keep it quiet!"*]

[*"I'm calling the police!"*]

The latter threat should have been the key to

survival for the giant. In the hands of the police, there would be safety from his pursuers. But he wasn't thinking that way. To him, all the world was a strange and terrifying place. The only place where he might find safety would be among his own kind, and they were loudly and angrily spurning him.

He heard the pounding of feet behind him, and couldn't wait any longer. He did not attempt any dodges or clever darting down side streets. He lit out at a dead run like a sprinter. His state of mind did not permit him anything more elaborate.

As it happened, the giant was approaching the outskirts of Little Tencton. The street curved around and, in turn, served as a feeder into the interstate. The giant was, at that moment, dashing across an overpass. Below him, cars roaring by, was the highway. He had no particular plan. He just wanted to get away.

He just wanted to be left alone.

He wasn't to have the opportunity.

River stepped out from behind a lamppost that was along the overpass. In his hand was a syringe.

The giant stopped where he was, his eyes wide. He didn't seem to be breathing hard at all. River, for his part, was mildly fatigued, after running like a madman to circle around and cut the giant off.

His associates had performed their task perfectly. All that was left now was to rein in the giant.

He took a step forward, sounding as soothing as he could. [*"No one is going to hurt you"*] he said.

The giant didn't look as if he believed it for a moment. For every step that River took forward, the giant stepped back, and considering that the giant had a considerably longer stride, it meant that, given time, he would have easily outdistanced River.

But he didn't have the time.

Perkins and Penn had come up behind him, and now his retreat was blocked.

[*"Come with us"*] River said soothingly, and repeated, [*"No one is going to hurt you."*]

The giant hesitated, looking in all directions. It was impossible to tell whether he was weighing his options, or instead taking on the air of a trapped beast. If it was the latter, then he was going to be extremely dangerous to approach.

And at that moment, a sound floated through the air from a distance. The sound of police sirens.

It had been the plumbing salesman who had called from his car phone, alerting the police to the "Big Trouble in Little Tencton," as the newspapers would blare the next day. Naturally it had been the salesman; the Tenctonese population had been more than happy to be left alone.

The reasons for the police arriving, however, were not nearly as important to River, Penn, and Perkins as the fact that they were, indeed, coming. Suddenly their time had run out, and the chase that the giant had led them on was being abruptly terminated.

The giant seemed to make a decision. To the shock of the others, he suddenly knelt and lay the infant down on the sidewalk.

Penn took it as an indication that the giant was surrendering, and started forward.

But Penn had proceeded from a false assumption. The giant had simply resolved that the time had, indeed, finally come to take that long-delayed stand.

His attack was startling in its ferocity, overwhelming in its speed. Penn had gotten within arm's length, and that was more than enough for the giant. His huge arm snaked out, and for the second time within recent memory, Penn was airborne.

This time the giant's aim was on target. Penn

crashed into River, and the two Newcomers went down in a tangle of arms and legs.

Perkins, for his part, had circled around behind the giant, and he made a desperate grab for the baby. His reasoning for doing so was sound. A frontal assault on the giant would be suicide. If he could get his hands on the infant, he'd have leverage to use against the behemoth. Make him surrender. He was certain that the giant would do anything to avoid injury to the child.

The giant spun and spotted Perkins just before the human got his hands on the infant.

Seeing the child directly threatened in that fashion was more than the giant could take. Cornered and frightened, lashing out at everyone and everything, the giant was pushed over the brink.

His huge fist swung like a club, propelled by the giant's full weight and full fury.

The last thing Perkins thought as he saw the fist coming was, *This is going to hurt.* Actually, it didn't. He died before pain managed to register as his head practically exploded from his shoulders. Blood and gore fountained, splattering the giant's jumpsuit. Some of it landed on the infant, who was as serene as ever.

River and Penn were on their feet, and watched in morbid fascination as what was left of Perkins crumbled in a heap. Even the giant looked momentarily surprised at the result of his unrestrained strength, and the two smaller Newcomers took that opportunity to charge.

They came in fast from either side, hoping to confuse him. The sirens of the police were getting louder. Penn wrapped himself around the giant's right arm, but the giant shook him loose and then kicked him in the knee. For a human, a blow to that joint was painful enough. For a Newcomer, it was agonizing. Penn went down, clutching at his knee and moaning.

But River had gotten as close as he needed to, and with a frantic lunge he jammed the syringe into the giant's thigh.

All he needed was a second to inject the contents. The giant roared, not so much at the syringe—the prick of the needle was insignificant to him—but at the proximity of River. He shoved at River before the Newcomer could shove the plunger home.

River staggered back. The needle still stuck out of the giant's leg and River took one last shot at it. He charged forward, dodging under the giant's outstretched arms, and grabbed at the needle in order to send the contents racing through the giant's system.

The giant stumbled back, trying to get away.

He had forgotten where he was, and how much distance there was between himself and the guardrail.

The edge of the overpass had been designed to aid people of normal size. When the giant hit it, staggering back, his center of gravity was so high that the guardrail merely acted as a fulcrum. His feet left the ground and, with an infuriated roar of protest, he flipped over the rail and was gone.

River charged to the edge of the railing and looked over. He expected to see the giant's broken body lying on the roadway below. Instead, his face fell.

He couldn't believe it.

The giant had landed on the canvas-covered cargo of a passing truck. He was lying there, looking somewhat stunned, as the truck roared off headed south.

[*"Damn"*] muttered River.

Well, things hadn't been a total loss, at least. At least they still had the infant.

The infant would probably serve their purposes.

Not only that, but it guaranteed that the giant would come to them. There was no way that he would just leave the child behind. Sooner or later, he would seek it out, and then they would have him.

Penn was staggering to his feet as River turned toward the infant. He started toward the bundle, which was lying, without so much as a whimper, where it had fallen.

And then the police siren became deafening, and a black and white roared up over the overpass, headlights blazing and dome light spinning.

Covering the distance between himself and the baby could quite conceivably mean getting nailed. The Newcomer made the decision in a split instant . . .

And ran.

The moment Penn saw River take off, he immediately followed suit. The two Newcomers sprinted like rabbits toward little Tencton, where they knew they could vanish amidst the population with no effort at all.

The two cops leaped out of the car, not bothering to radio for backup since they knew, beyond any doubt, that by the time any more police arrived, the two perps would be long gone.

One of the cops, Officer Stern, went over to the adult male body that had been picked up by the car's headlights. He knelt down beside the body, and it was only at that point that he saw the full damage that had been inflicted. He grimaced at the body, because it looked as if someone had taken a jackhammer to the guy's skull.

"This guy's dead," he said, somewhat unnecessarily.

The other cop, Officer Ryan, was looking in dread at the small bundle that lay wrapped up on the ground. He pulled the blanket aside without a clue as to what he would see.

A face smiled up at him . . .

A face that he couldn't believe.

His mouth moved for a moment, and then he actually managed to get some sound out. Barely above a whisper, he said to his partner, "Hey, Dave, you gotta see this."

Stern went to Ryan's side, and together they stared down in amazement.

The darkness was suffused with a gentle glow.

And all was silent.

CHAPTER 4

"I SLIPPED ON some soap in the shower."

Sikes sat in his car outside the police station, the morning sun glowing down at him with disgusting enthusiasm. He glanced one more time in the mirror and then spoke once more, varying the emphasis.

"I *slipped* on some soap in the shower." He paused. "I slipped on some *soap* in the shower."

Yes. That was it. Definitely put the accent on the word *soap*. Somehow it seemed to ring of greater sincerity. That's what he needed to be. Sincere. Honest. Straightforward. That was always the best attitude to keep in mind when you were lying through your teeth.

He heard someone call out, "Morning, Sikes," and he started to turn reflexively to respond. This was not a good move; it caused a sharp stabbing pain to ricochet through him like a pinball. So he continued to stare forward and wave halfheartedly.

He waited until whoever had spoken had had

enough time to get wherever he was going. And then, slowly, so slowly, he opened the car door and eased himself out of it.

He stood stiffly, then reached back with his foot and kicked the door shut. It sounded like it had closed securely. He sure hoped to hell it had, because there was no way that he was going to turn around and take a look.

He turned the collar of his leather jacket up a bit to try and obscure the odd angle of his head. In addition, he was holding out some hope that the black and blue bruise that was prominent on his chin was likewise hidden to some degree.

He entered the police station, his arms swinging loosely in as jaunty a fashion as he could muster.

Naturally . . . *naturally* . . . the first person he ran into was a Newcomer.

Officer Sandy Beach gave Sikes a very odd look that could best be described as fish-eyed. Sikes tried to avoid returning his gaze, which wasn't all that difficult. All he had to do was turn his body, since his head was not presently capable of independent motion. He started to walk past the officer, when Sandy called out, "Hey, Sikes . . ."

Sikes sighed. He stopped and turned his entire body to face Beach. Beach laughed coarsely, and then he made a tsk-tsk gesture with his fingers. It was as if he'd caught Sikes red-handed in the cookie jar.

"What?" said Sikes. He tried to sound impatient, as if he didn't have a clue as to what Beach might be snickering about.

Beach folded his arms, dropping any pretense of being coy, but still looking pretty damned amused. "Tried to jockey a Tenctonese woman, eh?"

All right. This was the moment he'd been rehearsing.

"No. I *slipped* on some soap in the shower."

53

Beach grinned widely, and Matt cursed himself inwardly. That hadn't sounded convincing, even to Sikes. Probably because he'd put the accent on the wrong word. That was it.

"Sure," said Beach.

Sikes was about to continue his protest of innocence, but decided that there was no point. He might as well save his strength. If Beach was able to see through it that quickly, the chances were that this was going to be a pretty long day.

He turned and walked away, and Beach called out behind him, "Better get in sync! Or you'll end up in the hospital!"

Sikes made a mental note that when Beach—who was newly married—had a child, Sikes was going to be first in line with the jokes. If it was a boy, it was "Son of a Beach." A girl, and she was a "Beach on Wheels."

He had a dreadful feeling that he was going to be making lots of mental notes of revenge as the day wore on.

He walked quickly, his angled head and bruise not catching all that much attention from the human officers. They probably just assumed that he had been in a fight. Certainly someone in Sikes's line of work, and with Sikes's temperament, could be expected to walk into work with an obvious war wound or two every now and then. Sure. That was it. If only the damned Tenctonese could just keep their opinions to themselves . . .

His desk, which faced George's, was cluttered as always. And just as always, George's desk was immaculate and—even more irritating—George was at it, early as usual. How the hell did the guy do it? For that matter . . . why did he do it?

George was eating what appeared, at first glance, to be a doughnut. But at second glance it was quite clearly something repulsive, so much so that Sikes couldn't even get up the nerve to ask what it was. So he settled for a simple, "Hey, George," as he settled down at his desk.

George took one look at him and knew instantly. "Matt . . ."

Oh God, don't say it.

Ignoring Matt's unspoken plea, George continued, ". . . did you and Cathy try to copulate last night?"

To George Francisco, *tact* was a word that sounded like the past tense of tack. Other than that, it had no place in his vocabulary or his personality.

Sikes's frustration with himself, with Cathy, with George, and pretty much with every Newcomer who had ever lived, tried everything he could do to repress his hostility. "No! There was a bar of soap on the floor of the shower. I didn't see it. I took a step to get the shampoo and . . ."

George was staring at him with that irritating detective stare that had proven so useful in breaking down the obfuscations of suspects and perps. It was a decidedly uncomfortable feeling to have it directed at him.

He waved impatiently, causing a mild spasm in his neck. "Oh, never mind."

George was able to file comprehension of the term *never mind* right up there with *tact*. He tilted his head slightly, studying Sikes as if he were a microbe. "Hmmmm," he said thoughtfully. "Your injury is consistent with that of males who rush into sex without proper preparation."

Sikes was really starting to get pissed off. Proper preparation? That's what you made sure to take care of if you were painting a room or something. What the hell did that have to do with the sex act? Lovemaking should be spontaneous, should be . . .

He realized that he really, *really* did not want to

discuss it. Not with George, or Sandy Beach. Or even with himself.

He was so desperate to change the subject that he actually forced himself to stare at George's breakfast. "What's that disgusting thing you're eating?" he demanded.

George held it up proudly, as if he'd just snatched the brass ring on a merry-go-round. "Weasel."

Sikes's eyes widened. Quietly his hand felt for the rim of the garbage can, just in case he needed to heave. He'd already eaten breakfast, and he was starting to fear it might make a return engagement.

Undaunted by the slightly pasty shade that Sikes must have turned, George continued cheerfully, "Weasel, but pressed into a ring. They're new. You have your doughnuts. Now I have mine."

He knew better than to try and offer it to Sikes. Sikes was never interested in sharing. He dipped the "doughnut" into his tea and continued, "Excellent for dunking. They make a jelly weasel, too." He took a satisfied bite and smiled.

Sikes made a mental note not to stop in at a Dunkin' Donuts anywhere within ten miles of a heavily Newcomer-populated area. He gripped the garbage can firmly. If George said one more thing extolling the virtues of any doughnut made from anything other than nice, simple dough fried in lard, he was definitely going to heave.

And he might just do it in George's direction.

Sikes was spared that experience, however, because before George could continue with his praise of the jelly weasel, Albert walked up.

Albert Einstein was the Tenctonese janitor at the station. A short time back he had gotten married to a lovely young Newcomer named May Flowers who stood now beside him holding his hand. May looked so happy that her good mood threatened to burst out of her and spread through the squad room, ruining a perfectly good gloomy day for the somewhat intense police officers.

Albert Einstein wasn't paying any attention to Sikes this day, however—something for which Sikes was immediately grateful. "George, we want to ask you—"

But it was too good to last. He noticed Sikes belatedly, and he was staring with concern at Sikes's injuries.

"Sergeant Sikes . . . your neck. Did you try to copulate with a Newcomer?"

If his neck hadn't been in such pain, Sikes would have slammed his face against his desk.

George leaned back in his chair, looking extremely satisfied that Albert had come to the same conclusion that he had. "He says," George told him with clear skepticism, "that he fell in the shower."

This was all that Sikes was going to take. He did not like, in the least, being called a liar . . . particularly when he'd been lying. It made him feel as if he wasn't any good at it, and he had always prided himself on his ability to deceive. Hell, most of his relationships depended on it.

"That's what happened!" he said angrily. "And if you don't want to believe me, that's—"

And then he moaned because he had been looking much too quickly from George to Albert and back again. As a result, his neck spasmed again, and this time the pain was something fierce.

Albert was drawn to suffering like an auditor to a write-off. "I can help you," he said confidently.

At least he was confident. Sikes was not remotely so. Albert was walking behind him as Sikes said suspiciously, "What?"

"Just relax."

To Sikes's horror, Albert quickly put him in a

headlock. His eyes widened in panic. He looked to George for succor, but George was just sitting there impassively, with some fur from the damned weasel sticking out the edge of his mouth.

"Albert, no!" Sikes cried out. He was terrified that the youthful Newcomer was going to rip his head off.

Albert snapped Sikes's head around, quickly and efficiently and with a large measure of self-confidence. Sikes let out a compressed shriek of "Niiiiaaagh!"

He waited for pain to rip through every pore of his body. His skin would doubtless feel as if it were being flayed off. Every nerve ending was . . .

Was . . .

Nothing.

To Sikes's astonishment, there was nothing. Well, not quite. There was something. But it was nowhere on a par with what he had been feeling before.

Albert took a step back. "How's that?" he asked, his open hands still poised at either side of Sikes's face. For a moment it seemed to Sikes as if Albert was preparing for the possibility that Sikes's head might roll off its shoulders.

Slowly he brought his head in a circle. "Better," he admitted, and then quickly amended, "It's still sore, but I can move it."

As if delivering a public service message, Albert said sagely, "Sexual ignorance is a very dangerous thing."

"So is making comments like that around some-one who's armed," said Sikes. "Remember, Albert, I do have a gun."

"Yes, Matt, I think we all remember that," George said pointedly.

Sikes glared at him.

May wisely took that moment to take the conversation in an entirely different direction. "George," she said, "Albert and I want to have a child."

George looked amazed. A grin split his face from ear to ear or, at least, what passed for ears on a Tenctonese head. "Really? That's wonderful!"

Sikes was still rubbing his neck to work out the last of the kinks. "How?" he asked in a slightly distracted fashion. "You gonna adopt?"

May looked at Sikes as if he'd just dropped down from Mars . . . which was pretty ironic, considering who was looking at whom. "I'm going to conceive," she said matter-of-factly. "Why?"

Now Sikes felt completely flustered. He had been so certain that adoption was a reasonable assumption, based on what he had learned about Tenctonese physiology. That was the problem with these damned people. Every time he thought he had a handle on them, they came up with some new philosophy or some new little biological trick that sent him off kilter once more. Sometimes he had the paranoid feeling that George and his friends were making this up as they went, just to keep the earth guy off balance.

May was still staring at him, clearly expecting an answer to her question of "Why?" And now Albert and George were also regarding him with open curiosity.

"Uh . . . well." He scratched his chin and immediately winced, because he'd rubbed the sore spot. He tried to think of ways this day could possibly get worse, and nothing came to mind . . . which was a bad sign, since Sikes was a pessimist. Nevertheless, he pressed on gamely. "I mean, I know about New-comers. It takes two men to get one woman pregnant."

It wasn't a statement so much as a question. He

Peter David

looked expectantly at the three of them, and almost as one, they nodded. He felt a slight measure of relief. It meant that they weren't suddenly going to change the rules on him ("Two men? Matt, what an absurd notion! Where did you get that idea?" his paranoid fantasies had George saying.) Slightly buoyed, he continued, to make sure he understood things. "A Binnaum, the catalyst, right?"

Albert nodded.

"And a . . ." Here his command of Newcomer terminology wore out. ". . . a . . . whatchama-callit . . ."

"Gannaum," George said helpfully. He beamed. "You've been paying attention, Matt. Very good."

"Yeah, well, with everything that's been going on the past year, it'd be hard not to learn something," Sikes said. "But . . . okay, look. Albert's a Binnaum. He's supposed to go around, y'know, popping other guys' wives."

Albert and May winced slightly at the coarseness of the terminology, and now George was looking at Matt with an air of disapproval. "I mean," Sikes said, "Gettin' 'em ready so their husbands can make 'em pregnant."

At that, May smiled. She patted Albert on the forearm. "Yes. I'm so proud of him."

Sikes tried not to laugh. A job where you go around boffing other guys' wives while everyone looks on and smiles, and your own wife looks at you like you'd just pulled three orphans out of a burning building. Sometimes he thought he'd been born into the wrong species. Just to make sure he fully understood, he said, "*Albert* can't make anybody pregnant. He hasn't got the right . . ." He sought a better word and couldn't find it, and finished, ". . . juice."

"True," said George, not at all put off by Sikes's

60

phrasing. "That's why Binnaums rarely marry. May would need to mate with a Gannaum after Albert had catalyzed her."

May looked as if she was jumping out of her skin with excitement. She clearly had something else to say, and now she was coming out with it. "We want that Gannaum to be you, George."

George looked stunned. "Me?"

And Sikes felt relief swim over him. Relief on a variety of levels. Not only was he relieved that his understanding of Newcomer biology was not deficient, but also relieved that they were now back on his turf . . . namely, predicting how females were going to react in certain situations.

Sure, he'd made mistakes every now and then, but he knew George's wife, Susan, fairly well. Susan was not accustomed to being married to someone who went around having sex with other people's wives. And Sikes knew, with as great certainty as if a huge hand had materialized and written it out in flaming letters on the wall, just precisely how Susan was going to behave when she heard about this "blessed event."

"Ohhh boy," said Sikes.

George, utterly oblivious to his partner's reaction, found himself at a loss for words. But it wasn't out of any sense of concern over what Susan would say. In fact, he was so overwhelmed by sentiment that Susan hadn't even entered the equation for him yet. "I . . . don't know what to say . . ."

"I was Binnaum for your children," said Albert enthusiastically, which was no surprise to Sikes, because Albert said everything enthusiastically. "You'll be Gannaum for ours. It's so beautiful!"

George looked with fondness, and even humility, at the excited young couple before him. It brought back to him so much of what he was feeling the first time that he and Susan had decided to create a child, the young male who would grow up to be Buck Francisco. Emotion swelled through him, almost more than he could contain. Certainly the middle of the squad room was not the appropriate place for such displays, so he internalized as much as he could. With effort, he managed to say, "Albert . . . May . . . it will be a great honor. Thank you."

Warmly, the three of them touched temples in the traditional Tenctonese method of close exchanges.

Sikes stared at them in the way that one sees a four-car pile-up about to occur and knows that he is helpless to stave it off. "Ohhhhhhh boy," he said again.

He might as well have said nothing because they weren't paying attention to him at all, since they were so enraptured in the sentiment of the moment. They broke from their intimate interaction, and then May cleared her throat and said, "We better get back to work."

Albert was grinning widely, taking joy not only in the anticipation of being a father, but also in the genuine joy that he had evoked in George. George, for his part, nodded in agreement with what May had said, and the two young Newcomers moved off. As George sat back down behind his desk, he realized his face was wet. He pulled out his handkerchief and dabbed at the tears, knowing that it was important to maintain decorum in the squad room. Earth males were not particularly comfortable with sentiment so openly displayed. Just another one of those little emotional oddities that he'd learned to live with, if not actually understand.

He noticed that Matt was staring at him with a most peculiar expression. He lowered the handkerchief and looked back at his partner questioningly.

"Hey, uh . . . Studley," began Sikes. "Don't you think you ought to run this by the missus?"

It took George a moment to translate for himself just what in the world Matt was saying. English was, after all, a learned language. With two odd terms of address, (Studley, the missus) and the slang verb (run this by), it took him a moment to grasp Matt's question.

Then he understood. But he still did not comprehend.

"What do you mean?" he asked.

"Most wives . . . my ex, for example," he said, remembering with more than a touch of dread what had happened after his rather inappropriate behavior at a police convention in Chicago, "aren't particularly thrilled when their husbands have sex with other women." He had picked up a pencil as he spoke, and now, as a minor visual aid, he made a circle with his thumb and forefinger and was casually sliding the pencil back and forth through the space as he spoke.

Now George comprehended. But he didn't believe it, and he gave Sikes a look that could best be described as faintly patronizing.

"Matt, Susan does not have your human propensity toward jealousy."

Matt's pencil drooped.

"Don't give me that, George," Matt said, and then added, "She's a woman," in the same tone of voice he would have used to announce that the pin of a hand grenade had just been pulled.

George sat back, thinking for a moment. His partner was generally a good judge of human psychology. Now he was rendering judgments on Tenctonese psychology, and for that, of course, he was ill-equipped. Still, George owed him the courtesy of trying to give as much weight to his words as possible. He tried to view the subject from all sides, looking for an analogy from his previous experience. "I admit," he said slowly, "I don't know any Tenctonese wives who have faced this situation . . ."

Matt slapped his desk and then extended his hand, palm up. "There you go." He lowered his voice to a tone that was both confidential and filled with dread. "She's not gonna like it," he warned.

George was still having trouble accepting that something as eminently human as jealousy could possibly factor into this. Then he realized something that might give a small degree of merit—not much, but a small degree—to Sikes's warnings. "The only thing Susan *might* object to . . ."

Matt waited.

"I have to maintain a high level of bah\na fluid," said George.

It was a statement that had no meaning to Sikes at all. He stared at George questioningly, uncertain of what the ramifications of this "high level" stuff were.

Realizing that Sikes hadn't grasped the significance of it, George added, "We won't be able to have sex for a month."

Matt's face fell. "She's *really* not going to like it. I mean . . . . she has to be celibate for a month, so that you can store up enough joy juice to erupt like Vesuvius after thirty days? With another woman? There's not exactly an up side for Susan in all this, George. Do you see that?"

George waved dismissively. "Albert is practically family. He helped father our children. Susan couldn't possibly object!"

At this point, Sikes gave up. He knew he was right. The only thing to do now was to sit back and let George walk straight into the lion's den. And Sikes knew, beyond any doubt, that poor Francisco was going to get chewed up and spit out.

At that moment, Captain Bryan Grazer approached them.

Sikes had never been that wild about Grazer. Oh, once upon a time, Grazer had been a good cop. Okay, hell, a great cop. But since rising to the captaincy, Grazer had seemed far more occupied with the notion of furthering his own advancement than actually tending to the mundane, unglamorous job of catching bad guys. A cop liked knowing that his captain was going to be there to back him up, come hell or high water. But Sikes had the distinct feeling that if the water were getting high, Grazer would let any cop under his command go to hell. It seemed very likely that Grazer would cut any of his people loose if it became politically inexpedient to support them.

But Sikes kept his opinions to himself and tried not to let it affect too much the way that he dealt with the man. Especially since Grazer could make his life miserable if he wanted to.

Grazer was rapping a file folder against his leg as he walked, and when he got to their desks, he said a curt, "Francisco, Sikes," by way of greeting, and then handed the file to George. Grazer was not one for cheerful morning amenities. He wasn't even inclined to give Sikes a pat on the back about the good work they had done on their previous collar. That was old business, and it was time to move on to the new. "You got a homicide in Little Tencton."

George flipped open the file, skimming it with his usual speed. "The victim, William Perkins, was human . . ."

"Killed by a Newcomer," said Grazer.

Already Matt's antenna were up. Whenever you had a human slain by a Newcomer, you had potential for an explosive situation because of the racial aspect. It meant that whoever had done it was going to have to be nailed fast. And that wasn't likely. In Little Tencton, finding a Newcomer to rat on a Newcomer was always difficult. And finding a human who could accurately pick out one Newcomer from another was virtually impossible. If Sikes had a nickel for every description he had that went, "He was bald and had spots on his head," as if that was going to be of any use whatsoever, he could have retired ages ago.

So it was with nothing short of amazement that he reacted to the captain's next words when Grazer said, "According to witnesses—a plumbing salesman, in particular—the perpetrator was a giant."

It was a godsend. They were going after a Newcomer with a major distinguishing feature.

George, naturally, could not refrain from looking a gift horse in the mouth. He frowned and said, "That's odd. I've never heard of giantism among Tenctonese."

It was just like George, Sikes thought, to try and wreck a perfectly decent lead just because it was something outside of his own experience.

Meantime, George continued to read the file. "Perkins worked security for Dual Pharmaceuticals. We can start there." Then something else in the file caught his eye. "I didn't know that." He looked up at Sikes and Grazer and said, "Dual is owned by Hadrian Tivoli."

This was an earth-shattering revelation, the importance of which went right by the two human officers. They looked at each other, as if trying to get silent verification from the other that he wasn't the only one to whom this meant absolutely nothing.

Amazed that they could be unaware, George added the customary title in front of the name. "*Doctor* Hadrian Tivoli."

Matt tried to look as if this jogged his memory. Encouraged, George further prompted by saying, "He patented a genetic cure for diabetes back in '94."

"Right!" said Matt triumphantly. *"That* Hadrian Tivoli."

George looked to Grazer to see whether the captain now remembered. Grazer, for his part, was staring at Sikes, and Sikes made a face that indicated very clearly that he still had never heard of this Tivoli guy. But in matters like this, it was best to convince George that everyone was playing on the same field so that they could move on.

Grazer took the opportunity to move on as well. "An infant was found at the scene of the crime. Before you go to Dual, take a look at her."

There was something in his tone that prompted inquiring looks from Sikes and Francisco. And all that Grazer could say by way of explanation was, "She's . . . different."

He actually seemed shaken by it.

Moments later, Matt and George understood why.

The police station had set up a nursery, a small facility to be used for those situations where small children were brought if they'd been lost. It seemed more humane than making a child stew for hours in the squad room, in the midst of the flow of human sewage that cops were constantly bringing into the station house on their way to booking and processing.

There were two cribs, a TV and video player, a few games and old toys that had been donated by a local parish. And there was a changing table which, at that moment, was occupied.

Sikes and Francisco entered quietly, uncertain of

whether the baby they were supposed to see was
sleeping or not. Then they spotted a woman attendant by the changing table, finishing the diapering of
someone. Sikes could see the hint of little legs
kicking around.

"That her?" asked Sikes.

The attendant turned. She had on a police ID that
identified her as Willis.

She had a look of quiet amazement in her eyes.
Instead of saying anything, she simply nodded and
then indicated with a tilt of her head that they should
come over there.

They did so, but stopped about a foot away. Their
expressions shifted into flat-out astonishment when
they saw what was on the changing table.

The child was not a child, at least nothing in the
traditional sense. She wasn't human. But she didn't
look quite Tenctonese. Her head was abnormally
large in proportion to her body, and it was perfectly
hairless. But there were no signs of spots either. Her
large eyes seemed to be many colors at once, and
they studied the two detectives with open curiosity
that was tempered with what seemed an overwhelming intelligence. Her gaze seemed to drill into the
backs of the detectives' skulls, penetrate into their
private thoughts and examine them, turning them
over and over the way that a child would find endless
fascination in the most mundane of objects.

Her arms lay quietly at her sides. Even the mild
movement of her legs had ceased. She was perfectly
still, and it seemed to Matt, in his imaginings, that he
was looking at something not only not from this
world, but not from this dimension.

It almost seemed that the child was glowing. But
that was certainly a mere trick of the lighting in the
nursery. There was more to it than that, though. It

was as if the infant was illuminated from inside by some sort of spiritual light of inner peace. Peace, contentment, knowledge . . . it was . . .

"Unreal," breathed Sikes.

George was no less captivated than Matt, but he made a conscious effort to remain businesslike. He turned to Willis and said matter-of-factly, "Has a doctor examined the baby?"

Willis shook her head. "We're waiting for someone from county. Sometimes it takes a day or two."

George could not hide his surprise. It seemed obvious to him that a circumstance like this would require top priority for all parties. "A day or two?"

Willis gave a sad shrug. "The health care cuts . . . they're shorthanded." It was clear from her expression that she was not happy about it, but she was resigned to the notion that there wasn't a damned thing she could do. She turned her attention back to the infant. "She seems in good health."

That was an understatement. She appeared not only to be the healthiest individual in the room but quite possibly on the planet. George studied her, and although he tried to remain clinical, he was not successful in keeping the wonder from his voice. "Look at the size of her cranium . . . the absence of spots . . . those eyes . . ."

Willis seemed a bit disconcerted by the intensity of George's reactions. It was clear that she thought she had worked out some of the baby's oddities herself. "I thought that might be normal for certain Newcomers."

Matt looked to George for confirmation, but George shook his head. "I've never seen a Newcomer child like this. Try to get a doctor here."

Willis spread her hands in a "What do you want from me?" gesture, but Sikes and Francisco had

69

already walked out of the nursery. The attendant looked back down at her small charge.

The baby actually seemed to be laughing inwardly.

Sikes and Francisco walked down the corridor, both of them clearly waiting for the other to say something. Every step they took away from the nursery helped to diminish the incredible impact that the child had had on them.

"The way that kid was looking at us . . ." Sikes finally ventured, but he realized that he didn't have the words to continue along that line. Instead he said, "You think her parents abandoned her? I mean . . . let's face it, George. That kid's a little spooky, and some people simply might not be able to deal with it."

George shook his head firmly. "It's not that the Tenctonese pregnancy isn't a conscious choice. Children are always wanted."

"Yeah," said Sikes grudgingly, fully aware of everything involved in producing a Tenctonese child. Kids didn't come to Newcomers as a result of impetuous grabbings in the back of a car, or perhaps a leaky condom. They were indeed fully planned projects from the get-go.

And that prompted him to snicker. George looked at him.

"What?"

"Well . . . I was just thinking about Albert and May," said Sikes. "Look, George, if you're smart, you'll break it to Susan as gently as you can. Better yet . . . take a getaway for the weekend. Have a real good time. Get some sheets smoking, and after you do, you can drop it on her that that's going to be it for a while. If you're really lucky, she'll be lying there basking in afterglow, and you can get her to agree to just about anything."

George looked at Sikes skeptically. "I'm simply going to tell her," he said.

Sikes gave a loud sigh. "You can't save a patient who doesn't want to live," he said.

George smiled patronizingly. "Believe me, Matt. Susan will be overjoyed. Don't you believe me?"

"George," said Sikes, patting his partner on the shoulder, "I believe you as wholeheartedly as you believed I slipped on soap in the shower."

CHAPTER 5

THE ADVERTISING AGENCY of Fairchild and Associates was located in one of the trendier parts of town. It was a small firm, but it was growing, particularly since they had landed the account of a nationally known chain of ice cream outlets.

Susan Francisco was bent over a drawing board, working up a layout for a projected series of newspaper ads. She was trying to develop a new and interesting way to work a coupon into the advertisement. She stared at it for a moment, and then began making adjustments when she heard a familiar clacking of high heels. She shared the small office with an extremely flamboyant copywriter named Jessica Partridge. ("My professional name, darling," she had once said. "Jessica Beerblatt just doesn't have it, *capeesh?*" Susan had not been entirely sure just what "it" was, but she gamely took Jessica's word for it.)

Jessica didn't simply enter a room. Usually, she

enveloped it. This time was no exception as Jessica swept into the office, dressed in a dazzling array of lavenders and silks that on anyone else would not have worked. But on her . . .

. . . Well, truthfully, on her it didn't work either. But Jessica was so powerful a personality that she seemed above trivial notions such as taste or style. In fact, she created her own style.

"Susan!" she called out as if she hadn't seen her coworker in years. She made puckering noises from afar. "Kissy kissy."

-Matt Sikes had once happened to be by when Jessica came bursting in in her usual fashion. That "kissy kissy" thing of hers had prompted him to nickname her Miss Piggy, a reference that Susan didn't quite understand.

"Hi, Jessica," she said, trying not to let her ostentatious office mate distract her too much from the job she was concentrating on.

"I love that dress!" she said, pointing at the simple white with blue trim outfit that Susan was wearing. But before Susan could voice thanks, Jessica continued unabated, "But the orange scarf . . ."

Susan touched the scarf with concern. It had been a gift from George, and she tended to wear it more out of sentimental value than with any thought given to matching her ensemble. Susan was insecure enough to feel that she was always one step behind when it came to Earth fashions. "You don't like it?" she said.

"Ouch," said Jessica, implying that the very sight of such an obvious mismatch had wounded her. She reached up and took one of the two scarves that enveloped her—a blue one, matching the trim on Susan's dress—and handed it to Susan. "Here. Take mine."

"No . . ."

"Go ahead, take it," said Jessica more insistently.

Susan did so, very carefully removing the scarf she was wearing, folding it and putting it in her purse, and replacing it with the one that Jessica had presented her. She hated to admit it, but it did go better with the dress.

Jessica studied her appraisingly. "You know, if you had ears, I have the perfect earrings for this outfit."

"How about if I wear them in my nose?" said Susan.

At that, Jessica laughed heartily. The problem was, Susan had been serious. Earrings through the nose were not an uncommon fashion trend among Tenctonese women. But the clear amusement that Jessica displayed upon hearing Susan's suggestion somehow made Susan feel uncomfortable to admit that she hadn't been joking. So she joined in the laughter, just to show that she was very aware of what a great kidder she was.

And then Jessica switched gears, stifling a wide yawn. For a moment, Susan thought that somehow she was boring her. Then Jessica stretched and said, "I'm soooo tired." Her voice dropped to a confidential tone. "I was up all night talking Patty Lockner off a ledge."

Susan was horrified. Patty was a sweet young woman who was Ms. Fairchild's assistant. She was always so upbeat and persevering. She hardly seemed the suicidal type. "She was going to *kill* herself?"

"Oh, don't be so literal," said Jessica.

Susan blinked. "Oh. Uhm . . . well, I was just remembering when George had to talk someone off a ledge, and . . . well, it was pretty literal . . ."

"Cops' wives." Jessica sighed. "No, Suze, sweetheart. Patty was just very, very depressed. She came home and found Doug with another woman."

Now this was serious dirt. The interrelationships and affairs of humans were so diverse and so involved that Susan found them endlessly fascinating. She leaned forward. "Really?" she said breathlessly.

"He was in bed," Jessica paused dramatically, "with his dental hygienist."

This time Susan chose to try and make a joke deliberately. "What an odd place to clean his teeth."

This prompted both of the women to giggle uncontrollably. The fire was fanned more by Jessica's loudly assuring her, "Baby, she wasn't anywhere *near* his teeth." It took them quite a few minutes to bring themselves in check.

"You want to hear something really crazy?" said Jessica. "You're kidding around, but Doug actually tried to act like he really was there on business, at least, some business other than funny business. He tried to give Patty some bushwa . . . said the hygienist was there to fit him for a temporary crown."

"No!"

"Do you believe the gall?" said Jessica tartly. "I'd've crowned the guy permanently if it'd been up to me."

Susan shook her head. "Human men are so strange."

There was no way that Jessica was going to let Susan feel that she was somehow removed from the irritations that beset every woman she had ever known. "Human? Come on, sweetheart. Get with the program. All men are the same."

"George would never do something like that," Susan said, firmly.

Jessica sat down in her chair, spinning it around so that she straddled it. "Of course he would," Jessica told her. "There isn't a man alive who wouldn't do anything . . . *anything* . . . to satisfy that little snake in his pants."

"What snake?"

"The magic monkey. The wonder weasel. You know, the little snake." She thrust her hips forward slightly.

Then Susan understood. She gasped in mortified laughter. "Jessica!" She wasn't sure which she was more embarrassed about—calling it a snake or referring to it as "little." She thought about correcting this unfair adjective immediately, but decided that it wouldn't be appropriate.

Jessica was undeterred. "My Frank is the same. I have to watch that hose head every minute of the day."

There was no way that Susan was buying in to this. "Not George," she said with utter serenity. "He'd never have sex with another woman."

Jessica rolled her chair forward slightly. "Baby," she said with the air of a woman who's seen it all, "let Jessica teach you the facts of life. Are you listening? Can you hear with those things?"

Susan nodded.

"Men," said Jessica, with unmistakable disdain in her voice, "are nothing but horny toads."

"Horny toads?" Between the snakes, monkeys, weasels, and now toads, Jessica certainly seemed to be obsessed with wild life.

"That's right," said Jessica. "And there isn't a one of 'em who wouldn't cheat on his wife if he had the chance."

Susan didn't believe it for a moment.

She and George had far too much history between them. They had been brought together under the most difficult of circumstances. Their existence on the slave ship had quickly taught them something: that you had to pick who you trusted very, very carefully, because trusting the wrong person—a snitch, perhaps, or an undercover agent of the Overseers—could have very fatal consequences.

Susan trusted George. Every fiber of her being told her that. And she knew that no matter what, he would never be unfaithful to her.

Never.

Except . . .

Well, Jessica was far more conversant in the ways of males than Susan. And . . .

But those were earth males. George was not a human.

Except he spent eight to ten hours a day, or more, involved with humans every single day. Wasn't there the slightest possibility that some of that might rub off on him?

No.

Never.

Except . . .

CHAPTER 6

THE OFFICE OF Dual Pharmaceuticals was ultramodern, a tower of glinting black glass and steel. At the upper stories, passing clouds were reflected in it. It reminded Sikes of the Ewing Oil Building in the TV show "Dallas."

As they got out of the car, George seemed somewhat nervous. For a moment Sikes thought that maybe his partner had been giving some serious thought to the whole business with Albert and May, and was finally getting apprehensive about approaching Susan.

But instead, George seemed completely preoccupied with the stupid building.

"I wish I'd shined my shoes," he said apprehensively. Sikes glanced at George's shoes. They were already more polished than any shoes Sikes had ever worn in his life, and that included his wedding day. George turned to face Sikes and asked, "Is my tie straight?"

"What's the big deal?" asked Sikes.

George's attitude made it clear that, as far as he was concerned, this should be self-evident. "We're meeting Hadrian Tivoli. If you were going to see Jonas Salk, you wouldn't want to look your best?"

"Oh, well, sure, Jonas Salk . . ."

"There? You see?" said George, triumphantly.

"Now he was . . . what? Third baseman for the Dodgers, right?"

"Who?"

"Jonas Salk. Batted .380 in the World Series?"

George blew an irritated whistle through his lips. "Never mind," he said in exasperation.

He took quick strides and Matt practically had to run to keep up with him. "George, for cryin' out loud, I was kidding. Okay? Salk, the vaccine guy. Right?"

"Yes," said George, with some slight relief. "It's good to know you're not completely devoid of historical knowledge, Matt."

"No, not completely. All I'm saying, George, is that we can't lose sight of the fact that we're here to question somebody in connection with a murder investigation. I don't care who it is we're questioning, we've got to maintain professional distance. We can't let ourselves get caught up in whatever glamour or reputation that person might have. Otherwise there are going to be questions that don't get asked and maybe, just maybe, crimes that don't get solved."

George fixed him with an icy stare. "The time we questioned that female rock singer, Sheila E., I believe she called herself. Your participation in the interrogation was limited to several buckets of drool, as I recall."

"Yeah, well, that was different."

"How?"

"She was hardly wearing anything."

"Since I anticipate that Dr. Tivoli will be fully dressed, I assume that I'll be able to control myself."

"Sure, George. Whatever you say." Sikes was too busy pulling up pleasant memories of that particular case involving Sheila E.

They entered the lobby. There were messengers hustling in and out, and some employees already heading out to an early lunch. The odd pairing of Francisco and Sikes brought glances of mild interest from some people going in or out, but no reaction beyond that.

There was a guard table at the far end of the lobby, and two guards were seated at it. Sikes and George noticed immediately that one of the guards had clearly had a rough time of things lately. He was wearing a large bandage over his nose.

Sikes was already flashing his shield as he and Francisco approached, but he decided to start things in a more conversational manner. "What happened to the honker, pal?"

"I slipped on a bar of soap in the shower," said the guard.

Sikes grinned significantly at George. "You see? It does happen every now and then, doesn't it."

George rolled his eyes.

Sikes turned back to the guards. "I'm Sergeant Sikes. This is my partner, Francisco."

The guard with the unadorned face extended a hand. "Hudson River. I'm Dr. Tivoli's chief of security. This is my associate, Bic Penn."

Sikes nodded deferentially to both of them. By this point in his life he'd gotten rather practiced in not bursting into laughter upon hearing Newcomer names. It made the investigative process that much easier when you didn't laugh in people's faces.

"We called ahead?" said George.

River nodded and gestured toward a private elevator. "I'll take you to him."

They stepped into the elevator, with River leading the way. He pushed a button that was labeled simply "P" and the elevator started upward.

"So is this part of some sort of fund-raising thing for the police?" asked River neutrally.

"Not exactly. It's a homicide investigation," said George.

River looked taken aback. "Homicide? You mean someone was killed."

"Yeah, that's generally how homicide investigations start," said Sikes, hoping he didn't sound too sarcastic and knowing that he did.

"Would you mind telling me the details?"

Sikes stared at him. "Are you going to be accompanying us to our meeting with the doctor?"

"Yes."

"Then why should we repeat ourselves?" said Sikes, reasonably. "We'll fill in the Doc and you all at the same time. How's that for efficiency?"

River merely nodded.

The elevator doors opened onto a spacious office, with an interior design that was very much along the lines of the exterior of the building. A Newcomer receptionist was seated outside, and Sikes began to wonder if he was the only human in the entire building. The receptionist gestured for them to enter the inner office, and they did so.

From behind a large desk rose the formidable form of Dr. Hadrian Tivoli. He appeared to be middle-aged (it wasn't always easy to tell with Newcomers), and he had a force and presence that simply could not be ignored. Hudson River stood to one side as Sikes and Francisco firmly shook hands with the doctor.

Remembering Matt's cautions, George tried not to

gush. He was only partly successful. "I want you to know what an honor it is to meet you, Doctor," he said, pumping Tivoli's hand.

"Thank you," said Tivoli. His voice was low and seemed to rumble throughout the office. He indicated the two chairs in front of the desk and said, "Please."

As Sikes and Francisco sat, he continued graciously, "Would you like some coffee? Herb tea?"

"No, thanks," said Sikes. He glanced at George, who was still sitting there with an enormous respectful grin on his face. It was clear to Sikes that he was going to have to keep the show moving. He pulled out a notepad and flipped it open to where he had jotted down the few facts they had about the case. "Now as we mentioned to you on the phone, William Perkins, a security guard in your employ, was found dead in Little Tencton last night."

"Yes. A shocking business," said Tivoli.

Sikes glanced around to see River's reaction. His face was immobile. He turned back to Tivoli. "Do you have any idea what Perkins was doing the night he was murdered? Who he was with?"

"I have very little contact with the security staff," replied Tivoli. He indicated River. "Hudson might know."

But River shook his head slowly. "Perkins was off duty. His time was his own."

Well, River certainly didn't sound all that choked up, Sikes observed. Guy just learned one of his underlings was killed, and handled it pretty damned well. Could be that Tivoli had already filled River in on what the investigation involved, and River was just being coy on the elevator. Or maybe River just didn't like humans and really didn't care about Perkins's demise.

Now George stepped in. "Witnesses say the man

who killed him was a huge Newcomer. A giant. They say that two other Newcomers and Perkins were chasing him."

Tivoli looked at them skeptically. "A giant?"

Sikes was still not quite willing to move his attention away from River. "Was Perkins ever seen with anyone fitting that description? Did he ever mention anyone?"

"No," said River. "I'm sure I'd remember. A conversation involving a Newcomer giant . . . that would stick in my mind, I know."

George sensed his partner's interest in River's responses. He'd generally learned to trust Matt's instincts when it came to such things. "The suspect was carrying a Newcomer infant that was left at the scene. Do you have any idea who that child might belong to?"

River looked a bit bored by the whole thing. "No."

"Haven't the parents come forward?" asked Tivoli with genuine concern. It reminded George of the true humanitarianism that flooded through the veins of this very great individual.

"Not yet," said George. "The child is . . . unusual."

"How so?"

"Her head is disproportionately large with no spots. She appears highly intelligent, but she doesn't move or make any sounds."

Tivoli leaned back, giving it some thought. His fingers steepled under his chin. "Has she been examined? Maybe it's a congenital syndrome."

"We're still waiting for a doctor."

Tivoli rose from his chair. He turned his back to them and walked slowly toward one of the large windows that overlooked Los Angeles. He stood there, staring out, his hands clasped behind his back.

The esteemed doctor appeared to have zoned out

for the moment, and Sikes took the opportunity to pursue his questioning of River. Every question had been a dead end, but he couldn't shake the feeling that there was something there. "You ever have any trouble with Perkins on the job?"

River shook his head. "He was a model employee."

Sikes tried to frame a follow-up question, but nothing came to mind. Neither River nor Tivoli had really given him a useful enough answer on anything to develop a follow-up question. It's not that they had been hiding anything that he could tell, or had stonewalled him. It's just that they had not been especially helpful in providing information.

He pulled his card out of his jacket pocket and handed it to River. "If you think of anything that might help us, give me a call." He didn't hold out much hope for it. River didn't strike him as the kind of guy who would suddenly say, "Wait! How could it have slipped my mind? I completely forgot to tell Sergeant Sikes about Perkins's ties to organized crime!"

"Sure," said River, taking the card.

Tivoli, meantime, turned back and said slowly, "If the parents aren't found, we could provide care for the infant here. Our research is focused on genetic defects in both humans and Newcomers. Perhaps we could help her."

George smiled gratefully. It was exactly the sort of thing he had expected Tivoli to say. "That's very kind of you. The baby's going to be placed temporarily in a foster home. But I'll tell Social Services of your offer."

"However you wish to handle it, Sergeant," said Tivoli. "After all, you are the professionals."

* * *

" 'You are the professionals.' Wow," said Albert. His eyes were wide as, back at the police station, George related the details of his meeting with the esteemed Dr. Tivoli.

Sikes, for his part, was busy doing his system of filing, which consisted of taking all the papers that he didn't know what to do with, and shoving them into a desk drawer until he could get around to it.

"Thoughtful and yet humble," George intoned. "That's how the truly great ones are."

"Yeah, and right after that, he turned water into wine," said Sikes.

George looked at him reprovingly. "Sarcasm wasn't called for, Matt."

"Well, something was," replied Sikes.

George picked up a phone message that had been left on his desk. "I think this is for you, Matt. Put on my desk by mistake. Someone named Kris is asking about your date for the Perelli dinner?"

"Oh yeah," said Sikes.

"I assume you'll be sitting with Susan and me."

Sikes looked up and couldn't quite hide his surprise. "You're going?"

"Certainly," said George.

"But you've never even met the guy!"

"You've spoken most respectfully of him," said George, reasonably. "Also, his reputation as a police officer precedes him. I think it only proper that every able-bodied ranking officer turn out for his retirement dinner."

"Uh-huh."

Sikes seemed very distracted by the entire notion, and George was about to ask why when Albert interrupted with an amused, "Whoever Sergeant Sikes's date is, I bet it won't be the Newcomer he was trying to copulate with last night."

George looked at him curiously. "Will you be taking Cathy as your date, Matt?"

"I didn't say I was trying to copulate with her last night, George!"

"There was someone else?" George asked in surprise.

"For the last time, I—"

"Slipped on a bar of soap in the shower," Albert and George intoned together. Albert grinned and moved off to complete his duties for the day.

"As for Cathy, well . . ." said Sikes, "I haven't decided yet."

"I hope you won't be holding the difficulties you encountered last night against her."

Sikes leaned forward, almost into George's face. "I'd watch what I'd say if I were you, George. You gotta go home and tell Cathy about your little mercy boff with May. And we'll just see how *your* jaw looks in the morning."

"You," said George calmly, "have no faith. None at all."

"Oh yes I do, George. I just have faith in different things than you."

"I have faith in Susan."

"So do I," replied Sikes. "So what we got here, George, is a crisis of faith. And woe to you, unbeliever, for most surely, you're gonna be in over your spotted head."

CHAPTER 7

Like a homing pigeon, he had returned.

Through the streets of Little Tencton lurched the giant. Returning to the site where he had lost his precious cargo had been easy. The truck had gone a far piece on the interstate before pulling over to a rest stop. And while the trucker had been inside, the giant had simply climbed down from the freight area and climbed into the cab.

The cab of the truck had been even smaller than the cab of the vehicle he had previously driven. But he had managed by the simple expedient of ripping out the seat so that he had extra room. It had required that he drive in a semicrouched position, his back up against the interior of the cab. But he had barely even noticed the physical demands put upon his huge frame. Nothing was important to him except recovering the only thing in the world that mattered to him.

He had ditched the truck by the side of the road a mile before arriving back at Little Tencton. Some deep need for stealth had kicked in, warning him that driving the stolen vehicle any longer than necessary meant possibly attracting the notice of the police. Not that being seven feet tall was the easiest thing to hide either. But at least he could hide among alleyways and shadows. You couldn't hide a truck, no matter how clever you were.

Now he roamed the night streets, driven by the irresistible, all-consuming need to find what he had lost. He stumbled about aimlessly, lost and alone. He knew better than to try and bang on doors or seek help from other Newcomers. They had already made painfully clear to him that there was no one he could turn to.

He had not come to Little Tencton with any sort of plan. Instead, he was only motivated by a craving he could not fulfill. And as hours passed, and it became more and more evident to him that he did not have the tools or resources to satisfy that craving, he became seized by black and blinding despair.

He stumbled down the darkened streets and then, shaken by helpless rage, he lashed out at the first thing that was at hand. In this case it was a steel mesh trash can. He grabbed it up, wielding it high over his head, and then turned and threw it. It sailed through the air and crashed into a parked car, cracking the windshield and scratching up the paint job on the hood.

It also set off the car alarm. The car began to scream, a high-pitched, annoying shriek. The sound assaulted the giant, and he staggered momentarily under it.

Everything had turned against him. Humans. Tenctonese. And now even inanimate objects like cars were tormenting him. It was too much for him to take. With an infuriated bellow, he grabbed the underside of the vehicle.

It was a small car, which didn't do anything to diminish the strength involved for what happened next. The giant grunted, roared, and then pulled his full strength into it. The car tilted slightly, and then faster. The axles squealed, and the giant flipped the car over. It landed, like an inconvenienced turtle, on its roof, amidst a grinding of metal. Its wheels were facing upright and were spinning slightly from the impact.

The alarm continued unabated. If anything, it had even more to howl about now than a mere broken windshield.

A block away, Hudson River and Bic Penn—no longer in their security guard uniforms—turned away from the side street they were about to go down. They had heard two things, the shrieking of the car alarm combined with the unmistakable bellowing of the giant. The alarm seemed to be echoing everywhere, but the scream of the giant had pinpointed it.

"Over there!" shouted River, and he dashed in the direction he'd pointed. Penn was hot on his heels.

They arrived in time to find a Newcomer bum poking tentatively at the overturned car. He was examining the destruction with the fascination of a child discovering a dead animal. Penn and River looked around desperately. They knew that only the giant would have been capable of such a feat of strength and anger. But their target was nowhere in sight.

River pointed and said, "Let's try down there."

They took off at a fast run down the side street. River knew it was a long shot. The giant might already be a mile or so from the scene.

They did not notice the alleyway that they ran past. An alleyway that was filled with garbage and debris . . .

And in the darkness of the succoring shadows, the giant sat. His long legs were curled up against his chest, his massive arms holding them close. He stared up at the night sky . . .

And sobbed piteously.

CHAPTER 8

GEORGE FRANCISCO ALWAYS looked forward to the family interaction that occurred around the dining room table. After a typical workday of dealing with —as Sikes so generously called them—the scum of the earth, George needed these nightly groundings back in the simple virtues of family.

Yes, that was all they were. A nice, simple, typical family.

George emerged from the kitchen into the dining room, a plate of raw meat carefully balanced on one hand, silverware clutched in the other. He called over his shoulder to his son, "Buck? There's a jar of thymus sauce in the fridge. Would you bring it? Oh, and a spoon for the roundworms," he added as an afterthought.

He glanced around. "Where's your mother? And Emily?"

* * *

Upstairs in the bedroom, Susan checked her appearance in the mirror one more time.

All that discussion about the loyalty of husbands had gotten Susan somewhat edgy. She knew, beyond any question, that she had every reason to trust George and no reason not to. Still, the problem that women had with their husbands straying was certainly not something that Jessica had fabricated. Before she'd gotten a job, Susan had seen many daytime television programs—talk shows, soap operas—and spouses sleeping with people other than their mates appeared to be a preoccupation.

She wondered if there wasn't something that she should be doing to make sure that George didn't get—what was the word?—a roving eye.

Originally she had put on a totally comfortable sweatshirt and jeans. But now she had changed to one of her shorter skirts and a loose green blouse that she knew George liked in particular. It wasn't exactly a come-hither outfit, which wouldn't have been appropriate during a family dinner. But it was enough to draw some appreciative looks from her husband, that was certain. And later on the evening, well . . . who knew?

She smiled into the mirror and then walked out of the bedroom and down the hallway.

She heard George's voice floating up the stairs. "Susan, are you up there? And Emily?"

"Coming down, George!" she called back, and paused at the door to Emily's room. She rapped authoritatively. "Emily. Dinner."

Instead of the door to Emily's room opening, the bathroom door opened instead. Emily emerged with a towel wrapped around her, having just stepped out of the shower. "Two minutes, mother. I'll be down in two minutes."

Emily seemed to be walking a little oddly, as if

reluctant for her mother to see her back. Susan frowned and said, "Are you all right? Have you injured yourself?"

"I'm fine. Really." She sidled past her mother, and then Susan saw them. The startled gasp from her tipped Emily to the fact that her secret was out, and she turned to face her mother.

"I know, I know."

Susan's hands went to her mouth. "My little girl!" She spread her arms out. "Come here. Let me—"

"Aw, mother," pleaded Emily, stepping back. "Let's not make a big deal about this, okay? Pleeeease?" She entered her bedroom and closed the door firmly, leaving Susan feeling flushed with mixed emotions—a little sad, a little joyful, and a little old.

George looked up as Susan trotted down the stairs into the living room. He noticed immediately that she looked very alluring this evening, and was about to say so when he was distracted by the expression on her face. Usually he could read whatever mood she was in, but this time he was getting very conflicting messages.

She did not leave him in confusion for long.

"You're not going to believe this. I just saw Emily getting out of the shower . . ."

"I don't find that difficult to believe at all. Emily is a very clean child," said George.

She gestured impatiently because George wasn't understanding immediately. "Her potniki spots are coming in."

"No!"

The potniki spots were something very crucial for every Tenctonese woman. Matt Sikes had discovered that the previous night. His close encounter with Cathy's potniki had ended up with his getting a stiff neck and blackened jaw.

93

Susan indicated the small of her back. "She has a beautiful little swirl right here."

She sat as George finished putting out the silverware. He had totally forgotten to compliment Susan on how good she looked. By this point he was caught up completely in this startling new development. "What color? The same as her head?"

Buck walked in. He was cradling his baby sister, Vessna, in one arm. Vessna, her firm little grip already well-developed, had her tiny fingers wrapped securely around the spoon for the roundworms. Buck was carrying a jar of thymus sauce in his free hand, and he set it down on the table. He worked on pulling the spoon from Vessna's grip, and was amused when the infant wouldn't give it up immediately.

In answer to George's question, Susan said, "No. More auburn."

George sat opposite her and said wistfully, "Just like my mother."

Emily trotted in, her body still damp from the shower and her clothes sticking to her. George looked up at her and said proudly, "Our little girl is becoming a woman."

Emily moaned loudly and shot a furious glance at her mother. Susan shrugged and smiled.

Buck, having placed Vessna in her bassinet, glanced around. "What do you mean, Dad?"

He pointed at Emily. "Her potniki are coming in."

The young Tenctonese girl stomped her foot in irritation. It was so aggravating. Here she was, genuinely annoyed, and her parents found her annoyance . . . cute.

"It seems like only yesterday you got your droonal flanges," Susan said in a melancholy voice.

Emily sat down with enough force to rattle the silverware. "Could we *please* talk about something else?"

Her mother reached over and rested a hand atop hers. "It's nothing to be ashamed of."

Not to put too fine a point on it, Emily repeated, "Puh-*leeze.*"

George took some food, scooping it onto his plate, and decided to take his daughter up on her pleas. Besides, there was certainly something of interest to everyone to be discussed. "All right," he said agreeably. "I have some wonderful news."

Emily looked heavenward and breathed a silent *Thank you* for her father's decision to change the subject.

"Albert and May," continued George, "want to have a baby."

"Oh, that *is* good news!" said Susan cheerfully. "Are they going to adopt?"

"No," said George. He remembered Matt's warnings, but ignored them. After all, who knew Susan Francisco better? The unmarried, divorced, and bruised Matt Sikes? Or Susan's own husband? "They've asked me to father the child."

He had been looking down as he cut his food, but he sensed—even before he looked up—that the temperature to his immediate right where Susan was sitting had just dropped by about ten degrees. He turned his gaze on her.

He had never seen an expression like that one on her face before. And he wasn't exactly thrilled to see it now.

"What do you mean, George?" Each word was spoken very individually, with a slight pause between each one.

It was as if she were giving him the opportunity to say, "They've asked me to father the child, but of course, I said no."

Which, of course, wasn't at all what he was going to say.

"I'm going to serve as Gannaum." He tried to sound as pleasant as inhumanly possible. But there was just enough of a hint of fact in his voice to make it clear that this was not a topic that he was throwing open to the floor for discussion.

Buck grinned broadly. "Cool." Emily was also smiling.

Susan looked around at them, feeling that if they looked so chipper about this, then maybe there was some positive aspect to it that she had not quite caught on to yet. "Wait a minute," she said, feeling a desperate need to clarify things. "You're going to have sex with May?"

"No duh, Mom," said Emily, using that annoying irony that only preteens can muster. "How else?"

Encouraged by the positive and enlightened reactions of his offspring, George said to them—but also, and mostly, to Susan—"Isn't it wonderful that I can help them like this?"

"I don't think it's wonderful," said Susan, so quickly that the words spilled over each other. "I think it's highly . . . inappropriate."

Her entire family stared at her.

George couldn't believe it. The thought that Matt could have so accurately, and easily, been more correct about Susan's reaction than George possibly would have credited, was simply overwhelming. Unable to muster any sort of coherent reply, he simply echoed her last word. "Inappropriate?"

And that was when, as far as George was concerned, his beloved wife completely lost her mind.

Her voice went up in alarm as she said, "Actually, it's . . . perverted! Gannaums don't go around servicing the wives of Binnaums . . . who aren't supposed to get married anyway!"

"It happens," said George lamely.

"When?! Name me one time!" She stuck an upraised finger in his face.

He pushed her hand aside and admitted, "All right, it's unusual. But I don't see why it's perverted."

She slammed her fists down with such force that she rattled everything on the table. "You're having sex with Albert's wife!"

"Albert had sex with you!" shot back George. "You didn't object to that!"

Emily and Buck were astounded. Whenever their parents argued, it was usually about boring stuff like money. But arguing about sex! This was incredible! Usually stuff like this only happened on television. Their heads snapped back and forth, looking from their mother to their father and back again, as if they were at a tennis match.

"Albert didn't have sex with me!" Susan said firmly. "He catalyzed me."

"Call it what you will. The same body parts were involved."

Then Susan made a mental leap that George really wished she hadn't made. If she'd reacted this badly to something that he felt was nothing horrible, how was she going to take the really unpleasant part of this whole business. The answer was not very well.

"What about me?" she demanded. "To impregnate May, you'll have to accumulate bah\na fluid. We won't be able to have sex for a month!"

"Can't we sacrifice for our friends?" he asked plaintively, hoping to appeal to some remnant of the nice, sane Susan that he'd married.

"Some sacrifice! You're out playing around with another woman!"

" 'Playing around'?" Finally, George couldn't control himself anymore. He had managed to contain his temper thus far, but now his voice rose in volume. "You sound like a human!"

Susan blanched. "That's a terrible thing to say!"

"You know what I think?" George pressed, finally forced to admit that which horrified him ... namely, that Matt was right. "I think you're jealous!"

Susan threw her napkin down and jumped to her feet. "My friend Jessica warned me this would happen! You men will do anything, say anything, to satisfy that little snake in your pants!"

She stormed out of the room. And now George was on his feet, shouting, *"What snake?!"*

He charged up the stairs after her and got to the top just in time to hear the bedroom door slamming. "Susan, I can't believe you have this attitude!" He stood outside the door, trying to strike a balance between anger and rationality. "I'll be sacrificing, too! I don't understand your thinking here. Do you actually believe that I'm so ... so desperate to sleep with May, that I'd willingly spend a month of not having sex with you?"

"All I know," said Susan through the door, "is that I sat there at work today saying that you'd never have sex with another woman. And then tonight you announce that you're willing to ... to backburner me for a month so that you can have sex with Albert's wife! Is she prettier than me, George? Or is it that you're just going to have enjoyment knowing that it's someone other than me?"

"And I sat at work," retorted George, "telling Matt that you'd be understanding, and—"

She threw the door open and stared at him aghast. *"Matt* knows about this?"

"Well, yes, but ..."

"Oh my God! Who else did you tell, George?! How many of your policeman pals know how I'm going to be humiliated? Or maybe they'll just all be able to tune in to the evening news!" And she slammed the door in his face once more.

He stood there, staring at it.

Knowing that it was not going to be opening again for the rest of the night.

He hated sleeping on the couch. It always gave him a stiff back.

"If Matt notices that I'm sitting oddly," said George grimly, "I can always tell him I slipped on some soap."

CHAPTER 9

"YOU SLIPPED ON soap?"

Cathy tried to keep the laughter out of her voice and failed miserably. She sat on the edge of the couch in Matt's apartment and giggled helplessly. Sikes sat at the opposite end, his arms folded, patiently waiting it out.

"I'm glad you think it's so funny," he said.

"Did they believe it? I mean . . . did *anyone* believe it?"

"Of course."

She looked at him skeptically. "Even George?"

"Even George," he said defiantly.

"Uh huh."

"Look, Cathy, why'd you come over here tonight? I mean, not that I'm not happy to see you," he added. "I mean, heck . . . why pass up an opportunity for some more bumps and bruises, huh?"

"That's not fair, Matt," she said sullenly. "I warned you what might happen."

"Yeah, well . . . I know." He sighed.

"I guess you just didn't take the warning seriously."

"Maybe you should come with a notice from the surgeon general printed on your side."

"No," she sighed. "Humans don't seem to take that warning seriously, either."

They were silent a moment, and then he said again, "Cathy, why did—"

"I come over?" He nodded. She said gamely, "I wanted to make up for what happened the other night."

"How? Wait, let me guess. You're going to let me handcuff you to the bedpost. Right?"

For a moment she actually seemed to consider it, but then she shook her head. "I don't really think I'd get any enjoyment out of that. Would you?"

He conjured a mental picture of Cathy lying naked and helpless, chained to the bed. She was writhing in ecstasy. He saw himself climbing on top of her . . .

And then, in the throes of rapture, she accidentally ripped out his throat with her teeth.

"Nah," he said. "That wouldn't really be fun. But . . . so what did you have in mind."

"Let's go in the bedroom."

"My five favorite words," he said, unhesitatingly.

They went into his bedroom and he obeyed her instructions as she told him to remove his shirt.

"Now lie flat on your belly," she said.

"You sure?" he asked. "Lying flat, I can't . . ."

"Yes, I know. But I can." To his surprise, she cracked her knuckles.

Not sure exactly what to expect, Sikes lay down on the bed as she had told him. And then she straddled him and dug her fingers deep into his shoulder blades.

"I am," she said confidently, "the best massage

artist you're going to find in this entire apartment building. Plus, I know precisely how to help injuries of your sort."

"You mean shower injuries?"

"Exactly."

Her expert fingers worked the flesh, and Sikes relaxed.

"It's not just your neck, you know, Matt. Your shoulders are one huge knot. You have got to be the single most tense individual I've ever given a backrub."

"You ever massage another cop?"

"No."

"That explains it."

She moved from his shoulders and up to his neck. His head went completely limp under her ministrations.

"Better?" she asked softly.

Sikes murmured in the affirmative. "You got the healing touch, Cathy."

"I'm a doctor," she said, matter-of-factly.

He smiled. He hadn't meant it as a confirmation of what she did for a living. She took everything literally. That was one of the things he lo—

Whoa.

Was he going to say, "Loved about her?"

Even though it had only been his private thoughts, he found to his surprise that he couldn't bring himself to even think the word. That probably meant he had a long way to go when it came to actually saying it.

But her comment about being a doctor had set his mind in another direction. A direction that might be able to help him on his case.

"Listen, Cathy, do you know anybody over at county?"

She nodded, and then realized he couldn't see it. "A couple people. Why?"

"Somebody abandoned this Newcomer baby. We're trying to get a doctor to see her."

She made a clicking noise. "They're swamped at county." She thought a moment, and then said, "If you want, I'll take a look at her."

"That'd be great. Thanks."

She lifted her hands and flexed the fingers for a moment. Then she slid off him and said, "Okay, sit up. How do you feel?"

He sat up and shook himself out like a big cocker spaniel. "Incredible. Where'd you pick that up?"

"I simply found that I had a knack for it. I had this patient once who thought I could make him feel better just by touching him. Apparently he'd seen *E.T.* about a hundred times. So I just started working him over with my fingers and he practically melted under my touch. I took some lessons, developed some of my own techniques, and presto."

"Magic fingers."

"How's your bruise?"

She took his chin gently in her hands and examined it. She was pleased and her guilt a bit alleviated to see that it was fading.

"If you kiss it," said Sikes, the soul of innocence, "you'll make it better."

She looked at him doubtfully. "Really?"

He nodded sincerely. "Ummhmmm."

She leaned over to kiss his cheek, and just as she did so, he turned his head quickly so that their lips met. She pulled back to see that he was grinning like a naughty little boy. "Matt," she said scoldingly.

He moved closer to her. "Take off your blouse. I'll give *you* a massage. You're not the only one with magic fingers."

She stared at him. "Matt, the first time, I could understand your actions because, well . . . you probably didn't fully believe what could happen to you. But a second time? Good lord, Matt, you don't really want to be hurt?" Then she gave it some thought. "Do you?" she asked. "I mean . . . I know some humans like that . . ."

"I'm not one of them," he said sincerely.

"Well, then . . . in that case, have you forgotten the last time you touched my spots?"

"I won't touch your spots. I just want to fondle your breasts."

He sounded very reasonable in his tone. Cathy considered it. "Well, I suppose there's no harm in that."

She started to unbutton her blouse, and then paused. She didn't have all that much experience with her breasts as sex objects. Although they were of particular fascination to earth men, she knew, there was nothing especially alluring about them to other Tenctonese. So as far as she was concerned, they didn't particularly factor into the sexual equation.

But Matt . . . well, he had had a good deal more practice in using them to obtain gratification. And maybe it was possible that he might get her worked up using them.

"No," she said firmly, and buttoned her blouse again. "I still might be aroused. It's just too dangerous."

He leaned back, unable to contain his disappointment. "So what's this mean?" he said in exasperation. "I'm never going to be able to touch you?"

"You've got to be trained."

Sikes moaned and flopped backwards onto the bed, his arms outspread as if he'd just been crucified.

Cathy could sympathize with him. If someone had come up to her, told her that everything she knew about medicine was wrong, and that she had to start all over again, she would certainly be as frustrated and disconcerted as Sikes was. But she had to convince him nevertheless that it was the only way. Otherwise their relationship was never going to head in the direction that she suspected they both wanted it to go.

"Look, Matt, they're starting a Human/Newcomer sex class at UCLA. Let's sign up."

Sikes covered his face with his hands. "A class? They're going to teach me how to have sex?"

"How to have sex with *me,*" she emphasized.

"Oh, no. Forget that. No way."

She was taken aback by the stridency with which he protested. "Why?"

He sat up and ticked off the reasons on his fingers. "It's personal. It's private. And it's embarrassing."

Slowly she rose from the bed. She thought very carefully about the way things were going with them and where she wanted them to end up. Although she felt more at ease with the subject than Matt did, it still wasn't the easiest thing in the world for her to talk about. But finally, in a low voice, she said, "Matt, I don't want a platonic relationship with you."

"Who's talking platonic?" He sounded confused. Clearly he still didn't understand. Tough, self-reliant Matt Sikes was having real trouble accepting something that, to Cathy, was self-evident.

She turned and faced him. "Unless we take this class, that's all we can have!"

Slowly understanding crept into his eyes. But it was very reluctant, and she wasn't sure that he was going to embrace the only course open to them.

"Matt," she said, and her voice dropped down an octave, sounding thick and throaty. "You know . . . I fantasize about coming over here, ripping off your clothes and making love to you . . . up one side of this room and down the other."

He gaped at her.

"Yeah?"

She nodded.

"I'll take the class," he said, unhesitatingly.

She clapped her hands in glee, went to him, and kissed him lightly on the top of the head. "You won't be sorry."

"I bet I will," he said ruefully. "Promise me I won't be forced to do anything embarrassing."

"I can't, Matt," she told him. "You have such a low threshold of embarrassment that the least little thing could get you flustered."

Sikes didn't look particularly thrilled with that assessment, and Cathy took the opportunity to change the subject quickly. "By the way," she said, "I just thought you should know I managed to sell those tickets to *Phantom*. I got a fairly good price for them."

"Oh, Cath. Now I feel lousy," he said.

"No reason for you to, Matt," she said. "There was a conflict. You weren't available. And, well, frankly . . . and I hope this doesn't overinflate your ego . . . there just wasn't anyone else I wanted to go with. So . . . that's that."

She didn't seem especially broken up about it, and yet Sikes felt like a creep. Especially since he knew more than he was letting on. And poor Cathy had simply assumed that he was leveling with her.

"Well, y'know," he heard someone who had his exact same voice say, "as it turns out, there was a last minute cancellation. So I happened to come by an extra ticket to the dinner—if you'd like to be my date for the evening, that is."

She smiled that beautiful smile of hers. "Oh, Matt! How lovely! Are you sure it's okay?"

"Sure I'm sure. I said I'm sure, and I'm sure. Is it okay with you?"

"Absolutely."

"Then it's a date."

Happily she embraced him. But even as he sat there, the warmth of her pressed against him, he couldn't help but feel a sense of dread about the whole thing.

He hoped . . . he *prayed* . . . that, in the several years since he'd seen him, Perelli had changed in his opinions.

Otherwise the evening could turn out to be a fairly uncomfortable one for all concerned.

Uncomfortable, hell.

It would be a disaster.

CHAPTER 10

SIKES WALKED INTO THE police squad room the next day, whistling cheerfully. He passed Sandy Beach, who called out to him, "Switch to baths to play it safe, Sergeant?" and then he laughed.

"You'll get yours, son of a beach," Sikes muttered to himself.

As always, George had beaten him to the squad room. The Newcomer was staring at the computer screen, his fingers flying across the keyboard. He barely afforded Sikes a glance as the human said, "What'cha doing?"

"Witnesses claim the suspect—this giant—fell off the overpass onto a produce truck," said George briskly. "I'm compiling a list of all food transport companies that route through Little Tencton."

Sikes nodded. "I was just about to suggest we do that."

George "harrumphed" noncommittally as Sikes sat down at his desk. Matt was pleased to see that, this morning at least, there was no sign of weasels—dunkable, jelly-filled, or otherwise. "How'd it go last night?" he prompted.

George did not respond, studying the computer with far greater intensity than was remotely required. This, in and of itself, was pretty much an answer to Sikes's question. But he did not let up, because for once, he had the upper hand in a conversation with the knowledgeable, and sometimes self-satisfied, Francisco.

"Did you tell Susan about Albert and May?"

Finally George glanced up. "Yes. I did." He went back to his work.

When no further reply was forthcoming, Sikes said impatiently, "And . . . ?"

George took a deep breath. Immediately Matt knew that he was lying. George didn't realize it, but every time he told any sort of lie, he always took extra air into his lungs, as if a lie was far more difficult for him to speak. He looked up gamely, unaware that grave doubts had already been cast on his next words. "Sorry to disappoint you, but she wholeheartedly approved."

Sikes sat back, putting his hand against his cheek in mock surprise, *à la* Jack Benny. "No kidding . . ."

In a wildly transparent move to change the subject, George said, "How'd it go with Cathy? Have you seen her since . . . your slippage?"

"Saw her last night, as a matter of fact," Sikes said easily. Now he, on the other hand, considered himself to be a consummate liar.

Francisco looked at him from side to side. "No new bruises. I guess you've had to exercise some restraint."

Studying his fingernails in as nonchalant a manner as possible, Sikes said, "Sorry to disappoint you, but we were hot and heavy last night."

Now George was as skeptical as Sikes had been moments ago. "And you lived to tell about it?"

"Yeah. No big. Cathy just needed to get used to . . ." He paused dramatically. ". . . the human touch."

Mimicking Matt's Bennyesque approach, George put his hand to his face. "You mean you 'went all the way'? 'Got lucky' to use your copulation euphemisms."

"Luck had nothing to do with it," said Sikes. "Y'know, George, the way you're talking, we should really be discussing this over malteds down at the soda shop."

"Hi, George. Matt."

The voice that came from behind them froze Matt's blood. It also froze his smile, as he turned and said, "Hi, Cathy."

As opposed to the soft, approachable Newcomer he'd seen just last night, today Cathy looked dressed for business. She was carrying a black medical bag. It took the flustered Sikes a moment to remember that her showing up here was, in fact, at his request. Unfortunately, since he didn't have the brains of a chicken (he decided), he hadn't thought far enough ahead to anticipate that his remarks to George might get crossed up by Cathy.

He stood quickly, putting an arm around her shoulder and steering her in the direction of the nursery. "She's, uh, gonna take a look at the baby," he explained quickly to George while keeping Cathy moving.

"That's very nice of you." George's polite tone did nothing to mask his curious expression as he saw Matt trying to hustle her off.

It didn't do any good. Apparently oblivious to Matt's haste, Cathy suddenly turned back around to face George. She bobbed up and down slightly on the balls of her feet. "Did Matt tell you?" she said cheerfully. "We're signing up for a sex class."

Through gritted teeth, Sikes said, "Cathy . . ."

George affected an air that successfully made it look as if he were surprised. "I thought you two already copulated."

"Do we have to talk about this?" Sikes said, wanting to melt through the floor.

Cathy frowned at George. "What gave you that idea?"

And in a sudden burst of frustration, Sikes shouted, "You know, it'd be great if you guys learned that some things were private! I mean, you don't just go around discussing people's intimate lives in public! All this stuff about did we copulate, didn't we copulate—it's making me crazy! And I'm getting sick of that word, too! If you're going to talk about it constantly, use some . . . some Tenctonese word for it, or at least some good old English word like fu—"

And he became abruptly aware that his voice was the only sound in the squad room.

He glanced around.

Every eye in the place was focused on him. Grazer had come out of his office and was staring. And, just to make it really exciting, a priest and two nuns were standing off to the side, looking at him with fish-eyed amazement. What they were doing there, Sikes had no idea, except that maybe God had stuck them there simply for the purpose of maximum humiliation.

"Fun," he finished.

They were still staring.

And Cathy, to his eternal gratitude, said, "Matt, they're going to need me back at the hospital soon. Can we look at that baby?"

"Yes," he said very quickly, and hustled her out of the squad room before any further disasters could befall, although he was hard pressed to think of a greater one.

He waited for Cathy to say something as they walked down the hallway to the nursery. But she did not seem so inclined. Was she mad at him? Frustrated? Hurt?

He stole a glance at her face and saw that she was looking at him, with her mouth in a crooked, amused smile. Immediately he relaxed.

"A little premature in our boasting, aren't we, Matt?"

He shrugged. "I like to think of it as aggressive wishful thinking."

"Tell you what," she said. "Next time, clear with me ahead of time what you're going to tell people so that I can be sure not to contradict you. How's that?"

"Next time it won't be wishful thinking. Okay?"

"Fine." She squeezed his hand slightly and they were still holding hands when they entered the nursery.

Then she saw the baby lying in the crib, and Cathy's grip closed so tightly around Matt's that he thought she might break his fingers. As delicately—and then, as firmly—as he could, he disentangled her grip from him. She barely seemed to notice, her entire attention on the child.

She walked over to the crib and stared down. The child regarded her with those calm eyes that seemed ancient beyond the infant's years.

"She's beautiful," she whispered to Matt. Then she extended her medical bag and said, "Hold this." He took it and she reached down, as if touching a soap bubble, and lifted the baby from the crib. She brought the baby over to the changing table so that she would have more room to examine her.

She paused a moment, taking a deep breath, and then her fingers ran lightly across the top of the child's skull, tracing the general shape. Then she opened her medical bag and removed a tonglike device with a metered scale in the middle of it. She briskly used it to measure the length and width of the baby's head. Then she shined a flashlight into the ear cavities of the child, and even shined the light in the baby's eyes. The baby blinked rapidly against the light.

Cathy put down the flashlight, and then picked up the baby's feet, pulling her finger across the bottoms. The baby's legs bent reflexively.

Apparently having regained her professional detachment, she manipulated the legs a bit more, and then placed the flashlight in the baby's hand. The tiny hand clamped around it immediately.

"Good Babinski reflex," murmured Cathy, making a mental note to herself. Then she took the baby by her chin and moved her head from side to side, as if in wonderment. "Incredible," she said.

As she was reaching into her medical bag once more, Captain Grazer entered. He barely looked at Sikes, apparently deciding that if the business from before was going to be discussed, it would best be done at another time.

"What's the verdict?" said Grazer to Cathy.

She didn't reply, her attention still riveted to the baby. She was pulling a double-bellied Newcomer stethoscope out of her bag. So Sikes stepped in and said, "She's not finished."

Grazer nodded slightly, and then started to say something else when Cathy looked at him severely and said, "Shhh!!"

Taken aback, Grazer quieted down as Cathy put the stethoscope to the baby's chest and listened.

Sikes watched carefully. This part should have been routine. Clearly, though, it wasn't. There was bewilderment on Cathy's face as she moved the stethoscope around on the baby's chest. Then she removed it and placed it against her own chest, as if to make sure that it was working. She nodded, clearly satisfied with what she heard, and put it back on the baby. And then, after a moment, pure shock crawled across her face.

She stepped back, staring at the child as if the baby's head had suddenly whirled around 360 degrees.

"What is it?" said Sikes, now extremely concerned.

"She . . ." Cathy looked as if she were trying to remember the words. "She has only one cardiovascular system."

"What?!"

That last was from George, who had apparently finished with whatever he was up to at his desk and had followed them to the nursery. He was as shocked as Sikes would have been if, say, a human baby had been announced as being perfectly alive and healthy . . . but without a drop of blood in her veins.

"You mean she doesn't have two hearts?" Sikes said in surprise.

Cathy was shaking her head as if disagreeing, but her words made it clear that it was from pure puzzlement. "No. Only one."

Grazer, who fancied himself an expert on the affairs of all things Tenctonese, said firmly, "That's impossible. She's a Newcomer."

"Maybe she isn't," said Cathy, clearly trying to sort it out as she spoke. "One heart, no spots. And the motor skills are more consistent with the development of a human infant."

Sikes stared at the angelic infant girl. "This is not a human baby, Cathy."

"No," said Cathy, as if from a distance. "The ear

configuration ... the cranial shape ... definitely Newcomer."

Now Grazer was starting to get frustrated. Clearly there was doubt on his face that Cathy knew what she was doing. "You just said she wasn't a Newcomer," he said in a faintly patronizing tone.

Cathy ignored the sarcasm. "I meant not entirely a Newcomer." She paused as if about to leap off a high dive into a pool drained of water. "I think she might be a hybrid."

There was a moment of dead silence.

"A hybrid?" said Sikes, finally.

She nodded, having cleared her first major hurdle merely by voicing the word. "Half human ... half Newcomer."

"That's impossible," said George flatly. "A Newcomer would have just as much luck producing offspring by mating with a platypus as he would with a human."

Cathy looked at him coldly. "Care to trot out your degree in genetics, George, to support that claim? The fact is, Tenctonese have been known to adapt genetically within a single generation. Interbreeding is just a matter of time."

Grazer looked flushed with excitement. "You're saying that I've got the first interspecies baby in my precinct?"

"I don't know for sure," said Cathy, starting to feel in a little over her head. "I've got to run some tests."

Clearly, Grazer hadn't even heard her. He was listening to those little voices in him that were screaming, *Opportunity of a lifetime!* He spun and faced Sikes and Francisco. "You find the parents!" he commanded, as if the idea had not already occurred to the detectives ages ago. Then he turned back to Cathy and bubbled, "I'm calling a press conference!"

Cathy blanched. "Wait! No." She put up her hands as if trying to ward off a blow. "I can't be sure until I run those tests."

"It's good enough for me!" he said. "Actually, I . . . had already come to the same conclusion. I didn't tell you because I didn't want to color your findings."

"And besides," Sikes put in, holding his thumb and forefinger an inch apart, "he was this close to inventing a cure for the common cold and didn't want to split his attention."

George looked extremely concerned. "Captain, with all due respect, I wouldn't call any sort of conference. The ramifications could be profound. People are easily frightened, particularly when it comes to Newcomers, and I wouldn't be surprised if violence were the direct result of any announcement of a possible hybrid."

If Grazer heard him, he gave no indication. "Find those parents!" he said again, and then charged out the door.

Sikes, Cathy, and George looked at each other.

"We got a biiiig problem," said Sikes.

When the press arrived, the problem became that much bigger.

Within hours, the police station booking area was absolutely crammed with reporters. When Grazer wanted to, he could be tremendously efficient. Unfortunately, those things that most caught his attention frequently were the least relevant to genuine police procedures.

Matt and George had been out for several hours, checking with child welfare clinics and pursuing a few leads that turned out to be utterly fruitless. They returned to find utter chaos. They had to elbow their way past the various television cameramen and print reporters just to find a small area of unoccupied space in their very own precinct station.

One newsman roughly elbowed Sikes out of the way. "Move it, fella," he shouted over the din. "I have a press pass!"

"And I have a lousy temper," snapped back Sikes.

"Now, Matt," George said. "You promised. No more breaking the legs of newsmen."

Sikes looked at George gratefully for the unexpected support. The newsman, looking a bit more apprehensive than before, carefully stepped around the two officers.

"Thanks, George," said Sikes.

Francisco shrugged, looking very human as he did so. "There's no excuse for rudeness," he said.

A podium had been set up at the front, with an array of microphones clustered around it. After a few more moments of barely controlled pandemonium, Grazer emerged with a clearly uncomfortable Cathy in tow. He put up a hand to forestall any questions until he could get to where he wanted to be, namely center stage.

"Thank you for coming, ladies and gentlemen of the press," he said pompously. He was so puffed up with himself that it was amazing that his feet remained on the floor. "I appreciate it, and I think you'll find that your time is not being wasted. The LAPD has turned up something that, I feel, is going to have ramifications, not only on a local basis but quite possibly, worldwide."

In the back, Sikes grumbled, "Here we go."

"A routine investigation into an incident in Little Tencton," said Grazer, "resulted in our recovery of an abandoned infant girl. The child is now in safekeeping here at the station, as we have endeavored to make do despite the crushing budget cuts inflicted on all aspects of the child welfare system."

"Great, a political statement," Sikes said. George nodded.

Grazer, however, was just warming up. "From the moment I laid eyes on her, I realized this was no ordinary baby. It seemed impossible, but I couldn't help feeling I was looking at . . ." He paused dramatically. ". . . the first interspecies baby."

Jaws dropped collectively through the room. Pleased at the initial response, Grazer pressed on. "I called in Dr. Frankel here, and she confirmed my suspicions."

Now Sikes started to take a step forward. *"He* called her in?" he whispered angrily.

But George, wisely, put a hand on Sikes's shoulder, stopping him. "Don't mix in this, Matthew. Keep your distance. Believe me, you're not going to want to be a part of what happens."

He looked at George. " 'What happens'?"

"Just watch," was all that George said.

Cathy, for her part, was now trying to get a word in. "Please, if I may . . ." she began.

But Grazer cut her off. This was his show, and the ringmaster wasn't letting on any other acts until he felt like it. "Of course, I *have* ordered further tests to be absolutely certain," he said.

Now, though, it was Grazer's turn to be cut off, as all the reporters began shouting at once. Questions overlapped each other into one large, loud, indecipherable mess. Grazer took a step back, looking momentarily stunned, like a surfer who'd just been knocked off his board by an unexpectedly huge wave. Then he smiled gamely, waiting for the din to die down so that he could field questions in a coherent fashion.

"Ain't he in heaven," Matt said.

George nodded. "Like a pig in chips."

Sikes turned and looked at him. "In what?"

"Chips. Isn't that the expression?"

He thought about it. "Close enough," he decided.

Meanwhile, things had calmed down just enough for Grazer to select someone to toss him a question. "Any idea who the parents are?" called out the reporter.

"No, not yet," said Cathy.

"But," Grazer added, as if about to deliver the word from Mount Sinai, "we are investigating several promising leads."

Matt said to George, "Promising leads. Dead ends. It's the same thing, really. Just semantics."

Then Grazer picked out another waving hand, and that's when George said, "Here we go."

"What do you mean?" asked Matt.

"I recognize that reporter," said George. "His name's McGee. His bias has been fairly evident in his reportage of previous Newcomer affairs."

"Dr. Frankel," called out McGee. "Doesn't this confirm what the human Purists have feared all along? That the Newcomers will alter human evolution?"

Grazer looked as if he'd just been slapped in the face. This was not the kind of question he'd anticipated. Abruptly he was all too willing to let Cathy field a question.

"Let me emphasize," she said, "it's too soon to be certain she *is* a hybrid."

There was no good way to answer the question, but that was one of the less preferable. It sounded as if she was backtracking, trying to avoid something unpleasant despite the fact that she was simply reiterating the position she'd had from the beginning. McGee smelled blood. "But couldn't this signal the end of the human race as we know it?"

"There are over four billion humans on this planet," Cathy said reasonably. "Less than three hundred thousand Tenctonese . . ."

"So your answer is yes!" shouted McGee. "It's just a matter of time!"

And Grazer again lost control of the situation as all the reporters started shouting simultaneously all over again.

"I don't like this, George," said Sikes worriedly. "Things could get really ugly."

"That McGee has always been a problem for Newcomers," said George. "He and that wire service reporter out of Chicago. They always act like they see monsters everywhere."

At that moment, a dispatch officer came up to them and handed them a message.

"Patrolmen just responded to a call in Little Tencton," he told them urgently. "That giant Newcomer you've got an APB on . . . he was caught stealing from a fruit stand."

"One of those promising leads we hear so much about," Matt said to George. He turned to the dispatch officer. "Tell 'em we're on our way . . . and we want that guy alive."

And they dashed out of the squad room, leaving Grazer sinking fast in a sea of waving arms and shouted questions.

CHAPTER 11

At the Fairchild Advertising Agency, Jessica stared at Susan with incredulity.

"Let me get this straight," she said. She started ticking off the points on her fingers. "He hasn't been sleeping around but he's going to. And he announced his intention to do so."

"That's right."

"At the dinner table. In front of the kids."

"Right." Susan sat there, her chin in her hands.

"And he thought that you'd approve. That, in fact, you'd be happy for him."

"He actually seemed a little hurt that I wasn't."

"And the kids were on his side."

"I think so." Susan looked up. "What does 'No duh' mean?"

Jessica shrugged. "And while he's getting geared up to boff this tootsie, you have to be high and dry for a month."

"Yes."

121

Jessica sat back and heaved a loud sigh. "Y'know, just once—just *once*—I'd like to be wrong. I mean, I'm use to men living up to—or maybe I should say, down to—my expectations. But then, every so often, something comes along that sets a new standard. I thought I'd heard everything until now. Of all the bald-faced—sorry," she amended when she looked at Susan. "Of all the nerve. You poor thing."

Susan sat back in her chair, pulling on her own fingers nervously. "Maybe I'm overreacting . . . ?" The question was directed partly at Jessica and partly at herself.

Jessica shook her head firmly. "Overreacting. Honey, I'd've kicked him in the prostate."

"George doesn't have a prostate," Susan pointed out.

"Well, what*ever* he has, I'd've kicked him in it."

Susan sighed again. She'd been sighing a lot, it seemed. She had slept the way she always slept when George wasn't with her: badly. Usually it was because he was out on stakeout or some such thing. She thought that there was nothing worse than lying there, staring up at the ceiling, unsure of whether her husband was safe, and when—or if—he'd come back.

But certainly lying there, knowing that he was as near as the living room but as far as anger could keep him, had to be right up there in terms of pure heartache.

"I just don't know what to do," she admitted.

"Baby, there's only one thing to do. You fight fire with fire."

Susan looked up at her, puzzled. This had to be earth vernacular. She could not believe that Jessica really was suggesting she torch George.

"When Frank tries to pull his bushwa on me," said Jessica conspiratorially, "I buy something tight and sexy. I may be forty-eight, but I've still got great gams."

If this was supposed to clarify things, it didn't. "Sweet potatoes?" said Susan, hopelessly befuddled.

For a moment, Jessica stared at her uncomprehendingly. Then it clicked. "Not yams," she said, trying not to laugh. Susan felt badly enough without having her confidant snickering at her. "Gams. Legs. Anyway, Frank gets all hot and bothered and I just freeze up. He doesn't get what he wants until I get what I want."

"You mean you manipulate him by withholding sex?"

"Yeah. What else have I got?"

"Jessica, I don't know. I mean . . . remember, if he goes through with this, we aren't supposed to be having sex anyway."

"Even better," said Jessica. "You'll be letting him know that you can make the month's abstinence a living hell for him. Strutting your stuff and he can't take advantage of it? It'll drive him crazy. Not to mention that you'll also be reminding him that when he comes crawling back to you after he's had his little fling, you can turn the rest of your married life into a sexual torture chamber."

"But why would I want to do that?!" said Susan. "What kind of way is that to live? That sounds terrible. Using sex as . . . as a weapon. How can anyone exist in a relationship that way?"

"Honey, what planet are you—no. Forget I said that." She sat down close to Susan and said firmly, "Listen, you play doormat to a man, and believe me, all you'll get is the bottom of his shoe."

Susan looked bewildered. "It's all so . . . so foreign."

"Baby, this is war," said Jessica with utter conviction. "And I'm not going to let you lose it. You gotta say to yourself, Nobody loses a fight when a Francisco is involved."

In Little Tencton the car screeched to a halt next to a black and white police squad car. Matt and George leaped out and approached officers Chase and Morra. They looked as if they'd been rooted to their unit, either unable or unwilling to move. Apparently they were quite pleased that they'd been told to keep their distance and wait for Francisco and Sikes.

"Where is he?" said George.

Chase pointed and replied, "Down the street."

Moving in the direction that Chase pointed, Sikes said, "You got him cornered?"

"Uh-uh," Morra told him. "He's got us cornered."

Sikes didn't understand what Morra was talking about until he got within range of the disturbance. Then he understood only too well.

There was a huge Newcomer sprawled across the roof of another black and white patrol car. The patrolmen were still inside because the giant was holding the doors shut with his powerful arms, keeping the frustrated cops from getting out. They could, of course, have shot directly through the roof with their guns. But there was a good chance the bullets might not penetrate, which meant they'd be injured or killed in a ricochet. Besides, cops weren't allowed to fire their weapons unless they'd been fired upon or otherwise believed that their lives were in immediate danger. There was nothing in regulations about being held prisoner inside your own unit. Nearby a fruit stand had been overturned. One did not need a slide rule to figure out what had happened.

Chase and Morra backed up the two detectives as they approached and then stopped several yards back. Sikes whistled. "Look at the size of him . . ."

"Guy's missing a few parts upstairs," Chase ventured an opinion.

Sikes and Francisco looked at each other. They didn't even need to discuss how to handle the situation. It was fairly obvious.

Slowly, so as not to appear the least bit aggressive, George called out to the giant, [*Come down off the car. No one is going to hurt you.*]

He had hoped to get some sort of coherent response, just to see whether they were dealing with a being who could be communicated with, or some raging behemoth. If it was the former, then perhaps things could be dealt with in a reasonable manner. If the latter, then it was quite possible that someone was going to get badly hurt . . . or worse.

His initial hopes were dashed as the giant's only reply was an earsplitting roar of anger. But George was too much of a veteran to let his trepidation show. [*No one is going to hurt you. Come down off the car*] he said, trying to have a mixture of firmness and sincerity in his voice.

He stopped five feet away. The giant just glared at him and held even more tightly to the car.

Morra, who seemed more amused by it than anything, removed his hat, and scratched his head. "What are we going to do?" he addressed the question to the assembled officers.

"He tried to steal fruit," said Sikes reasonably. "He must be hungry."

He looked for confirmation at George, and the Newcomer nodded. He drifted over toward the overturned fruit stand and picked up the largest red apple he could find.

And then, because George was, after all, still George, he checked the posted price on the cart and carefully placed fifty cents in the spot from which he'd taken the apple.

Sikes rolled his eyes. Then, bringing his mind back to business, he moved off to one side so that he and George would be flanking the giant, should the big guy suddenly show a disposition toward moving.

George held up the apple, keeping it steady until the giant's gaze was locked onto it. [*Are you hungry?*] George asked him. [*You can have all the food you want. Just come down.*]

He kept repeating it over and over like a mantra. The giant was spellbound by the combination of the proffered food and the almost hypnotic quality of George's voice. Sikes pulled out a set of handcuffs, making sure to do so without any overt fuss. He did not want to distract the giant at this crucial moment.

The giant was clearly considering George's offer. His eyes narrowed, but not in any sort of sinister or canny manner. George realized that the creature was exhausted. Who knew how long he'd been on the run, or what emotional demons were tearing at him.

And hungry. He was unquestionably hungry.

Slowly, the giant slid off the top of the car. Sikes forced himself to hold back as the giant's feet touched the street.

Nearby, various passing Newcomers were passing no longer. They had stopped whatever they were doing in order to watch the fascinating drama being played out in the streets of Little Tencton. Not that anyone was offering the cops any help, of course. Things simply didn't work that way in Little Tencton.

Sikes gestured that the two cops in the car should sit tight. He didn't want them leaping out and becoming two more bodies in the way. He waited until the giant was in perfect position, with his back to the human police officer and all his attention focused on the apple.

And that was the moment that Sikes attacked.

He grabbed the giant's arm, twisting it around with all the strength he had so that he could get the cuffs on him.

Unfortunately, all of Sikes's strength didn't even come close to what was required in this instance. The giant bellowed and swatted Sikes, sending him flying. He crashed into the top of the police car and rolled across the roof, thudding to the ground on the other side.

With the giant distracted by Sikes, George took the opportunity to rush the giant. The giant turned back and grabbed at Francisco, but George was too quick. He darted underneath the behemoth's flailing arms and sprang onto his back.

The giant whirled, but George desperately hung on. Roaring defiance, the giant stumbled back and slammed up against a lamppost. The impact was bone-jarring, and for a moment, George almost lost his grip.

But then he crisscrossed his arms even tighter, and moments later had his legs intertwined around the giant's waist. The move shoved air out of the giant's chest and left him gasping, trying to suck in new air that was being denied him through George's hold around his throat.

Sikes staggered to his feet and saw his partner holding on for dear life. But now George was no longer quite as desperate—with the giant's air choked off, George went on the offensive. He jammed his thumbs under the giant's ears.

The giant's eyes opened wide in alarm. Sikes, a few feet away, recognized what George was doing immediately. It was a Newcomer sleeper hold, incredibly effective. The question was, would it work on so massive a Newcomer?

The behemoth staggered forward, taking one titanic step after another. He closed on Sikes, and George shouted, "Matt! Get back! Don't help me!"

Sikes needed no urging, because he saw what was happening. The giant's knees began to buckle, his eyeballs rolled up into their sockets. And with a final groan of protest, the giant fell forward like a tree, crashing to the ground so hard that Sikes was certain he felt the street vibrate under his feet.

The giant thrashed spasmodically a few more times, but that was after the fact more than anything else. Consciousness had already fled him.

George lay atop him, panting from the exertion. Finally, satisfied that the giant really was out of it, he relaxed the hold. Sikes was by his side, helping him to his feet. "Are you all right?" he asked.

The Newcomer detective examined the sleeves of his jacket. The impact had shredded both of them rather badly, and he sighed. Terrific. More things for Susan to be angry with him about.

"I'm fine. Yourself?"

"Yeah," Sikes said, nodding briskly.

The moment he'd ascertained that Sikes was all right, George turned back to the giant. Considering that the giant, given the opportunity, would have ripped him apart, George was extremely concerned about his welfare.

The uniformed patrolmen were handcuffing him both behind his wrists and around his legs. Sikes, upon seeing the precautions, could only breathe in relief, but George called out loudly, "Don't hurt him!"

The cops stepped back once their job was done, and they all stood in a small circle around the behemoth. The moment seemed familiar to Sikes for some reason, and then he realized why. It was like the old cartoon "Gulliver's Travels" that Sikes had seen when he was a kid. The Lilliputians, going to extreme lengths to truss up the unconscious man of Brobdingnagian (to them) proportions, only to have him wake up and snap the bonds without even giving it any thought.

Recalling how that scene had played out didn't exactly do a lot for Matt's confidence.

In quiet awe, George said, "I've never seen a Tenctonese like this."

"And he's hard to miss," said Sikes. "Where do you suppose he's been hiding?"

"I don't know."

"Neither do I. But I can tell you where he's going."

CHAPTER 12

Captain Grazer studied the afternoon newspaper with tremendous satisfaction. Damn, it was a good picture of him.

Front page, above the fold. It didn't get better than this. There was the headline in as large a type as he'd seen recently—at least as big as when the Pope came to visit. "NEWCOMER BOMBSHELL," it read, followed by a smaller headline that stated, "HYBRID INFANT REVEALED BY POLICE CAPTAIN."

He looked up at his wall, trying to figure out where he would hang a framed copy of this. There were twenty copies of the newspaper piled up on a chair nearby, for whatever uses he could come up with.

The phone had been ringing off the hook. Suddenly he was *the* source on Newcomer affairs. Undoubtedly, when any articles were written subsequently, he would be one of those "authorities" who was always contacted and liberally quoted.

Oh yes. This was going to be a major step upward.

Then there was a knock at the door. He looked up and saw a khaki officer with a Newcomer couple standing in the doorway, looking just a bit nervous over the brouhaha that was going on in the station.

"Captain," said the officer, "these are the folks that social services sent over."

Grazer rose from behind his desk and extended a hand. The male Newcomer shook it firmly as Grazer said, "Captain Bryan Grazer."

"Franz Kafka," replied the Newcomer. He indicated the female beside him. "This is my wife, Hans Brinker Kafka."

He looked at her with interest. "They gave a female a male name? Don't get that too often."

She inclined her head slightly. "All earth names have no real significance to us, Captain. The name Hans has no more meaning to me than the name Bryan Grazer."

He smiled at that, but then his smile drooped slightly. Something about her voice made it sound as if she wasn't particularly thrilled to see him.

Franz Kafka indicated the stacked newspapers. "We read the item of which you seem to have so many copies. Quite a flattering picture of you."

"Thanks," said Grazer.

Then Kafka's eyes narrowed. "I hope you've given real thought to the likely result of your actions."

Now Grazer was mystified. "I don't understand."

"You will," said Mrs. Kafka sullenly.

And then, in a tone that indicated that as far as they were concerned, this conversation was over, Kafka said, "And now, if you would be so kind, we'd like to see our foster child."

"Of course," said Grazer. "Right this way." But he watched the Newcomers carefully as they preceded him out of the office.

He'd understand, they said. Now what in the world did they mean by that?

The giant sat huddled in a cell that seemed in stark contrast to his remarkable size.

Throughout the day, officers had been trickling by the holding cell area, every single one finding some flimsy excuse to stop by. The real reason was obvious, of course. But if the giant was aware that he was on display—an object of curiosity, or even fear—he gave no sign. Instead he sat there, his hands to his spotted head, bent over in almost a fetal position. Inevitably, when some cop would come by, he or she would speak in a low, hushed voice, as if in the presence of something beyond comprehension.

Which it was.

Indeed, it struck a cord of fear. Where there was one giant Newcomer, there could be more. Newcomers could be a handful under normal circumstances. If they were suddenly popping up seven feet tall—potential juggernauts of destruction—it made police work that much more dangerous.

And who was to say that the abnormal growth would be limited to seven feet?

During much of the day, Albert Einstein had stayed on the outskirts of the police traffic. He didn't want to contribute to the general circus atmosphere that was pervading the giant's incarceration. But, by the same token, he felt drawn to the pain that radiated from the giant. Pain so strong that he felt he could touch it.

What finally prompted Albert to action was one human police officer, a tall gangly fellow with an unkempt air. He walked in carefully, glancing right and left as if he wanted to make sure that he was unobserved. He didn't see Albert standing off to the side, obscured by the open door of the broom closet that he was entering.

And then, from the officer's shirt pocket, he pulled a small Instamatic camera, and aimed it at the giant.

Abruptly a broom blocked his vision before he could push the shutter release. He turned to face Albert, who was—for Albert—quite angry. Nevertheless, Albert's voice never rose above normal conversational tones as he said, "Please don't do that."

The cop chuckled patronizingly and brought his camera up again. Again Albert raised the broom into his view.

This time when the cop turned to look at him, it was with a very menacing gaze. "Knock it off," he said quietly.

But Albert, refusing to be intimidated, said, "Captain Grazer is very media-conscious. How do you think he'd react to a picture in some tabloid of the giant sitting in a holding cell? I'm sure he'll start asking around as to who took the picture. Do you think for a moment I'll cover for you?"

It was purely a guess on Albert's part that the cop was going to take a picture for publication. But the expression on the officer quickly confirmed it.

The cop looked right and left for a moment, and then in a low voice he said, "Look, I'll cut you in for twenty-five percent." When Albert's gaze didn't waver, he said, "Okay . . . half. Okay? It'd be worth a—"

"Tell me, sir," said Albert with genuine curiosity, "is however much money you get paid for this picture really going to be worth losing your job?"

There was a long, annoyed pause, and then the cop pocketed the camera. "You people all stick together, you know that?"

"Yes," said Albert reasonably.

133

With an annoyed snort, the cop turned and stalked away.

Albert looked back at the giant and, to his surprise, saw that the giant was gazing back at him. There was a moment of silent communication between the two of them.

"You're very sad," said Albert.

When this drew no response, Albert switched to Tenctonese. [*You're very sad.*] He paused. [*Are you hungry?*]

The giant simply stared at him, that same picture of misery etched on his face. Albert reached into his pocket and pulled out an apple, extending it to the giant.

[*Here*] he said.

The giant recoiled, growling like a frightened dog. Albert frowned, confused. Was the giant that untrusting that he would shun food offered him, in friendship, by one of his own kind?

Then again . . . considering the giant's size . . . maybe there was no one of his own kind. Not to him, at any rate.

At least when the Tenctonese had landed on earth, they had had each other to give support in the complex assimilation into Earth society. But here was someone who literally had no one except himself.

A true alien in every sense of the word.

Albert heard footsteps and, for a moment, feared that the cop with the camera was returning—perhaps this time with friends, who were going to try and "convince" Albert to play along. But he breathed a sigh of relief inwardly when he saw that it was Sikes and George.

"How's Tiny?" asked Sikes. If it was meant to sound jovial, it didn't quite succeed.

"What did he do?" Albert inquired.

"He's a suspect in a murder case," George said.

"Really?" Albert looked with new curiosity at the giant. Anyone as fearful as the giant didn't seem the sort to go on some sort of killing spree. "It must've been an accident. He wouldn't hurt anyone on purpose."

Sikes tried not to smile at the emphatic tone of Albert's voice. "Albert, how long have you known this guy?"

"You mean started talking to him?"

"Yeah."

"About two minutes."

Sikes shook his head. "And you're ready to be his character witness."

But George was curious about Albert's phrasing. "You said 'talking to him.' Did he say anything to you?"

"No. No, it's been kind of one-sided, actually. But I can just feel it. He's very sad. He's lost something."

George and Sikes exchanged glances. "The baby?" said Sikes.

"It would seem to be the only thing that makes sense," said George. He paused, and then said to Sikes, "I'm going to ask him who he is."

"Brilliant, Holmes," said Sikes.

George ignored the sarcasm, or perhaps simply didn't pick up on it. He approached the giant slowly, still being cautious enough to keep his distance from the bars. The giant had a long reach, and it would do no one any good if George suddenly found his neck creaking under the creature's embrace.

[*What is your name?*] asked George.

There was no response. Somehow, George hadn't expected one, but nevertheless he tried again. [*"Do you understand me?"*]

And then he got a reaction out of the giant.

For a moment he thought that it had come as a

result of George's prompting, but one look at the giant's face quickly corrected that notion. The giant had lifted his head, but he was not looking at George. Instead it was as if he were looking straight through the Newcomer detective; even straight through the wall behind him. Like a dog responding to a high-pitched whistle that only he could hear.

It was as if he were sensing something.

"I need more time with her!"

Cathy felt as if she were talking to a brick wall. She was carrying the baby, who was nestled in her arms with that same strange, impassive look. Grazer walked alongside, and at one point even gently prodded Cathy forward when she appeared to be slowing down. When he did that, she shot him a glance so poisonous that he withdrew his hand as if a snake had bitten him.

"I have to follow regulations," he said reasonably. "We can't keep the child."

They turned a corner and, at the other end, there was the Newcomer couple. Cathy studied them with wary eyes as Grazer said, "Dr. Frankel, these are the Kafkas. They'll be serving as foster parents. I'm sure they'll provide a good home," and then he grinned in that way he had when he was making a stupid joke, "as long as they manage to keep that cockroach problem under control, huh, folks?"

All three Newcomers stared at him.

"Forget it," he said.

In the holding cell, the giant was now on his feet.

Although George, Sikes, and Albert were all well out of range, they nevertheless found themselves reflexively stepping backward.

[*"What is it?!"*] George demanded.

The giant didn't respond. Instead he gripped the bars, his eyes wide, as if he were watching a lover dying of a pernicious disease . . . knowing that he was helpless to save her.

Cathy studied the Kafkas. They seemed like perfectly decent individuals . . . or, at least, Cathy discerned as much as she could, considering that she'd met them a bare ten seconds ago.

They were looking, spellbound, at the baby in Cathy's arms. Cathy looked down at the child as well, expecting to see her usual calm, serene manner.

But now, for the first time, the child seemed agitated. Her eyes were darting nervously about. Apprehensively, Cathy said, "I'll need to see her on a regular basis."

"Of course," said Kafka, extending his arms.

The giant screamed.

It was a sound unlike any Sikes had ever heard. In all likelihood, he would never hear anything like it again unless, of course, he was unfortunate enough to end up in hell to witness damned souls writhing in torment.

"What's wrong with him?!" he demanded of George.

George gestured helplessly and looked to Albert. But the janitor was as flabbergasted by the sudden alteration in the giant's previously passive mood.

"I don't know," said George, trying to maintain calm. But it wasn't easy.

The infant screamed.

It was silent, and yet deafening. Since the child had been so passive, so calm earlier, this was a horrifying contrast. Her once tranquil eyes were now

137

swirling with turmoil. She began to twist in Kafka's grip, her tiny fists balling up. Her body became rigid, seizing up almost as if she were in the throes of a fit.

Or like a junkie going through withdrawal.

Kafka looked down in surprise at the child's abnormal shift in mood. He made clicking noises to comfort her, but they seemed to have little effect.

"She seems upset," Cathy said, unable to contain her urgency.

Kafka nodded in agreement, but his assessment of what they should do was at odds with Cathy's. "Let's get her home," he said. "She'll be calmer once she's out of here."

"Maybe she should stay." Cathy started to reach for her. The child turned to her, twisting in Kafka's arms. There was pure terror in her eyes, and she started to reach for Cathy . . .

But Grazer stepped in between them, facing Cathy and saying firmly, "I can't allow that. Thank you, Mr. and Mrs. Kafka."

Cathy stood there, watching helplessly, as the baby was carried away down the corridor.

The giant, his huge hands on the bars, twisted and writhed as if the bars had been shot through with electricity. The door creaked and moaned under the strain of the giant's grip.

"Stop it! Knock it off!" Sikes was shouting.

"Matt, he doesn't understand you."

"How the hell do you know, George?!" demanded Sikes. "He doesn't respond to Tenctonese. Maybe he only speaks French. Hey! Vous! Knockez it off!"

His lame attempt at humor was Matt's way of covering the panic he started to feel building in him.

Because he wasn't sure if he was imagining it or not, but it looked to him as if the bars might be starting to bend.

In the corridor upstairs, the Kafkas walked very quickly toward the exit. Franz Kafka was still desperately trying to calm the distraught child.

[*"There there"*] he whispered. And still the child was in the grip of hysterics.

Cathy watched with a horrified certainty that this was wrong. She wanted to throw herself after them, tackle them, make them realize that the child couldn't, shouldn't, *mustn't* leave.

But she couldn't explain why. She didn't have the words for it . . . not to give to them, and not even really to explain to herself.

All she had was a gut feeling, and in a case like this, that simply wasn't going to cut it.

Sikes wasn't imagining it. The bars started to bend.

Quickly Matt pulled his weapon, George following suit. Albert took a frightened step back, his eyes wide with fear. Sikes wasn't sure if Albert was more afraid of the giant hurting them or of them hurting the giant.

"Hey, guy! Easy now!" cautioned Sikes. But he knew that the giant didn't comprehend, or else simply didn't care. The creature was going berserk, and there was a very great likelihood that if Tiny didn't get a grip—other than on a cell door—within the next ten seconds, he was going to wind up with several well-placed bullets in him.

The Kafkas walked out the door. The last view Cathy had of the baby girl was her anguished look

139

penetrating straight through Cathy's head, straight into her mind . . .

Straight into her soul.

The giant howled once more, the howl of someone who knows that he has lost.

Sikes couldn't distinguish the ululation from the giant's screams of pure rage. Gripping the gun with both hands, and praying that the monster would listen—understand the words, garner the tone, *something*—he shouted, "Back off! Right now!"

And the giant did exactly as he was told.

Sikes was dumbfounded as the giant suddenly released his grip on the bars. He was like a balloon from which the air had escaped. He sagged back, not looking where he was going. The backs of his legs bumped into the cell bench, and he slouched down onto it.

But it was as if his body had turned to liquid. The bench didn't hold him. He slid right off it, like a waterfall, and dropped to the floor. He curled his knees up, almost up to his chin, and wrapped both arms around them.

And said, of course, nothing.

Sikes and Matt looked at each other.

"You got an explanation for that, George? Or how about you, Albert? You're the character witness. What the hell just happened here?"

"A great loss," Albert intoned.

"Yeah, you said that," said Sikes impatiently. "But . . ."

"The 'but' is, Sergeant," Albert said quietly, "that losing something once is truly heart-wrenching. But losing it twice . . . that, Sergeant Sikes, is a little taste of damnation."

He slung his mop over his shoulder. "If you'll

excuse me," he said, and moved off down the corridor.

They watched him go, and then looked back at the now helpless giant.

And they wondered what would happen if, next time, the creature didn't back down.

CHAPTER 13

SIKES EXPECTED, FOR some reason, that the sex clinic would have large neon lights flashing on and off, with the words Open 24 Hours in capital letters.

Instead what he found was a rather sedate brownstone on the campus of UCLA. That didn't serve to make him feel all that much better.

As he walked across the campus, he felt completely out of place. Passing students would give him appraising looks. He kept waiting for one of them to point and start giggling, knowing in some arcane student way that he was there for the purpose of signing up for Remedial Alien Boffing. And the student would tell his friends, and pretty soon everywhere he went on the campus, people would be pointing and snickering to each other.

And once it was all over the campus, it would spread like wildfire across the city. Or even worse— one of those stupid magazines that published articles like "What's Hot on Campus" would catch wind of it, and his picture would be stuck onto glossy pages in between photos of some rap group and students enjoying spring break in Florida . . .

Get a grip, for crying out loud, he thought. *No one is paying attention to you; it's all in your imagina—*

"Excuse me."

He stopped, his hands deep in the pockets of his leather jacket, and turned to face a student. The young, long-haired individual was wavering slightly from side to side.

"Yeah? What?" asked Sikes.

"Are you a cop?"

Sikes frowned. "Yeah. I'm a cop. Why?"

"Oh. Okay."

The student started to walk away, and now Sikes was extremely confused. "Hey! Kid!" he called out. The student stopped and turned around. "Why did you ask?"

The kid shrugged. "Well, I figured either you were a cop or else you were selling drugs." And then he kept on going.

Sikes watched him go. Then he pulled sunglasses from his vest pocket, and a baseball cap from his back pocket, jamming the former on his face and the latter on his head.

If he was going to be subjected to stuff like this, at least he could cut down on the likelihood of being identified later on.

Cathy had left the station house shortly after the Newcomer child had been taken away. She said it was because she wanted to check on some lab results, but that could have been done over the phone. Sikes figured that she really wanted time to compose herself after the clearly grueling day she'd had, and he couldn't blame her. So he had arranged with Cathy that he would meet her right at the clinic.

But considering what she'd been subjected to,

Sikes really wouldn't have blamed her if she'd decided that going to this clinic tonight was going to be too much of a strain. No . . . no, he wouldn't blame her at all.

In fact, she probably wasn't even there. If Matt went home right now, he'd probably find a message on his answering machine or perhaps a note tacked to his front door, with Cathy's apologies for just not having the strength to haul herself out to UCLA.

That was it. He should really just head straight home.

He hesitated at the door to the clinic. Just to cover his bases, he would look in to make absolutely certain that Cathy wasn't there. Yes, absolutely. Look in, walk out. It wouldn't take more than a second.

He opened the door and peered in.

Cathy was looking straight at him.

There was a line formed at a registration table, and Cathy had made it as far as being second on line. She had been looking at the door with obvious apprehension, but the moment she saw Matt, her face brightened. She gestured eagerly to him that he should join her.

Sikes smiled as best he could, although he was certain that it came out looking far more like a grimace, and he touched the brim of his cap in acknowledgment. He made his way quickly across the room, making certain not to meet anyone's gaze directly.

He got to Cathy's side. She leaned over to kiss him on the cheek, but Sikes kissed the air a few inches away from her face, and then turned away as if suddenly engrossed with studying their surroundings. Cathy blinked in mild surprise, and then looked at the sunglasses.

"It's nighttime," she said.

144

"Yeah, I know."

"Then why are you wearing sunglasses? Are your eyes bothering you?"

"No . . . well, yes," he quickly amended. "It's these darned fluorescents."

She glanced up at the overhead lighting. "These are incandescents."

"That's what I meant," said Sikes lamely.

"Oh." Clearly Cathy took him at his word. She frequently did. Sometimes that could be of tremendous use. And then there were the other times—like now, when he was keeping the shades on primarily because it gave him a secure feeling of anonymity—that he felt like a bit of a cretin.

"There's my friend, Betty!" said Cathy. She called out to a passing Newcomer nurse. "Betty! Hi!"

Matt endeavored to thin out his molecular structure so that he could pass through the floor like a ghost. He wasn't particularly successful. Cathy, on the other hand, had complete success in getting her friend's attention. Betty walked over to them and said cheerfully, "Hi, Cathy!"

"Betty Banner, this is my boyfriend, Matt. Matt, this is Betty."

"Yeah. Hi." Sikes shook her hand as quickly as possible, and hoped that Betty would go away before Cathy said something clever like . . .

"We're taking a sex class together!" Cathy bubbled.

Sikes sighed and pulled off his sunglasses. "What's the use?" he asked.

"Congratulations," said Betty, patting him on the shoulder. "Good luck!"

"I'll tell you all about it!" said Cathy as Betty walked off. "'Bye! Give my love to Bruce!"

Sikes waited until Betty was out of earshot, and then through gritted teeth said to Cathy, "You and I need to have a long talk about what is and what isn't appropriate to discuss in public."

She looked at him in surprise. "But, Matt, I'd think it was fairly obvious what we were here to do."

"In that case, it wasn't necessary to broadcast it, was it?"

Before they could continue a discussion that neither of them wanted, the couple in front of them finished signing up and stepped aside. Cathy's hand tightened around Matt's, and she stepped up to the registration desk. Sikes didn't exactly hang back, but he didn't precisely jump to the forefront either. Cathy, however, pulled him forward a step or two in her enthusiasm.

Sikes stared at the woman behind the registration desk. She was wearing a small name badge that read, Hello, My Name Is, and Mrs. Krik was handwritten below it. She had thick white hair, glasses, and a hearing aid that she was, at that moment, frowning at and tapping lightly with one finger.

It didn't bode well.

"Name?" said Mrs. Krik. She was speaking loudly even though they were only six inches away from her.

"Cathy Frankel," said Cathy, and she turned to Matt.

He wasn't saying anything.

"And Matt Sikes," she added for him.

She checked off their names against a master list. "Mr. Sikes, how old are you?"

"Thirty-six," he said.

She looked up at him. "What?"

He raised his voice. "Thirty-six!"

She smiled and made a notation. And then she said, "How large is your penis when erect?"

Matt's jaw went slack. "What?!" His voice was barely above a harsh whisper.

This naturally prompted Mrs. Krik to shout, "What?!"

"How large is your penis when erect?" Cathy said, hoping to cut down on time and totally missing out on Matt's discomforture.

"Your penis," Mrs. Krik said loudly enough to be heard in Santa Monica. "When erect, how lar—"

"I heard you!" shouted Sikes.

He couldn't believe this. This was like that nightmarish time when he'd been fifteen years old and bought his first box of condoms. Standing there in the drugstore, with the woman behind the counter bellowing all the way to the front of the store, "Hey, Morris! I got a kid here who wants a box of rubbers! I can't find 'em! Where've we got 'em?" And then Sikes had to stand there for five achingly long minutes as every customer passed by and chuckled at him while the woman searched everywhere, through every damned box, saying loudly, "Now where are those rubbers?"

He wondered if it was, by any chance, the same woman who was sitting in front of him now, staring up at him with apparently infinite patience—and infinite willingness to holler her questions repeatedly until she got an answer.

"It's none of your business," Sikes said desperately.

"What?" yelled Mrs. Krik.

"Matt, it's important," said Cathy. "In sex, it all has to be precisely timed, and the speed of the penetration is based on the length of—"

"Okay, okay!" said Matt. He glanced behind him. Everybody behind him was shuffling, annoyed at the hold-up.

And just to make it worse, every Newcomer in the mixed couples behind him was a male. Male New-

147

comers were renowned for their . . . endowments.
Matt had never forgotten the time he'd shown
George a condom and described its purpose. George
had stared at the rolled-up piece of rubber and said,
mystified, "And it fits?"

Sikes had unrolled it to its full length and said,
"See? It stretches."

George had taken it from him, studied it, and
pulled it to its greatest possible length, and had then
repeated, in that same amazed tone, "And it fits?"

Indeed, although Sikes had never really wanted to
admit it to himself, one of the things he'd found
intimidating about approaching Cathy on a physical
level in the first place was her mentally contrasting
him to Newcomer males she'd experienced. Who
wanted to get himself into a situation where he was
virtually guaranteed to suffer in comparison?

And now, here he had to confront it right up
front . . . in a room full of people.

He sighed. "Ten inches."

This drew a derisive snort from the Newcomer
behind him, and he muttered something no doubt
unflattering in Tenctonese.

But Cathy was now saying with great skepticism,
"Matt . . ."

Now there was a thought.

"More or less," he said defensively.

"Matt," she said in an admonishing tone.

Mrs. Krik was still staring up at him, her pencil
poised above the form.

With a last-ditch effort to preserve what was left of
his dignity, Matt leaned forward and whispered
directly into Mrs. Krik's ear. At that range even she
could hear him. She wrote down his answer, and
then handed him a plastic specimen cup.

"We'll need a sperm sample," she said primly.

"What? Right now?"

Mrs. Krik pointed. "That's the men's room. You'll find some magazines in there."

Matt took the cup and stared at it.

The Newcomer male behind him said something else in Tenctonese that drew some laughter from behind him. In a low voice, Sikes said to Cathy, "What'd he just say?"

For the first time she actually seemed to empathize with Matt's embarrassment. "He said 'Maybe he'll need a bigger cup to accommodate him.'"

Matt turned to face the grinning Newcomer male. And then he hooked his jacket open just wide enough to display his gun in its shoulder holster. The Newcomer's eyes opened wide.

"This big enough for you?" said Sikes in a low voice, too low even for Cathy to hear.

The Newcomer nodded wordlessly.

Pulling the tattered remains of his dignity together, Matt went into the men's room.

There were several stalls there. One was occupied. He heard some very distinctive sounds coming from within, and knew damned well he wasn't going to be able to do anything until this guy was done.

He heard a foot slam against the stall door, and a magazine dropped to the floor in a rustle of paper. Sikes concentrated with all his might on combing his hair just so.

A minute later, the stall door opened. A human male, grinning lopsidedly and looking slightly punchy, stepped out. He was holding several porno magazines in his hand, and he tossed them on the counter in front of Sikes. "Here y'go," he said.

Sikes watched him head toward the door, and then his ever-present sharp detective's eye noticed something. "Hey. You forgot your cup."

The guy turned and looked at him blankly for a moment, and then he understood. "Oh. I don't have

149

a cup. I'm not with them," he said, pointing outside. "I just come here for the magazines."

He sauntered out.

Sikes contemplated arresting the guy, and thereby dodging the whole problem that he was now faced with. Ultimately, though, that would solve nothing. Cathy would just be annoyed with him, and besides, Sikes didn't want to have to fill out the paperwork on a collar like that.

Maybe he could have George do it . . .

Nah.

Why postpone the inevitable.

As he took the magazine and, feeling thoroughly humiliated, set about to take care of "business," he hoped that perhaps George was having an easier time patching things up with Susan. Because he knew that, no matter what George was claiming, Susan was, in fact, pissed.

Warily, George Francisco entered his living room.

He did so with the air of someone who felt as if he had to watch for land mines or booby traps. Clutched in one hand like a life preserver was a potted cactus with a red ribbon tied around it. It was Susan's favorite type of plant.

"Susan . . . I'm home," he called cautiously.

George wondered if, in coming to his wife with such an obvious attempt at reconciliation, he was going to appear too desperate to patch things up. Would she accept the plant in the spirit with which it was given? Or would she look at him disdainfully and say, "You thought you could make me happy with some potted plant?" He pictured her grabbing it from him and hurling it against the wall . . . or even worse, bouncing it off his head.

Maybe he should call ahead first. Maybe it'd be

best if he just backed out the front door while there was still time . . .

Susan emerged from the family room.

She was wearing a black dress that looked as if it had been spray-painted on her. In front of her she was carefully holding a tray on which were balanced a carafe of sour milk and two champagne flutes.

"Hello, George," she said, in a voice that elevated the room temperature by at least twenty degrees.

George wasn't falling for it. Not immediately, at any rate. This might still be a setup. The complexity of a woman's mind knew no bounds. He held up the plant and said, "I brought you a cactus."

She looked at it as if it had just been handed down by God, accompanied by a heavenly choir and a ten-minute light show. "It's beautiful," she sighed. "Set it down and have some sour milk."

"All right," he said, allowing himself to feel slightly encouraged. This was certainly a far better reception than he could have possibly imagined. He set the cactus down and stared at the incredibly tight black dress she was wearing. "Is that a new outfit?" he asked.

"Why, yes," she said.

She set the tray down on the coffee table, and then twirled in place once. George gaped in astonishment as he saw that the dress was cut very low down the back, nearly to the base of the spine. On a human woman, it would have been alluring. On a Newcomer woman, with its open display of the hypersensitive potniki spots, it was the equivalent of a human woman wearing a dress that consisted of simple nylon mesh from neck to crotch, and nothing else.

"Do you like it?" she asked coquettishly.

"I can see almost all your potniki," George said, trying to keep the amazement from his voice. He couldn't remember Susan ever being this overt before. Not that she had ever been a—what was the Earth term?—shrinking violet. But even so . . .

Susan approached him, draping her arms around his neck. "Is that so bad?" she asked. "Seeing my spots, I mean."

"No," said George, and he felt his blood racing. "Not at all." Then he paused, taking the plunge. Referring to events best left forgotten might not be the smartest thing under the circumstances, but he still had to clear it up. "Susan, that fight we had last night . . . it was ridiculous."

"Yes," she agreed readily.

"Let's make up."

Again, she said, "Yes."

They brought their temples together, sharing in the physical and spiritual enjoyment of their proximity. He started to slip his hand around her waist, but before his fingers could brush against her spots, she pushed him a step back.

It took a moment or two for George to register that she had broken contact. He shook his head slightly, as if to try and toss off a fog. "What?" he asked.

In a voice that was like ice, she asked, "Have you changed your mind about Albert and May?"

George had been so certain that that was a closed issue, that he was completely confused to find it suddenly thrown up in his face again . . . especially as he began to realize with a hideous sinking feeling that he had completely misread the situation. "I thought you'd changed yours?" he said with a bare touch of hopefulness.

This barely optimistic viewpoint was quickly dashed as she said firmly, "Of course I haven't."

"Susan," he said imploringly. His mind and body were in total havoc, one battering against the other.

His mind was telling him that it was important to get matters settled. His body was letting him know that the top priority right now was getting Susan into the bedroom so that he could peel her like a grape.

He reached for her, but she pushed him away. "No," she said firmly.

And then, as if the situation weren't difficult enough, they heard a thudding down the stairs as Emily trotted into view. "Mom, Dad, I fed the fish, I did my homework, and now I'm going with Jill to the mall."

George's mind said, *Good. Now your mother and I can have a satisfying exchange of ideas, without being concerned over raising our voices.*

George's body said, *Good. Now I can rip Susan's dress off and take her right here on the floor, without being concerned you'll walk in on us.*

And then George saw what Emily was wearing.

And George's mouth said, "Not like that you're not."

She was sporting a dress that, while it wasn't tight like Susan's, was nevertheless cut low down the back.

Susan, despite her abrupt cold-shouldering of George, immediately allied with him out of parental sense of presenting a united front. Besides, she wasn't thrilled either. "Come back here! Where did you get that dress?" she demanded.

"Jill gave it to me," said Emily, with an injured air. "It was too tight on her, and I liked it. What's the problem?"

"You're naked!" said George, waving his hands and feeling like some sitcom father.

"I am not," retorted Emily.

Susan pointed and said, "Your potniki are showing."

"So? What about you?"

"For one thing, I'm not marching around a mall. And for another, I'm a grown-up!"

"What difference does that make?" Emily's hands were on her hips in her best defiant manner.

George spoke as firmly as if he were making an arrest. "Little girls do not go around with their potniki on display."

"You march back up those stairs and put something on."

"What?! Mommmmmm!!"

"You heard me."

Emily stomped her foot. "It's not fair! How can you tell me not to do something when you do it yourself!"

"Because . . . because we're your parents!" said Susan in exasperation.

She looked to George for backup. George, for his part, knew that morally they were on extremely shaky ground. But there was one thing of which he was completely certain, and he didn't care a bit about any shadings of gray. "You are not leaving this house," he said firmly, "until you put something decent on."

Emily exploded with an infuriated "Ooooohhfff!" and stormed back up the stairs as if hoping that every step would shake the house apart.

Susan and George looked at each other.

Her expression indicated that she was frustrated, exasperated, vulnerable.

George's mind said, *Say something sensitive. Write off sex for tonight. Concentrate on being a nurturing husband.*

George's body said, *She's vulnerable. She's worked up. She's still in that dress. Make your move. Do it! DO IT!*

His body won.

George lifted the carafe and said invitingly, "How about that sour milk now?"

Susan stared at him as if he'd just sprouted a third eye.

"I'm getting out of this stupid dress," she said. And she marched up the steps, making a stomping noise that was quite similar to the one her daughter had produced mere moments ago.

Rattled and bewildered, George sank down on the floor next to the coffee table.

George's body said, *She's upstairs taking the dress off. Now's your chance! If—*

"Oh, shut up," said George tiredly. He started to pour himself a stiff shot of sour milk, and then changed his mind and drank it straight from the carafe.

He hoped that Matt was having better luck with his sex class than George was having with his sex life. Maybe, after Matt had finished with the course, George would ask him for some advice on how to handle Newcomer women. Because Matt would be freshly schooled, and George couldn't imagine that he, George, could be doing worse with his Newcomer woman than he was right now.

The classroom for the Human/Tenctonese sex class was lined with wall charts depicting a variety of interesting things: Human and Newcomer internal sex organs; Newcomer lovemaking positions (back to back, head to head); and the human digestive system.

The sex therapist was a middle-aged Newcomer woman with a general sort of earth mother air about her. She was wearing a loose-fitting brown peasant blouse and a long flowing skirt spread neatly across her lap.

The class was seated in a circle of chairs. There were chairs set up for nine couples—six where the males werc Newcomers, and three where the females were the Newcomer partner. There was only one empty chair in the group.

It was next to Cathy.

She looked at it with mild nervousness, but kept telling herself that Matt would never, ever, ditch her right at the beginning of the class. No matter how self-conscious he felt, he would never put her in such an embarrassing position.

She hoped that if she said that to herself enough times, she might actually believe it.

The therapist cleared her throat slightly, which settled down the low buzz of conversation in the class. They looked at her expectantly.

"Hello," she said, bobbing her head at the class. "My name is Vivian Webster, and I'm so happy to see all of you here tonight. You're really like pioneers, the first explorers in the new land of Newcomer/Human love. And with today's headlines, your being here couldn't be more timely."

She held up a tabloid and read the headline out loud. "Human/Newcomer baby shocks the world." Then she smiled gamely. "It seems that, on top of everything else, you've also got to worry about birth control."

This drew some appreciative laughter.

It was at this moment, naturally, that Sikes walked in.

As self-conscious as he was, at first he thought that the laughter was directly in response to his entrance. But then he saw that everyone had their backs to him and were clearly amused by something that the teacher had said. It relaxed him, but not overly.

Then the teacher spotted him and looked up

questioningly. Everyone else followed her gaze and, within moments, every eye in the place was on Sikes.

He stood there with his little cup, moving his feet uncertainly. "Uh . . . where should I put this?"

Vivian pointed toward a table. "Just set it there." And then, seeing how uncomfortable Matt was, she endeavored to put him a bit more at ease by adding, "And don't put it anywhere near the coffee maker. We don't want a repeat of the time someone confused it with Cremora."

This drew a healthy laugh, switching the focus from Matt back to the therapist. Sikes was, of course, quite aware of what she had just done, and was extremely grateful. Chalk one up for the therapist in the Sikes book of appreciation.

He set it down on the table and moved quickly over to Cathy, taking the empty seat next to her.

In a low voice, Cathy said, "I was getting worried about you."

"This month's interview was with Joe DiMaggio. I got distracted. Sorry," he said.

She looked surprised. "Joe DiMaggio? I took a pottery class with him! If you'd like, I'll introduce you."

He sighed. The Newcomer gag names were wearing thinner every time he heard them. "No, thanks," he said. "I wouldn't know what to say."

"Oh. All right."

Vivian, in the meantime, ignored the whispered exchange and said, "I like to start each class with a series of exercises." She gestured for them to get to their feet. "Let's all stand."

They did as instructed, with Sikes looking as uncomfortable as he felt.

"The process of learning to make love requires the letting go of inhibitions. I know many of you are self-conscious, but let's start breaking down some of those barriers right now. Everybody hold hands and form a circle."

They did so. Sikes found himself holding Cathy's hand with his left, but with his right hand he was holding hands with a Newcomer male. Even better, Sikes quickly realized that it was the Newcomer male who'd been standing behind him in line. The Newcomer was staring at him with a certain amount of dread.

"Say 'hi' to the stranger next to you," said Vivian cheerfully. She did everything cheerfully. Sikes was starting to hate her.

"Hi," said the Newcomer, making an effort. "I'm Noel. Noel Parking."

"Sikes," said Sikes, trying not to make eye contact.

"Now," Vivian called out to the class, "The basis of Newcomer foreplay is humming. Can any of the human students tell me why Newcomers hum?"

"They don't know the words?" suggested Sikes, more to himself than anyone else.

The comment got no laughs at all. It did, however, get a rueful smile from Vivian. "There's one in every group." She sighed. "The reason Newcomers hum, class, is . . . well, I'm sure you've heard the expression, 'Let's make beautiful music together.' Newcomers find that the humming literally brings them in tune with one another. When they've reached the peak of humming, they will shift notes and tones in perfect unison without problem, because they are so completely in sync with each other. Imagine, if you will, an entire symphony orchestra playing a piece without sheet music or even a conductor. Instead they're so in touch with each another that they simply operate as a unit, instinctively. Once the humming link has been achieved to perfection, then one can move on to the next phase of sex. So, let's practice humming. Close your eyes . . . and let's all hum."

Setting the pitch, she began to hum. The others followed suit.

Everyone had their eyes closed, trying as best they could to be sensitive not only to their own sensibilities, but also the general tone that was being hummed by the class. Their eyes were closed, their attention was focused.

Everyone except for Sikes.

He chanced a look at the others, looking through narrowed lids at the idyllic expressions on everyone else. He knew he was supposed to have his mind squarely on what was happening. But instead, all sorts of things were whirling through his head.

Why was he the only one who was self-conscious? Was there something wrong with him? Was there something wrong with everyone else? Was this all really worth it? What was he committing to by undertaking the class? If a Newcomer was tone-deaf, did that mean he or she had to be celibate their entire life?

And finally, ultimately, as humming filled the room, all of Matt's conflicting concerns boiled down to one, clear imperative.

It was simple.

It was clean.

It was tidy.

And it overwhelmed anything else.

Get me the hell outta here, he thought.

But he stayed.

For a while.

CHAPTER 14

GEORGE WAS NOT particularly looking forward to seeing Sikes the next morning since Matt had been so dead-on accurate in his prediction of the intensity of Susan's reactions.

Sikes was not particularly looking forward to seeing George the next morning since George had this tendency to discuss Matt's sex life with a candor that was disconcerting and a volume that was stentorian.

So naturally they both ran into the one individual who they wanted to see even less than each other.

George, walking through the coffee room, bumped (almost literally) into Albert. Albert looked up at him eagerly and said, "George . . ."

George knew precisely what Albert was going to ask, and yet hoped against hope that, in fact, Albert was going to discuss the weather or Vessna's help or anything other than . . .

"Did you talk to Susan yet?"

160

George maintained his brisk stride. Albert paced him, utterly oblivious of George's unconscious attempt to leave him behind. George smiled gamely. "You know, I forgot."

Another individual might have been wounded at such a response. At that point in time, there was nothing more important to Albert than the conception of his child. For George to sound almost cavalier in his handling of the situation might have prompted, at the very least, annoyance in some people.

Not Albert.

"Oh," he said, allowing the one brief flash of disappointment that his character would permit. Then he nodded understandingly. "I'm not surprised. With the giant and the strange baby—it's been a very distracting couple of days."

"Thank you for understanding, Albert," said George, feeling like dirt. "I'll speak to her tonight."

Through the bedroom door, he added silently, *just like the previous nights since you got me into this. When was any honor so completely distressing.*

Albert was still at his side, chatting about the giant, as they approached George's desk. Sikes was already seated, which George found to be extremely interesting. The only time that Matt ever beat George in was when something was on Matt's mind —something that, invariably, he didn't want to discuss. George could take an educated guess what it was. Normally he would have immediately felt prompted to try and draw Matt out on whatever was bothering him, but this day, he was more than happy to keep his mouth shut. If he didn't probe Sikes about what was bothering him, Matt might not inquire about the increasingly tense situation between himself and Susan. An unspoken *quid pro quo* might be reached.

A nice strategy that was promptly blown to hell and gone as Albert said cheerfully, "Good morning, Sergeant Sikes. How was your sex class last night?"

Sikes looked up, paling slightly. Behind him, someone somewhere barked a laugh. His head snapped around, but he wasn't able to see who it was. Then he turned back to Albert, but his gaze was leveled malevolently at George. "How do you know about that, Albert?"

Even Albert, who was not exactly a master of picking up nonverbal cues where humans were concerned, knew that he had blown it. "Uh . . ."

George guiltily looked down at his shoes.

Sikes sat back in his chair. The one convenient thing about Albert and George was that, between the two of them, they were as subtle as a television evangelist. Maybe they couldn't keep secrets from each other, but neither of them could even come close to keeping secrets from Sikes. He didn't have to be a detective to figure this one out. Hell, a meter maid could have put it together where these two bozos were concerned.

"Thanks, George," he said acidly. "Just blab it all over town." Then, with an irritated air, he stood. "Come on. Grazer wants to see us."

George nodded, grateful for the chance to put some distance between himself and Albert. He headed toward Grazer's office, Sikes right behind him.

As they approached the office, Grazer's aide tried to block their way. "He's on the phone," she said. "Come back later."

"We're not yo-yos, Hilda," said Sikes, in no mood to have to bounce back and forth between desk and office. "He wants to see us, so here we are."

He walked past Hilda, George right behind her,

although George did take a moment to mumble a brief apology.

They strode in and Grazer looked up at them, his ear to the phone, and he made a frustrated gesture that they should wait outside.

"It's noisy out there," Sikes said, leaning against the wall of Grazer's office. George assumed a stance that was roughly on par with the military "at ease."

"Yes, sir," Grazer was saying through gritted teeth, still waving in futility like a crazed bird. "Perhaps it was a bit premature, sir . . ."

Grazer had the phone pressed so hard against his ear that the side of his head was getting white. And now Sikes understood. He glanced at George and saw that his partner likewise comprehended. The captain was smack in the middle of getting his butt severely chewed out by someone in authority. And considering Grazer's activities in recent days, there was obviously only one thing it could be about. He looked at George, who mouthed the words, "The baby." Slowly, grinning, Sikes nodded, and wished for all the world that he had a tape recorder for this immortal moment.

"No, sir," said Grazer. "No, I . . . yes, I understand that I have to see the big picture. But you see, I thought that . . . no, obviously I wasn't, sir . . . Yes, sir . . . I mean, no, sir. I won't make any more statements to the press without your permission . . . without your *written* permission, yes, sir . . . yes, sir . . . oh, and, sir, I just wanted to say—and I think this is very important—that—"

He stopped because the *click* on the other end was so loud that even George and Matt could hear it. Grazer actually stared at the receiver for a moment, which surprised Matt since he didn't usually see people do that outside of TV programs or movies.

Then, slowly, as if defusing a bomb, Grazer settled the receiver back in the cradle. He looked up at the two detectives.

"I was, uh, just chatting with Chief Amburgey. This hybrid baby stuff seems to have set a lot of people off. Assaults on Newcomers are way up."

"No! Really?" said Sikes. "I can't believe it! Can you, George?"

George put his hand to his chest. "My hearts. The shock." Matt grinned. For the perpetually polite George, that was truly blistering sarcasm. It was a hint of just how upset by the entire situation George was.

"So in other words," Sikes jumped back in remorselessly, "you just got your ass reamed."

Barely able to contain himself, Grazer said angrily, "Shut up, Sikes! What the hell are you doing here?"

"You wanted to see us."

"Oh. Right." He took a breath to compose himself. "You ID'd that giant yet?"

"We're running a tissue type, but the BNA computers are down," Sikes said. "We should get it later today."

Grazer leaned back and picked up a signed baseball that he kept on his desk, flipping it back and forth from one hand to the other. "The public defender's office ordered a psychiatric evaluation of this giant, whoever he is. They think he's *non compos mentis*—unfit to stand trial. A few bricks shy of a load. A few cards shy of a deck. So instead they want him—"

"To be made a police captain?" asked Sikes innocently.

"Drop it, Sikes," Grazer warned him. "They want the giant remanded to a mental institution."

"Ah. What did you once call that?" said Sikes.

"Oh yeah . . . a one-way monorail ride to the Magic Kingdom."

"Not my idea, Sikes," said Grazer tersely.

Sikes shrugged. "So remand him."

Grazer stopped flipping the baseball. He looked quite clearly irritated that, apparently, Sikes wasn't getting it. "That Nuke is the only lead to the identity of the baby. Is he related? Did he kidnap her? The public wants some answers."

"Hey, Bry, *we* didn't call that press conference," Sikes said. "Don't start shouting at us when you want us to save your butt from getting burned some more."

"You were supposed to find the parents of that baby!" he shouted.

Matt was about to yell back, but the more conciliatory George stepped in. "Captain, maybe if we brought the baby back here . . . showed her to the giant . . . he might respond in some way. Give us a clue."

"I don't care what you do!" bellowed Grazer. "Just find her!"

Matt clapped George on the back. "You heard the man, George. He doesn't care what we do. Just the words I like to hear. Let's go."

And they went.

But as they went, George couldn't help but frown in concern over what Grazer had said. It had confirmed all his worst fears.

And the most unnerving aspect was that at least George had the protection of his badge and gun, of his authority as a police officer, and of Matt backing him up.

His wife and children could not say the same.

He envisioned them going about their day-to-day business, and wondered bleakly how long it might be before George went from police officer to being the husband or father of a victim of violent racism.

It was not a pleasant thought.

Buck Francisco had gotten used to being one of the very few Newcomer kids in school. Or at least he had thought that he was used to it. But every so often, just when he believed that everything was going to be normal, something new happened to temporarily dash that hope. He was starting to think that maybe he was kidding himself. That "normalcy" was an idealized state that quite simply would never be attained.

As he walked down the corridor, he was aware of human kids looking at him and whispering. When he had first come to Earth, he had joined a Newcomer gang, striking a defiant attitude and lashing out at everyone and everything. But the ultimate folly and self-destruction of that had eventually become clear to him. The percentage of Newcomers in Earth's population was almost insignificant.

He had come to realize that it was important to maintain dignity in dealing with humans, yes. Keep your self-respect, your pride. But the way that you did that was not to attack every pointless whisper, every sideways glance. You had to pick and choose your battles or else you were just a scattergun. A loose cannon. There was no point to that, and it was certainly no way to live your life.

He did what he had done so often in the past. He simply took the whispering, the murmurs, the snickering, and turned them into a simple mental humming. It had no more meaning or importance than bees buzzing—less, in fact, considering that bees could sting you whether you wanted them to or not. Words could only sting you if you permitted it.

He opened his locker, and he heard a particularly

loud peal of laughter that he knew was at his expense. Angrily, he tossed in his books, pulled out the biology text, and slammed the locker door so hard that the sound ricocheted up and down the hallway like a bazooka blast. The only purpose that that served, of course, was to draw more attention to him.

So much for Mister Calm Under Pressure.

Buck took a deep breath to calm himself down, and then walked down the hallway to the biology classroom. The door was open partway, and he heard the voices of several girls in the class, fairly loud as they spoke to be heard over one another's giggling.

"I think it's neat," said one, whose voice Buck immediately identified as belonging to Cindy Bahr. "It's like having a baby with E.T."

"Would you go to bed with one?" came another voice that Buck couldn't place immediately.

"Oh yeah!" said Cindy eagerly. "I hear they're really hung."

Buck sighed. This promised to be an extremely long afternoon, which in turn was going to be part of a long week, month—possibly even an entire lifetime of feeling dragged. There are simply some days where one feels as if he's going to be in high school for the rest of his life.

Just ignore them, he told himself. Go in there as if you don't know what they're talking about and you don't care.

He stepped in and started briskly across the room. Cindy and the girl she was talking to, who Buck now recognized as a blonde named Frannie, spotted him and quickly shoved a tabloid into Cindy's desk. It wasn't fast enough for Buck to miss the headline, which was "OUTER SPACE LOVE CHILD."

It was kind of a shame, really. Under ordinary circumstances, Cindy's attention was something that Buck might easily have coveted. By human or

Tenctonese standards, she was quite attractive. But now her very glance made him feel dirty, and he was only grateful when she looked away self-consciously.

Trust Frannie to keep the problem going. "Hey Buuuccck," she called. "Cindy wants to bear your child."

Cindy squealed, her face flushing red, and she slapped Frannie's shoulder. "I do not!"

Buck shook his head. It was amazing. No wonder they were so quick to turn against Newcomers and subject them to attack or derision. They did exactly the same thing to themselves.

Buck moved to his lab table. As he put his book down, he suddenly became aware of two shadows looming over him. He had a sneaking suspicion who it was. Then a voice rumbled from overhead, "You touch any girl in this school and you're dead."

Again, Buck sighed. He felt as if he were doing that a lot lately. Apparently the premier school jock, Bruno Carson, didn't have enough to occupy what was laughingly referred to as his mind. Now he had to waste time displaying his masculinity by threatening Buck . . . who had never done anything to him.

Buck didn't even bother to turn to see who was standing next to Bruno. Ultimately, it didn't matter all that much. The various athletes tended to blend in one with another, as far as Buck was concerned. His common sense told him that he shouldn't even bother to respond. If he said nothing, if he gave them nothing to feed off, they'd probably just go away.

Then again—with types like these, the point wasn't always simply to deliver a message. If he did nothing, they might very well start trying to provoke him, just to get a rise out of him. In fact, their track record indicated that that was probably precisely what they would do. Why sit around and wait for that to happen?

"What's the matter, guys?" said Buck with false joviality. "Afraid they'll like space meat?"

Suddenly Buck was facing Carson. He hadn't particularly intended to. But Bruno Carson had grabbed Buck by the shoulder and spun him around with such force that, for a moment, Buck felt slightly dizzy.

Bruno's temper was as short as his buzz-cut hair. He had the IQ of a tablecloth. This didn't make him any less dangerous or Buck any less angry.

"Purists are right," Carson snarled into Buck's face. The foul smell of cigarettes on his breath that Carson had been sneaking in the men's room made Buck wince. "Slags oughta be put in camps."

Buck made a slight popping sound with his lips, and glanced right and left with apparently limitless patience. And then he raised his voice just enough to make sure that it carried throughout the classroom.

"This what they call penis envy?" he asked.

The walls of the room were lined with various specimens embalmed in jars of formaldehyde. Buck became abruptly aware of this because suddenly he was off his feet, at the receiving end of an infuriated shove from Carson, and he was unceremoniously smashed into one of the shelves, sending the specimens crashing to the floor. The powerful smell oozed through the classroom, causing students to gag and also become a bit nauseated by the dead animals splattered all over the floor. Frannie in particular made a loud noise of disgust, and Cindy was shouting at Frannie that this was all her fault even as she started opening windows to air the place out.

Buck didn't hear any of it. He stepped forward, anger boiling over. His foot came down on a frog with a loud squish, but he didn't notice it. He was far more intent on Carson's slablike fist that was winging his way.

He could have dodged it, but instead he chose to remind his tormentors of just how strong Newcomers were. He caught Bruno's wrist, stopping the punch cold.

Bruno strained for a moment, too intent and, frankly, too stupid to realize that Buck was barely straining against him. Buck twisted, keeping his balance despite the slime lining the bottom of his Reeboks, and tossed Bruno across the room. Carson crashed backwards over a desk as the student seated at it leaped to her feet to avoid him.

He kept going and smashed into the wall. Fortunately enough he wasn't injured since he'd only hit it with his head. From his undignified position on the ground, he bellowed, "Get him!"

Another two jocks leaped to their feet from the back of the room, converging with the third to bear down towards Buck. Buck stood there, fists cocked, poised on the balls of his feet, and bleakly hoped that he wouldn't have to kill them to stop them, since that would probably look pretty bad on his school record.

That was when an angry voice called out, "Gentlemen!"

They stopped dead in their tracks.

Standing in the now wide open doorway was the teacher, Mr. Bowen. He surveyed the damage, making no attempt to disguise just how appalled he was by what he was witnessing.

Bruno was on his feet now, pointing to Buck in a desultory fashion. "He hit me."

Bowen needed no time at all to assess the situation. "I can see very well what's going on here."

Upon hearing that, Carson folded his arms and grinned malevolently at Buck, with an unmistakable "You're gonna get it now, punk" attitude. So he was caught flatfooted when Bowen's next words were, "Mr. Carson, you clean this mess up."

Carson whirled to face him. "Me?!" Bruno looked apoplectic, and Buck thought that the jock seemed to have a good shot at spontaneously combusting.

Bowen took a step forward. With thinning hair and unimpressive build, Bowen was a head shorter than Carson. But with the pure fury that was quite clearly rampaging through him, he seemed to tower over the athlete.

"If there are any more incidents of this kind," said Bowen, "I'm sending you and your friends to Mr. Fischer's office." And then, his face darkening even further, he added, "It will also have a very negative effect on your grade in this class. And need I remind you of the grade point average you must maintain in order to participate in football and all your other little testosterone festivals."

Carson glowered at him, but he seemed to be withdrawing into himself. Bowen pointed to the hallway and said, "There's a mop in the janitor's closet."

After a moment's consideration in which Carson clearly tried to decide whether getting tossed off the team was worth slugging the teacher, he obviously decided that it was not. He walked out towards the janitor's closet to get the mop, although he paused long enough to fire off a furious look at Buck.

Buck didn't notice.

He was busy with a paper towel, wiping frog off his sneaker, and wondering just what in hell he was going to have to do to get accepted around this place.

CHAPTER 15

D AYLIGHT FLOODED THROUGH the single window of the interrogation room—daylight that was broken up by the bars of the window. One little patterned square of light from the earth's closest star.

How far the giant had come. His view was pretty much what it had been before.

Not that he gave any indication that he was aware of it . . . or aware of anything, for that matter. He sat hunched over in the interrogation room of the police station, apparently oblivious to the world around him. He was heavily shackled, but he seemed weighed down by far more than mere chains.

Standing next to the giant on either side were Sikes and Francisco. Once again George had made a few tentative efforts to communicate with the giant, but, as expected, had made no headway at all. He had lapsed into silent, thoughtful gazing at the sullen creature. Sikes, for his part, was staring at the door. Two uniformed cops were standing there. One was

172

holding a tranquilizer gun, clutching it tightly, and idly flipping the safety on and off.

It was the giant who reacted first. Before the sound of footsteps reached their ears, the giant had already raised his head. His face changed, his expression moving instantly from despair to desperate hope. The shift was so abrupt that the cop with the tranq gun reflexively took a step back and half raised the gun. Sikes made a gesture for the cop to lower the gun and get a closer grip on himself.

Then they heard the footsteps, as Sikes and George had already figured they would. The giant's internal radar when it came to that baby was already quite evident. At least, though, the giant seemed to have acquired a bit more self-control. He wasn't howling or groaning or in any way acting in a truly alarming fashion. Indeed, his face was a mask of concentration, as if he was doing everything he could to rein himself in. He had, however, gotten to his feet, once again prompting the cop with the tranq gun to raise his weapon, this time thumbing off the safety.

"He's all right," said George confidently, addressing the cop but never taking his eyes off the giant. The cop, however, wasn't especially quick to lower his gun this time. The giant's height and presence were rather unnerving, despite the fact that he was in chains.

The door opened. In the doorway stood Grazer. He peered in a moment to ascertain for himself that everything was secure, and then he gestured behind him. Franz Kafka entered, carrying the infant. The Newcomer then hesitated, clearly taken aback when he saw the towering being in front of him. To his credit, he reflexively held the baby closer, as if to protect her.

The giant's expression had not changed. Indeed, he seemed to be concentrating more than ever.

And suddenly, too late, George realized why.

Instead of thrashing around, he was devoting his full strength and attention to breaking out of his bonds. And now, perhaps fueled by the appearance of the child, he suddenly emitted a roar as a karate master would shriek when smashing boards barehanded.

The shackles virtually exploded off him, links flying every which way. Luckily for the giant, one length of chain hit the guard who was holding the tranq gun. It knocked the cop back, his finger squeezing spasmodically on the trigger, and the dart shot out the open doorway.

George and Sikes leaped at him, but in the enclosed area they had no room for artful maneuvers. Consequently it was strength against strength, and in that contest they weren't even real entrants. The giant shoved the detectives out of the way and charged towards Kafka. Kafka was frozen in place, rooted there by the terrifying sight of the giant bearing down on him.

Grazer shouted, "Tranq him! Somebody!" and the other cop was grabbing the fallen weapon.

Kafka did all he could, but at that moment, all he could manage was not to let himself scream in fright. The giant bellowed once more into the Newcomer's face in inarticulate rage, and then grabbed the baby out of his arms.

For one horrific moment, Grazer saw the next day's headlines: "Hybrid Baby Murdered While Cops Stand By." *"Tranq him, for God's sake!"*

But there was no clear shot. The giant held the baby tightly cradled in his arms now, and had fallen back behind a desk. The cop with the tranq gun knew that any sudden movement by the giant would cause the baby to catch the dart instead. It could drive right into the child's skull if the shot were unlucky, and even if it simply struck the infant's body, the dosage might still very well kill her.

And then George was blocking the shot as well. He was standing in front of the giant, his hands outstretched, and Sikes was next to him.

[*"Don't hurt the child"*] George said as soothingly as he could.

Sikes overlapped him, saying, "Give us the baby."

They moved closer toward the behemoth, who was backed up as far as he could go. They were concerned about his threatening the baby as an effort to escape; about his maybe hurting the baby but unaware that he was doing so; about his actually getting away, and the whole thing starting over again.

In short, at that moment they were concerned about everything except getting the huge mute to speak.

[*"Don't hurt me . . . "*] said the giant. [*"I am . . . fine . . ."*]

Sikes and George froze. "Was that . . . did that mean anything?" Sikes asked George.

Francisco nodded, but before he could translate, the giant repeated the sentence in halting English. And then he kept saying, "I am fine. I am fine," like a parrot or a broken record.

"We won't hurt you," said Sikes soothingly. He held out his hands. "Just . . . just give us the baby. Okay?"

Sikes knew damned well that the moment the baby was clear, the giant was going to get pumped with enough tranquilizer to send the Green Bay Packers' offensive line to dreamland. He noticed, from the corner of his eye, Grazer waving the cop with the tranq gun around to one side to try and get a clearer shot.

Sikes wasn't sure whether the giant had noticed or not. Nevertheless he held the infant more tightly

175

than ever. And then he said something that, even though it was in English, was incomprehensible to Sikes.

"Chorboke is coming," he intoned. "Chorboke is coming."

But though it had no meaning to Sikes, George looked as if someone had just hit him upside the head with a red-hot poker. "Who?" he said, with an air of someone who is hoping that he heard incorrectly.

Very carefully, overenunciating every syllable, the giant said, "Chorboke . . . he's coming."

Grazer, looking as if he wanted to take command of the situation, stepped past Kafka, who was still paralyzed against the door. But now he looked frightened for a different reason. His look of concern mirrored George's perfectly, and it was clear that the giant had said something extremely significant. Clear, that was, to everyone except Grazer, whose major anxiety revolved around how all of this would look if it hit the papers.

"Come on, now," said Grazer firmly. "Give us the baby."

"Wait!" said George, in a tone so firm and commanding that it was clear that the balance of priorities in the room had suddenly shifted. As far as George was concerned, the focus was entirely on the previously mute giant's words rather than his actions. Slowly, as if displaying some final hope that he and the giant were discussing two different things, he said, "Chorboke is dead."

The infant looked up at George with those same tranquil eyes. A tranquility that was even more disturbing when it contrasted with the seriousness of what they were discussing.

"No," said the giant, as if he were sounding the death knell of the Newcomers. "He is coming."

At that moment, Grazer signaled the cop. With the giant's attention fixed completely on Francisco, it was now an easy and safe shot. The gun spit out its second dart, and it struck the giant in the back of the shoulder.

The giant cried out in pain and anguish, and the baby's reaction was immediate. The fear and terror in the giant's face was mirrored in the baby's own.

"No!" shouted George, but it was far too late. All that he and Sikes could do was break the giant's fall because he was tumbling over to the side. Grazer quickly snatched the baby out of the giant's arms, fending off the possibility of the giant falling atop her and crushing her like an egg.

The baby, however, didn't seem at all concerned about her own welfare. She squirmed in Grazer's arms, clearly unnerved by the giant's collapse. There was no longer any sense of peace in her eyes, but rather pure, undiluted fear.

And Sikes realized, with dull horror, that it was more than just being upset about the giant falling down. It was as if she were sharing in whatever it was the giant was feeling, at any given moment.

"Let's get him back to the holding cell," said Sikes wearily. With the aid of George and the other two cops, they managed to shoulder the burden of the giant's weight. As they started to drag him into the hallway, Sikes muttered, "Y'know, Albert's so hung up about this guy. He's not going to be real thrilled when he finds out we had to knock him out."

But as they left the room, they almost stumbled over a body in the hallway—Albert Einstein, lying there peacefully asleep, a tranq dart in his upper thigh. Apparently the misfired dart had found a target after all.

George and Sikes looked at each other.

"I won't tell him if you won't," said Sikes.

CHAPTER 16

THE GIANT CAME to long before Albert did. And once he did, he was back to his unspeaking, sullen self. By the time Albert recovered consciousness, the giant was back in his holding cell, lying on the floor.

A single tear rolled down his face.

As Sikes stood there and witnessed it, he had the distinct feeling that he had never seen a more heart-wrenching portrait of misery than he saw right then.

Albert was leaning on his broom a bit more heavily than he ordinarily would, favoring the leg that the dart had penetrated. He shook his head slowly. "They shouldn't have hurt him."

It was a typical Albert comment. He had not voiced the slightest complaint about what had happened to him, and his mishap as an innocent bystander. His only concern was for the soul-sick giant. George nodded. "I know, Albert."

"He should be with the baby," Albert continued,

his gaze never leaving the cell's occupant. "They need each other."

Sikes glanced at him. It was a notion that he had already intuited, but Albert said it with such conviction that it made Sikes wonder if Albert had some sort of inside information. "Why do you say that?"

"I don't know," said Albert. "I . . . feel it."

Sikes nodded understandingly. If there was one thing that Newcomer males seemed to be into a lot, it was feelings. Indeed, Sikes found that particular aspect to be the most disconcerting, rather than the spotted heads or two hearts, or even the imbibing of sour milk. He gave Albert a sympathetic pat on the shoulder, and then said, "Come on, George."

He and George went out, leaving Albert and the giant in silent communion.

As they headed towards the squad room, Sikes studied George carefully. He saw that the Newcomer was distracted. Not only that, but he even recognized the look on George's face as the kind of look he had when he was thinking about something that involved the Tenctonese—usually something unpleasant from their past. Frequently Sikes didn't have a clue as to what George's concerns involved, but this time it was fairly self-evident.

"Who's that guy you were talking about. Chore . . . something."

"Chorboke," said George. The simple act of speaking the name seemed an effort, and he could do nothing to keep the revulsion from his voice. When he continued, it was with obvious difficulty. "He was a scientist on the ship."

"On the spaceship that brought you here," said Sikes, who then mentally kicked himself. *No, moron, on the "Love Boat" during the last big Newcomer pleasure cruise. Of COURSE the spaceship.*

But George, preoccupied by his concerns and not

particularly prone to sarcasm anyway, simply nodded. "He performed medical experiments on the
slaves . . . terrible things."

"Did he . . . on . . . ?"

Sikes couldn't even complete the sentence, but
George immediately understood. "On me? Or
Susan? No. No, if anything as devastating as a crash
could be termed 'lucky,' then we were lucky. He
didn't get around to us before our forced landing.
But if our journey had continued . . . who knows?"
He shuddered. "I never saw Chorboke but, like
everyone else, I feared him."

"You said he was dead."

"That's what we were told. That he died in the
crash."

He spoke with the air of someone who desperately
wanted to hold on to his beliefs about something
because to deal with other possibilities was simply
too horrible to contemplate.

They entered the squad room, and Sikes noticed
that Zepeda was standing by Sikes's desk, the phone
to her ear. Sikes felt a flash of annoyance; Zepeda
had her own desk, for crying out loud, and her own
telephone. What'd she need to be on Matt's phone
for? What was she . . . calling a bookie or boyfriend
or something?

Zepeda was jotting something down, and she had a
wide grin on her face. Then she spotted Sikes coming
across the room, and promptly crumpled up the
paper. This led Sikes to believe that it genuinely was
illicit betting numbers or some such thing, until
Zepeda pressed the Hold button and called across
the squad room, "Hey, Sikes! I was taking a message
for you. It's Cathy on line two. She wants to remind
you about sex class tonight!"

This, of course, had every head turning and grins

from every idiot in the squad room. Sikes tried to restrain himself from doing two things: charging across the squad room as quickly as possible, and throttling Zepeda when he got to his desk. He didn't succeed at the first, and barely held back from the second. Instead he squeezed the receiver tightly, imagining it to be Zepeda's neck.

"You had to shout that across the place?" he demanded in a harsh whisper.

Zepeda sighed in mock-apologetic manner. "Yeah. I had to. Sorry, Sikes. Character flaw and all that." Then she grinned. "Have loootttts of fun tonight," and she walked away.

As George approached his own desk, Sikes picked up the phone. "Cathy, hi. Look, I was gonna call you. My neck . . . it's gotten a lot worse. I can't even move my head."

Cathy sounded startled on the other end. "Oh, Matt . . . I'm . . . I don't know what to say. I thought for sure that it was improving. You'd better have it x-rayed, and a chiropractor might want to put you in a neck brace—"

"I'm way ahead of you," said Sikes quickly. "I already called my chiropractor, but the only time that I could get in to see him was tonight."

"Oh," she said, unable to hide her disappointment. "Well . . . well that conflicts with the class tonight. But of course, your health comes first. That comes above everything."

"I know," he said. "I'm really disappointed."

"I guess . . . well, maybe I could go and take notes. Better still, I could tape record it."

"Yeah! That's a good idea. You do that and we can get together later and listen to it. Just the two of us . . . in private. It'll be even better than in the class."

"I don't know about that," said Cathy, doubtfully. "But we'll make do. After all, this is all about adapting to each other's circumstances, isn't it."

"Exactly. Okay. Gotta go. Bye."

He hung up, and then immediately was aware that George was staring at him. In fact, he didn't even have to look at his partner to know that George was gaping at him in open disbelief. Immediately he started shuffling through a stack of papers, hoping that George would, for once in his life, have the good sense and grace to keep his nose out of Matt's private life. For that matter it would be nice if *some*one kept their nose out of his private life, since it seemed as if it was awful public these days.

"Where'd I put those witness statements," he muttered.

"You lied to Cathy." There was stark incredulity in his voice.

"No. My neck hurts." As if to bolster his claim, he rubbed his neck a moment and stuck out his chin.

But George would not be deterred, although he still displayed lack of mastery over slang as he declared, "It was an in-and-out lie! You don't even *have* a chiropractor!"

"George, I don't feel like discussing this."

Sikes still wasn't looking up, but that didn't stop George. He leaned down on his desk to bring his sight line level with Sikes, even though Matt was now hunched over some papers. "Why did you do it?" Surprisingly, there was nothing accusatory in his tone. He sounded more concerned than anything else, because he knew that it couldn't have been an easy or casual thing for Matt to have been less than truthful with Cathy.

Sikes bit his lower lip, and then it all came pouring out in a rush. Everything that he had wanted to say to Cathy but had been unable to because she had spent so much time after the class saying how wonderful it was and how pleased she was with Matt that he was willing to go through all the training and sessions for her.

"I can't take it!" he practically exploded. "Okay? I can't go to that class! All that . . ." His face wrinkled in disgust. ". . . that touchy-feely, disgusting, personal stuff! They made me hold hands and hum!"

Clearly George wasn't understanding the problem. To him it was a matter of simple practicality. "But Matt, these are things you need to know."

"I don't *care! I can't handle it!"*

He had gotten louder than he had intended. Again he was the subject of curious and bemused looks throughout the squad room. He lowered his voice and said, "Look, George, can I come over tonight?"

It was a shift in conversation that George had not expected. "Of course. Why?"

"I can't go home," said Sikes, sounding like a hunted man. "Cathy might see me. And I don't want to hang out in some bar."

George flinched a bit. "Won't I be aiding and abetting your lie to Cathy?"

"No, you're being loyal to your partner, George. Didn't you ever see *The Maltese Falcon,* for crying out loud? C'mon, whaddaya say. I'll bring over a six-pack—a quart of Old Yellow for you—it'll be fun."

"All right," George sighed. "You can even bring your malted falcon if you wish."

At that moment Zepeda called over to them from her computer. "Hey! Guys! Take a look at this!"

They walked over to her desk, Sikes telling himself that if Zepeda made one more crack about the sex class, the distributor cap on her beloved Porsche was going to vanish rather mysteriously. But no, at this point, Zepeda was all business. She was studying her computer screen, and she said, "I finally got through to the BNA computer. When I try to run a tissue type on your giant, look what happens."

Her fingers flew with confidence over the keyboard, and Sikes and Francisco leaned over her shoulder to peer at her keyboard.

The word Searching was pulsing at the top of the screen. And then the words OPSIL—CLASSIFIED appeared below it. Zepeda tried reentering the information, but every time she did, she kept getting the same message, running into an electronic brick wall.

"What the hell is Opsil?" asked Sikes.

Zepeda shook her head. "Beats me."

He looked to George, but he was also drawing a blank.

"Get in touch with the Feds," said Sikes. "See if you can find out." He stepped back and said, "I got a feeling this thing might be bigger than we thought. This might be one of those cases where we ain't gonna like where it leads us. Not like it one bit."

CHAPTER 17

SUSAN FORCED HERSELF to try and bring her mind back to her work.

She had already had a bellyful of the stares that she had drawn on her way in to the office. And there had been some fairly tasteless remarks, muttered just low enough so that she hadn't quite heard them, but loud enough that she knew something was being said. It was extremely frustrating, and more than a little humiliating.

She refocused herself on what her assistant was saying. Molly, a young, pert Newcomer who was fairly new to the firm, was going over the campaign she had developed, storyboard by storyboard. Susan was so distracted that she found herself shaking her head instinctively before she had the opportunity to understand, on a real level, why she was having problems with Molly's storyboards. Then she put up a hand and halted Molly before she could continue.

"Molly, NuGuy is a masculine hygiene deodorant," she said patiently. "Our emphasis should be on freshness and cleanliness. When it comes to the male body, people don't *really* want to be reminded of—"

(That little snake?)

"—what's down there," she finished, ignoring her internal interruption. She tapped the storyboard, which depicted a Newcomer male cheerfully spraying himself in the area of the crotch, wearing nothing but a smile, while a female lay in a bed in the background, wrapped in a blanket and clearly nothing else. "This is just too graphic."

Then she leaned forward and, despite herself, started staring closely at the male's lower regions. "What is this you've drawn in here? Hanging from around the male's . . . genitalia." She found, oddly, she didn't want to touch it to indicate, so she waved her finger over it. "It looks like . . . some sort of . . ." She looked questioningly at Molly. ". . . of bell?"

"You've never seen those?" said Molly, cheerfully. "Susan, where have you been? They're all the rage. When the male hums, it sends out a series of chimes that harmonizes and causes heightened excitement."

"And . . . they hang from there?"

"That's right. They're called Hum Dingers. Would you like me to pick one up for you? I know this place—"

"No," said Susan, trying to sound casual. "I guess I'm just a little old-fashioned." Then she added ruefully, more to herself than Molly, "George would say too old-fashioned."

Before Molly could ask what she meant, Susan's human supervisor, Art Delgado, walked in. Susan quickly pulled the tissue overlay down on the storyboards so Delgado wouldn't catch sight of them.

"Susan . . ." said Delgado.

"Yes, sir."

"I understand your husband's involved with this hybrid baby case." He stood in front of her, his arms folded.

"Yes."

"When he locates the parents," said Delgado, "would you let me know?"

Susan did nothing to hide her surprise and puzzlement. By way of explanation, Delgado continued, "Jenson Baby Foods is looking for a mascot for their new unispecies line. They want to buy commercial rights to the baby's image."

"Well, as long as George wouldn't get in any trouble," Susan said after a moment.

Delgado smiled and said, "See what you can do." Then he turned and walked out.

Susan sat there thoughtfully as Molly started to gather up her storyboards. Molly was shaking her head in amazement. "Why would they want to use that baby? It gives me the creeps."

That confused Susan. For a moment she thought they might not be talking about the same infant. "I've seen pictures. She's beautiful."

Molly nodded, allowing for that, but said, "It's not the physical look. It's the . . . well, it's the idea." She shuddered. "Making love to a human."

Susan was utterly taken aback. Molly, who always came across as thoughtful and considerate and sensitive . . . making a throwaway comment like that one. It bordered on racist. Hell, it crossed the border. It was racist.

"I . . . well, actually I know some people who are . . . involved that way," Susan said cautiously.

"Ecch," said Molly. "You mean voluntarily?" When Susan nodded, Molly just shook her head. "Some people. What are you going to do? They feel the need to experiment, regardless of whether it's a good idea or even in good taste. I mean, come on, Susan. The humans don't have any shortage of each other. We only have us . . . and there's not that many of us. We don't need to get ourselves thinned out."

"You realize," Susan pointed out, "that you're arguing for racial purity. That's the argument that the Purists always use to try and explain why we should be shepherded off into camps; you know, the necessity of keeping a species genetically pure. You really want to share a philosophy that some would use to exterminate our race?"

Molly just laughed. "Susan, you're a wonderful boss and a great person, but sometimes, you just don't get it."

"I guess not."

As Molly walked out the door of Susan's office, Jessica swept in. With people flying in and out of her office this much, Susan was starting to feel as if she lived in the center of a railroad terminal.

Jessica, naturally, spent no time getting down to details. With a flip of her red scarf, she said, "How'd it go with George? Did the dress work?"

Sorrowfully, Susan shook her head. "He still intends to sleep with May."

This served only to irritate Jessica, just as Susan had expected it would. She was about to tell Jessica to forget about it—that, if George was going to do this thing, then she was not going to humiliate herself by trying to browbeat him into changing his mind. But before she could get a word out, Jessica was already rolling.

"Oh, he does, does he?" she said heatedly. "Well, two can play that game. We'll give George a dose of his own medicine."

"What medicine?"

Jessica spread her arms wide as if she were on

stage, about to burst into song. "Tonight, we're gonna paint the town!"

"What color?" asked Susan, hopelessly befuddled.

Jessica laughed and slapped Susan lightly on the shoulder. "A 'girls' night out,' Susan."

Susan could not see how that would possibly solve anything. "What will that do?"

She waved an authoritative finger in response. "Let him imagine what *you're* up to. Let *him* squirm and worry. Believe me, baby, this always works with my Frank. And besides," and her infectious grin spread wider, ". . . it'll be fun."

CHAPTER 18

WHEN GEORGE AND Matt got out of their respective cars in front of George's house, the Newcomer walked over to his partner and said, "Now, Matt . . . Susan is having a, um . . . a difficult few days, so if—"

Sikes had popped the trunk of his car and was pulling out a grocery bag. "She still mad at you because of the whole thing with Albert?"

"She is *not* mad at me," George said. "She's just having a rough time recently, so if she's a bit . . . short-tempered, don't be surprised. That's all."

"Fine. I'm warned," said Matt, and he slammed the trunk shut. As they approached the front door, Sikes thought he heard something coming from the second story of the house. A slow, steady pounding. George was so preoccupied with his and Susan's situation that he really didn't notice it, at least, not until they got inside.

Buck was seated at the dining room table. With one hand he was feeding Vessna, and with the other he was making some preliminary notes for an essay he was going to write. He looked up as the two detectives entered. "Hi, Dad. Sergeant Sikes."

"Hiya," said Sikes agreeably.

But now the pounding was impossible to ignore, and actually pretty difficult to take as well. It was just a steady, continuous, unrelenting thumping. Sikes felt that he was trapped in an Edgar Allan Poe story.

George looked up the stairs, wincing against the pounding. "What is that awful racket?"

"Emily bought a ka\na drum," said Buck. He was sliding the thin tail of some animal into Vessna's mouth. Sikes didn't want to know what it was from. Vessna gobbled it hungrily as Buck reached into a small dish for more. "I think she's mad that you won't let her wear that backless dress."

Being aware that the trick to being a good parent was to be reasonable at all times, George walked to the bottom of the stairs and called, "Emily, we have company. That's enough."

He smiled at Sikes, then, to show how relaxed he was as a father. His smile started to crack a bit, though, as the ka\na drum not only did not abate, but in fact grew louder. He rapped on the banister a couple of times in an apparently idle fashion. But he was, in fact, endeavoring to control himself and only partly succeeding.

"Did you hear me?" he shouted, desperately trying to give her the benefit of the doubt.

Her response was to pound on it even louder, making her anger and—worse—her disrespect completely evident.

"Emily!" he shouted again, but it's virtually impossible to keep one's temper in check while one's

191

voice is raised, and George finally blew up. He bellowed, "If you don't stop this instant, there'll be no eucalyptus chips for a month!"

The drumming stopped.

George turned, trying not to let his embarrassment show. But he wasn't hiding it particularly well. Sikes forestalled it immediately by putting up a hand and saying, "Don't sweat it, George. I've been there, remember," in reference to his own grown daughter.

George nodded gratefully and then clapped his hands briskly. "So . . . let's make ourselves comfortable."

"I'm with you," said Sikes. He proceeded to pull beer and sour milk out of the shopping bag.

Buck glanced over from the table. "Hey, can I have a glass of milk?" he asked, hopefully.

George laughed and said, "No. Don't be ridiculous." Then, not wanting the teen to feel left out, he offered, "You can have a beer if you like."

Buck snorted disdainfully. "I'm too old for beer."

George heard footsteps coming down the stairs and braced himself. At first he thought it might be Emily, and he anticipated more rudeness. But then the slow, measured tread caught his attention, and he realized it was going to be Susan.

Would she embarrass him in front of Matt? No. No, he couldn't believe that of her. No matter how angry she was, no matter she was at odds with her husband . . . he couldn't envision her deliberately trying to humiliate him in front of his friend and partner.

He hoped.

She appeared at the bottom of the stairs, and to George's surprise, she was wearing the same slinky dress she'd sported the night before. He wondered if she'd completely lost her mind. Was she going to try coming on to him again? He wasn't fool enough to fall for that again. And in front of Matt, for heaven's sake? Not that George would have minded, especially, but Susan knew that Matt felt self-conscious about that sort of thing. And Susan prided herself on making her guests feel at home.

When she saw Sikes, she said with what seemed genuine warmth, "Hello, Matt."

"Hi, Suze. Uh . . . you look great." Which was an understatement. She was practically radiating sex.

"Thank you, Matt." Then her tone immediately became quite cool and she said, "I'm going out, George."

"Dressed like that?" said George in surprise. "Where are you going?"

"Jessica and I are having a girls' night out."

George looked in confusion to Matt. Sikes had his hand over his mouth, making a clear indication that he was not going to get involved in this for any amount of money.

"What does that mean?" demanded George.

"Oh, we're going to meet some people," Susan told him, sounding very off-hand. "Go to a club. That kind of thing."

Once again George looked to Matt, feeling completely adrift in a bizarre sea of un-Susanlike impulses. Despite his silence, Matt's look said it all. *What the hell is happenin' here, George?*

"Are there going to be men there?" asked George.

"Maybe."

"Susan . . .!"

For a moment, George was rendered absolutely speechless, and Susan took the opportunity to blurt out everything that she'd been keeping pent up. It came out with staccato speed. "If you can go to bed with another woman, I ought to be able to socialize with other men." And then she did the exact thing that Sikes was afraid she'd do. She turned to him and said, "Don't you agree, Matt?"

"Uh . . . well . . ." said Sikes, whose only goal had been to keep his head down and out of the firing line, and apparently wasn't succeeding in even this meager endeavor.

Susan was relentless. "Do you know what George is planning on doing with May?"

"Uh . . . sort of . . ." Matt said, pulling at his shirt collar. It was actually a truthful answer. Even though he'd been aware of it in the conceiving of Vessna, he was still a little hazy on the whole "it takes three to tango" school of procreation.

Buck, lacking Matt's wisdom in knowing when to keep out of things, volunteered, "Mom, it's not like Dad's in love with her. He's just going to have sex with her."

It was Buck's lucky day that his mother was too focused on Matt to react to her son's cavalier dismissal of her concern. Instead she used it for more fodder in her assault on Matt's neutrality. "What do you think about that? Do you think that's right?"

"Well . . . actually, uh . . . no . . ."

"Matt!" George looked mortally wounded.

Immediately Matt tried to amend his statement. "Look, it's not really for me to say! I mean . . . let's face it, a lot of stuff you people do is pretty much skewed from the way we do things."

"Yeah, Mom, he doesn't know anything!" protested Buck. "He's human."

Matt glanced at him. "Don't help me, okay, kid?"

"Humans know more than you think," snapped Susan. "There's a lot they can teach us."

She headed for the door, tossed off a parting shot of "Don't wait up" to George, and stalked out the door.

"Susan!" called George, but it was too late. With Susan beyond the reach of his ire, George looked balefully at Sikes. "You were a big help," he said.

"She asked me!" Sikes said defensively. "Was I supposed to lie?"

Buck shook his head and looked pityingly at the two adults. Vessna, showing remarkable flexibility, was not the least perturbed by the noise and arguing. In fact, she was nodding off. "You guys are a mess," he said. He stood and picked up his baby sister. "I'm going to put Vessna to bed."

George gave a curt nod of thanks as Buck headed up the stairs. The moment he was out of earshot, Sikes said accusingly, "George, you told me Susan 'wholeheartedly approved' of you and May."

At first George was going to give a vehement response, but then he started to feel a bit sheepish about it. "I suppose I . . . might have exaggerated slightly."

"Yeah," affirmed Sikes. Then he looked at his partner sympathetically. "Okay, look, George . . . we could beat each other up because we're not paragons of honesty. But we gotta stick together, y'know? Especially if Susan's doing this girls'-night-out stuff."

"We do?" said George.

"Absolutely. She's gonna have a girls' night out? You have a boys' night in. We'll call some guys over for poker."

"Poker?" George searched his memory. "Isn't that a card game?"

He clapped George on the back and looked heavenward, as if addressing a heavenly choir. "It's a lot more than that, George. It's spiritual. It's . . . men." He started for the phone. "Phil just got divorced, so I'm sure he's free. And that Newcomer ballistics guy, Harry . . ."

"Bush?" George supplied.

"Yeah." Sikes started dialing. Phil's number he knew from memory. And since Phil was the local union head for the precinct, he'd have everyone else's phone number. "This is going to be great, George. Just wait'll the guys get here. The evening's really gonna take off."

"Take it off! *Take it off!*"

Bumping and grinding, the stripper made his way down the runway of the club. Dressed in a cowboy outfit, he strutted through the smoke, gyrating as colored lights flickered over his sweating muscular body. Most of his outfit was long gone, and he was gyrating in only chaps, a G-string and a red checkered bandanna.

The runway was lined with women, screaming and hollering, shouting suggestions, obscenities, and lewd observations. They were falling over each other to shove dollar bills into his G-string, for which in return he would plant a kiss on the giver.

The air was thick was cigarette fumes and sweat. Conversation was limited to screaming, because the music was so deafening and the women so rowdy that it was impossible to communicate in any other fashion.

Sitting at the edge of the runway, Jessica was watching, engrossed. Susan, clearly uncomfortable with the entire situation, was averting her eyes.

"Wheeewww!" shouted Jessica. "Get a load of those buns!"

Reaching the end of his routine, the stripper removed his bandanna, twirled it over his head like a lasso, and let it fly. It landed, naturally, on top of Susan's head. There was applause, but Susan felt only mortification as she shoved the bandanna off her head as if it were crawling with ants. It fell into her lap.

Apparently unaware of Susan's discomforture, Jessica shouted, "Lucky you!"

Holding the bandanna between the tips of two fingers, Susan picked it up and tossed it back onto the stage. The stripper grabbed it up and headed backstage, strutting all the way.

"Can we go now!" asked Susan, taking advantage of the momentary lull in the hullabaloo.

"There are three more acts," Jessica informed her.

"It's so stuffy in here. And so noisy."

"Relax. Enjoy yourself." Jessica took a swig of beer. Then she pointed and shouted, "Here! This guy! Here's what I wanted you to see! Look!"

A new stripper had appeared on stage. He was a Newcomer, dressed in a space suit that looked as if it had come out of the old *Buck Rogers* movie serials. He stood bolt still for a moment, and then pinpoint beams of light leaped into existence around him, crisscrossing him. The music swelled, the piece entitled "Also sprach Zarathustra" . . . although it was more popularly known to the women in the audience as the music from *2001: A Space Odyssey*.

He started to peel off the space suit. Jessica turned to Susan and said, "How do you like him?" But to her surprise, Susan was barely watching. She was staring down into her sour milk, playing with it idly rather than drinking it. "Susan, what's wrong with you?" she asked. "I thought your eyes would be riveted to the stage!"

"That sounds like it would hurt," Susan said.

"I mean I thought you'd at least be watching what was going on!" Jessica was leaning over, practically shouting into Susan's ear to make herself heard. When Susan responded to Jessica, she had to do essentially the same thing.

"I keep thinking about George!" she shouted. "I know he must be worried!"

"Baby, that's the *whole idea!*"

As the Newcomer continued his act, and as his apparel diminished, Susan still did not seem especially interested. "I don't know . . . this all seems so . . . dishonest. Why can't George and I just sit down and talk?"

"Because men don't understand talk!" said Jessica with the exasperated air of someone trying to convince a member of the Flat Earth Society that the earth was, in fact, round. She realized that the only way to get Susan to join in the fun was to lead her by the hand. So she took Susan's hand and shoved a dollar into it. "Here! Have some fun!"

Susan stared at the dollar blankly. Clearly she didn't have a clue as to what Jessica intended that she do with it.

"Give it to him," said Jessica, pointing at the stripper.

Susan looked up and really noticed, for the first time, the dollar bills that were already sticking out of the Newcomer dancer's G-string. "No! I couldn't . . ."

"Bushwa!" retorted Jessica, and she signaled to the dancer. "Hey! Flash Gordon! Over here, honey!"

"Jessica—!" protested an embarrassed Susan.

The stripper danced over and dropped to his knees in front of Susan, putting his G-string within reach. And she also saw the look in his eyes, or at least the look she imagined she saw. Challenging, provocative . . . and also appraising her.

"Go on! Go on!" urged Jessica.

Resolving to end this nightmare as quickly as possible, Susan tucked the dollar into his G-string, trying to place it as far from any especially provocative areas as she possibly could. "Atta girl!" Jessica shouted, and the stripper danced off as the audience hooted.

Susan felt unclean.

"Jessica, I want to go home," she said firmly.

Slowly Jessica shook her head in obvious disappointment, swirling the red stick in her drink. "What am I gonna do with you?" She heaved a long sigh and said, "Okay."

Susan immediately started to get up from her chair, and then Jessica stopped her and added, grinning, "After the next act."

They'd come in Jessica's car.

Susan was stuck.

She sat down again.

The heady sounds of pasteboards being flipped through, shuffled, and then hitting the table with that distinctive *flap flap* noise, filled the air in a hymn to the male experience.

Seated around the table were Matt, George, Phil, the union head, and Harry Bush, the Newcomer. The humans were on one side of the table, the Newcomers on the other. This was not out of any sense of segregation, but rather for convenience of the refreshments. George and Harry were not particularly interested in being positioned near the beer and pretzels, while Matt and Phil made it extremely clear that the farther away they were from the sour milk and dried bugs, the happier they would be.

"Man, this is great," sighed Sikes, dealing a hand of five card draw. "A night without women."

"Can't live with 'em," Phil said sagely, "and can't live . . . with 'em."

"I don't know," George said. "Susan's an excellent card player."

Sikes rolled his eyes. "Man, has she got you whipped."

"I'm in," said Harry, tossing in a chip. Phil did likewise.

George frowned at his cards and said to Sikes, "Does a full home beat a flush?"

"House. A full house. Yes."

"Oh, good." He tossed in a chip. "What do you mean I'm whipped?"

Rounding out the opening ante, Sikes said, "Susan leads you around by the nose."

"I'll take two . . . today, please," said Harry.

Sikes continued to deal as he said, "It's not just you, George. Women are calling the shots everywhere."

"Amen," intoned Phil. "My ex-wife and her woman lawyer—boy, did they soak me good. And the judge just nodded *her* head and let 'em. Gimme three."

With two drinks already in him and feeling slightly more relaxed than usual, Sikes actually found the nerve to say, "Look at me. Cathy's got us enrolled in a sex class."

"A sex class?" Phil sounded appalled. "Used to be, a woman didn't like the way you made love, she kept her mouth shut."

Sikes realized that Phil had gotten an impression that he hadn't meant to give. "Whoa, Phil, she likes it, okay? She likes what I do. It's just . . . dangerous." He glanced at George. "How many cards do you want?"

"None," said George, half smiling at his cards.

Sikes took three.

As Harry threw a chip in, he said, "You don't need sex class. I can tell you everything you need to know right here."

This was quite conceivably the best news—in fact,

the only good news—Sikes had heard all week. "Everything?" he said.

Phil looked at the smug George and said, "Fold."

Harry nodded in response to Matt's question. He leaned forward, speaking in a low, conspiratorial voice. "A lot of women just want to sync up, get their kicks, and go to sleep. But we like to take our time. We like to touch. To be held."

Phil was giving an ear to this as well, purely out of curiosity's sake. But now he and Matt looked at each other, and then in unison said, "We do?"

"Yeah," affirmed Harry. "We don't care about orgasm. It's the time spent together that's important."

Matt coughed politely. Phil was just gaping,

George was simply nodding in agreement as he threw in a handful of chips. "I'm in."

"I'm gone," said Harry, tossing down his cards. As Sikes matched and raised George's bet, Harry leaned back and brought his foot up. "There's a place on a woman's foot . . . right here," and he pointed to his instep. "Press it with your thumb. She won't get in sync for hours. You can hug and cuddle all night long."

"All night. You mean like . . . hours and hours . . . of foreplay . . ."

"Of course." Harry looked puzzled. "Why? Isn't that what you needed to know?"

"Absolutely," said Sikes quickly. "I mean . . . hey . . . I'm not just some quick fling in the sack, y'know?" He couldn't believe this conversation. He looked at Phil, who obviously couldn't believe it either.

George wasn't helping. He tapped his cards and said, "Does a full house beat a straight?"

"Yes! Now will you just bet!"

George pushed forward a stack of chips tall

enough that he could have bungee-jumped off. "All right."

Sikes threw down his cards in irritation. "Aw, c'mon, George, I'm not going to walk into that!"

"So you're flopping, then?" asked George carefully.

"Folding! Yes! I'm folding! You are zero fun at this, George. Western Union doesn't telegraph as much as you. If you seriously think I don't know you've got a full house . . ."

George looked at him ingenuously. "No, I don't."

"What?"

Sikes turned over George's cards, which he had placed carefully down on the table. A two of clubs, a four of hearts, a seven, a jack, a king—a garbage hand.

"Then why the hell did you keep asking about a full house?!" shouted Sikes in exasperation.

Smiling like a toddler who had just walked across the room for the first time, George said proudly, "I wanted to bluff you."

"That's not how you play!"

"You get cards and try to win through bluffing?" said George, carefully.

"Yes, but—"

"Then that's how I play," George said with satisfaction.

"Sikes, remember," said Harry of the all-night-endurance, "press her foot."

Sikes rolled his eyes. "Why do I bother with you guys?"

As Sikes spoke, the phone rang. George went to answer it as the deal passed over to Phil.

George was saying, "Yes . . . thank you," into the phone, and immediately Matt's internal feelers went up. Something in George's tone was very disturbing. And his concerns were borne out when George returned to the table, but did not sit down. Instead he faced Sikes and said, "That was Zepeda."

"She got something on this Opsil—?"

"No. But she thought you'd want to know. There's a Purist demonstration at the sex clinic. It's getting violent."

CHAPTER 19

CLOUDS HAD PASSED in front of the moon, throwing the scene outside the sex clinic into dark, forbidding relief. The area was partly illuminated by street-lamps, but flying rocks had busted some of these. Police flashlights danced across the area like hand-held goblins, and the eeriness of the scene was further heightened by the red glow cast from the flashing domes atop the police cars.

Everywhere there was shouting and screaming and vituperation. A mob of Purists were surging about, barely held in check by the cops who were doing their best with a combination of police barricades, batons, and linking of arms.

"Two, Four, Six, Eight, slags and humans will not mate!" they shouted over and over again, an evil mantra. Over their heads, impaled on large sticks, were Newcomer baby dolls being waved about.

The Purists' ire was specifically directed at the sex class students. They were being ushered out of the building, escorted by uniformed cops while their brethren were fighting to keep the crowd at bay.

At the outskirts of the madness, Sikes's car screeched to a halt. He jumped out, George at his side, both of them wearing their POLICE windbreakers to make it that much easier for the cops to identify them. If things got ugly—at least, uglier than they were right now—Sikes did not want to have to deal with the possibility of being clubbed from behind accidentally. He already stood a good chance of getting his head caved in; he didn't need to stack the odds even more in his favor.

A narrow funnel for people exiting from the building had been created. Cops had set up barricades and were standing there to reinforce the cramped aisle as people moved through it like escaping Jews through the parted Red Sea. Waiting at the opposite end were police vans to escort them to their cars, or to their homes for those who had walked or taken public transportation.

As people were siphoned through, Sikes ran up to a cop and flashed his shield. "Why're you bringing people out here?!" he demanded. "They'd be safer in the building!"

"Bomb threat!" replied the cop tersely, bucking momentarily as a Purist tried to push past to get at an evacuating Newcomer. "We got no choice!"

Sikes fired a quick glance at George, who was right behind him. George immediately knew what was going through Matt's mind, and simply nodded.

Without another word exchanged, George and Sikes ran the gauntlet. Dodging thrown bottles and rocks, they charged through the police-created funnel and in through the front door, pushing past the evacuees who were waiting to be escorted out.

They didn't have to go far. Just past the entrance-way, he saw Cathy, along with Vivian, the instructor.

Cathy, being who she was, was helping to usher people through and giving them words of encouragement so that they wouldn't panic in the face of such overwhelming hostility. Apparently it hadn't occurred to her that her safety was anything particularly important. At least, not as important as these others.

"Cathy, you okay?" demanded Matt.

She turned to him, clearly surprised, and it was only then that he saw the fear in her eyes that she was so marvelously managing to keep pent up.

"Matt . . . yes . . ."

Sikes guided Vivian toward George and said, "Take her out, George. I'll go with Cathy."

"Ma'am," said George deferentially.

Shielding her with his body, George eased her out into the funnel.

"Your neck . . ." said Cathy, looking at Sikes.

"Ready?" He took her by the arm, concentrating on sizing up the crowd.

"You're fine!" she said.

"Let's go!" He grabbed her by the arm and they moved into the funnel.

"You lied to me!" Cathy seemed oblivious to the danger they were in as rocks and bottles sailed past them.

"Let's talk about this later."

"Why did you lie?!"

"Cathy, come on!"

Just ahead of them were the last of the evacuees. The crowd intensified its shouting and taunting, as if sensing that this was going to be their last shot.

Matt looked right and left, looked at the faces twisted in hate, and felt a tremendous amount of embarrassment for his entire race.

And then he heard a scream.

Just up ahead of them in the funnel, one of the

larger Purists had managed to shove his arm through, over the shoulders of one of the cops. He had clamped onto the scruff of the neck of one of the Newcomers, and Sikes immediately recognized him as being Noel Parking. Parking was stronger than the Purist, but he was more terrified of the crowd, and the terror paralyzed him.

Sensing a potential victim, the crowd started to surge forward. Cops on the street started to converge to shore up the hole in the funnel.

And then, with a terrified yell, Noel was yanked into the crowd.

With a move borne far more of an instinct to help others than common sense, Cathy started to shove forward to try and help. Sikes grabbed her and pulled her back.

Too slow. Someone else, ducking under the barricade, grabbed at Cathy, snagging her by the leg. Sikes grabbed at her too late, and Cathy was hauled, screaming Matt's name, into the throbbing mass of humanity.

The crowd started to converge, and George—pushing Vivian forward, turned to see that he'd been cut off from his partner. He shoved Vivian forward into the arms of waiting cops, turned, and started to push through to get to Matt.

And Matt Sikes, without hesitation, hurled himself into the crowd like a linebacker.

The Purists were fueled by anger, but Sikes was spurred on by anger supplemented by fear and desperation. He shoved his way in, yanking people this way and that, kicking, biting, totally heedless of his own safety. "Cathy!" he screamed. "Cathy!"

He found her. She was five rows deep, and she was next to Noel Parking. Parking, now figuratively backed up against the wall, was fighting desperately, and his Newcomer strength was serving him well.

Then a bottle cracked across his head and he went down.

Sikes slugged one man in the face. Blood fountained from the Purist's nose as he staggered back, and Sikes grabbed Cathy around the waist. With one hand she anchored herself onto Matt, but with the other she was reaching out for Noel, trying to save him. And it became quickly apparent to Sikes that she wasn't going willingly without him.

Noel was trying to get to his feet. Someone kicked him viciously, and he rolled over toward Sikes and Cathy. He looked up at Sikes with terrified eyes, and Sikes yanked out his gun, aiming it at the infuriated Purists who were converging on him. Cathy leaned forward and grabbed Noel, yanking him to his feet. The three of them tried to back up, but there was nowhere for them to go, hemmed in on all sides. Cops were trying to fight their way through to them. The barricades were starting to collapse, and in the distance there was the sound of police sirens, but they were going to be too late . . .

And then there was an explosion like a thunderclap, followed by a second and then a third. It was absolutely deafening. Purists were clapping their hands to their ears, staggering under the pure noise and ferocity of it.

And then came a voice through a megaphone. As it spoke, booming everywhere, Sikes seized the opportunity to push his way through, dragging Cathy and Noel behind him. And as he shoved the two of them over the battered barricades, into the arms of waiting police officers, he recognized the voice.

"Ladies and gentlemen," it said with the calm drawled assurance of an airline pilot. "I'm not going to see any police officers injured. Now if it means shooting a few of you with this assault rifle, that's fine by me. I'm a month from retirement, so if they suspend me it's a vacation for me. Who's going to be the first to volunteer for target practice?"

There was uncomfortable murmuring from the crowd. This had taken a turn they weren't expecting. Then they started to get noisy again, apparently building up their nerve, feeding off each other.

George was at the wheel of Matt's car, having headed there the moment he saw Matt, Cathy, and Parking break from the crowd. Matt dashed down the funnel, pushing the two of them ahead. A human woman was standing to one side, and then she shrieked Noel's name, pointing and yelling. Sikes practically pushed the staggering Newcomer into the arms of his woman.

Parking turned, blood trickling down his face, and he looked at Sikes with surprise. "You had a gun . . . because you were a policeman," he said thickly.

"Ma'am, get him to an ambulance," Sikes told her. "They're over there."

Parking was reaching out, and he touched Sikes's temple. "Thank you . . ." he managed to get out, and then the woman pulled him away as they headed toward where Sikes had indicated.

"Matt, come on!" called out George. "This isn't over yet! We've got to get Cathy out of here *now!*"

Matt pushed the shaken Cathy into the back of the car, jumped in behind her, and slammed the door. The car took off with a roar, George cutting hard to the right. A thrown rock glanced off the driver's side window but only left a small nick in the glass.

As the car angled away, all three caught a brief glimpse of someone. He was speaking through a megaphone and holding an assault rifle with his other hand. Clearly he was the owner of the voice they'd heard. The rifle was still smoking from the three shots that he'd fired into the air and caught the crowd's attention and, as a side benefit, given Matt and the others the chance they needed to break away.

The man was dressed in plainclothes. His hair was thinning and black with speckles of gray. He had a large jaw and a wide, muscular body. Then the car turned out onto the main road and he was lost from sight.

"Who was that?" George asked, not necessarily expecting an answer.

He got one anyway. "That was Jack Perelli," said Sikes.

"The man you told me about?" asked Cathy.

"Yeah. Him." He looked at her, but the expression on her face said that the fact that he had lied to her was still very fresh on her mind.

"So that is the legendary Jack Perelli," George said from the front seat. "Very fortunate that he showed up when he did. You may owe him your life, Matt."

"Won't be the first time," said Sikes. He turned to Cathy. "You okay?"

"Yes. Just a little shaken. I owe you my life, too, Matt. Thank you."

It was the last words out of her for the rest of the ride over to George's house. And after Sikes dropped George off there, she was silent the rest of the way to their apartment building.

He parked outside it and killed the engine. For a few seconds the two of them just sat there, saying nothing. Finally, unable to stand it any longer, Sikes said, "Okay, I confess, I lied about my neck. Okay? I'd think that saving your life would make up for a lie."

She gave a small sigh. "Your saving my life makes me feel even more for you than I did already. But . . . it still bothers me, Matt. How can you care for me enough to risk your life but not enough to risk the truth?"

"Because you don't want to hear the truth!"

"And what is the truth?"

"The truth is that I can't sit around with a bunch of strangers and talk about my sex life! Sex is something you do. It isn't something you talk about!"

"How can you learn anything if you don't talk about it?"

"I'll read a book!" said Sikes in exasperation. "What's the big deal?"

"Matt, sex is the most intimate form of communication there is. You seem embarrassed about it."

He clapped his hands. "Bingo! To me, intimacy isn't something that I like to stand up in public and discuss. Intimacy is . . . intimate. You want to know what sex is? Sex is a nasty thing you do in the dark. And you're lucky if you get away with it!"

If he'd announced that he fantasized about sheep wearing negligees, he could not have gotten a more surprised look from Cathy. "Where do you get ideas like that?"

"What makes you think your ideas are any better?" he shot back. Then he sank down a little in the seat. "Let's try it my way," he said. "We'll take it slow. We'll take it easy. We won't discuss it with every Tom, Dick, and Harry . . ."

"Matt, it won't work," she said flatly. "We need to understand each other's bodies."

"Cathy, I've had sex a lotta times, and I never understood a woman's body."

"This is a defense?" she asked.

"No, it's a statement. Men don't want to know that much about it."

She shook her head sadly. "Matt." She took his

hand in hers and squeezed it. "With me, ignorance is not bliss. It's suicidal. You have to decide what you want."

She got out of the car and Sikes watched, feeling torn, as Cathy headed inside.

He thudded his fist against the top of the car and snarled, "That's just great."

CHAPTER 20

SOMEWHERE IN THE background, music was playing.

The city was spread out below Sikes, twinkling invitingly. A blimp cruised overhead for no apparent reason.

Sikes pulled anxiously at the jacket of his tuxedo as he paced the roof of his apartment building. He turned toward the young boy who was seated nearby wearing a sequined sweatshirt, and snapped his fingers. In response, the boy raised a mirror for Sikes to look into. Sikes straightened his hair, adjusted his tie.

He heard the telltale click of the door that opened out onto the roof. He turned and there was Cathy, wearing a long blue chiffon gown. Her fingers were interlaced in front of her. Her expression was one of love and understanding.

"Cathy . . ."

She smiled broadly. "Matt."

They moved toward each other. Sikes felt as if his

feet weren't even touching the ground. "All this has been my fault," he told her.

"No, mine," she replied dreamily.

They came together, hands clasping and intertwining. At that moment Sikes was painfully aware that what they felt for each other was far more important than the differences that threatened to keep them apart.

Off to the side, the boy in the sequined T-shirt lifted the tone arm on a record player. He dropped the needle down onto the spinning surface of an old 78. A moment later, the voice of Fred Astaire began to warble "The Way You Look Tonight."

Cathy and Sikes drew closer together, and then suddenly they separated. Their hands still clasped, they stretched in opposite directions, throwing their free arms wide dramatically. He spun her around, her dress swirling about her, and then the music carried them away.

Cathy sailed into Matt's arms and the two of them moved in time to the music. Matt had never taken dancing lessons, but it did not matter. He was a natural, leading Cathy with style, elegance, and grace. She was totally comfortable, totally at ease, and totally swept away in the romance of the moment. The rooftop became their ballroom, the small record player their orchestra, and the world their own.

Bubbles sailed past them, blown through a bubble wand by the impish looking boy. As they danced, the bubbles seemed to surround them. Lights sparkled off them, and it was as if they were dancing through stars.

Cathy whirled through Matt's confident arms, and then he swung her down in a stylish dip, followed by an elegant swing upward.

And then he was gaping at her in amazement.

She was human.

Her long auburn hair, thick and rich, accentuated her exquisite eyebrows. Her ears were small and round and perfect. In the background, Astaire was singing "Oh, but you're lovely, with your smile so warm . . ."

Energized by the miracle that had been handed them, Cathy and Matt resumed their dance with more power and enthusiasm than before. Someone had once said that ballroom dancing was two people doing vertically what they'd really like to be doing horizontally. That might very well have been the case with Cathy and Matt. For now, with the final barriers removed, any possible trepidation and uncertainty that had remained between them was gone. Now there need be nothing between them, spiritually, physically, or otherwise.

Sikes knew that he was flying now. Knew that nothing could possibly bring him down to earth. He was sailing through the cosmos with Cathy, who had crossed a galaxy to find him, and he could not remember a time when he had ever been this happy.

He looked down at Cathy, to see if she was as captivated by the moment as he. But she was looking at him in a way that he had not expected. There was . . . surprise. No. Not just surprise. Shock.

He mouthed the words, "What is it?" but found he couldn't make his voice come out. She shook his hands away, gaping. What in hell was wrong with her?

Or was there . . . something wrong with him?

He stretched out a hand and snapped his fingers. Instantly the smiling boy was there, once again holding a mirror in front of Sikes. He stared into it.

A stranger stared back. A Newcomer.

Slowly Sikes raised his hand to his face . . . and the Newcomer in the mirror did likewise.

He reached up and put his hands to the sides of his head. His ears were gone. Frantically his fingers searched his face and the top of his skull, looking for hair, along with the frightened mirror reflection.

There was nothing. Nothing except large brown spots decorating his skull in a random pattern.

Cathy the human was staring at Sikes the Newcomer with unremitting dread. Time seemed to slow down and distort, stretching endlessly off into nowhere. Sikes was rooted to the spot.

Out of nowhere, Jack Perelli was in front of him, speaking in mocking tones through a megaphone.

"I warned you, Sikes," he said, his voice drowning out the dance music. And now the music was shifting, and it was no longer Fred Astaire. It was the steady thudding of the ka\na drum, the relentless *thump, thump, thump.* "When they first landed, remember? I told you that it was going to happen. They're going to take over. They're going to ruin the human race. They may have two hearts, but they're heartless. They're soulless. They're not human, and they have no business being on this world. And you agreed with me, Sikes . . . remember? But it didn't stop you, did it."

Matt was clutching at the top of his head, as if it were one of those skin wigs that made you look bald, like he'd had when he was a kid. He was trying to pull it off. But he couldn't. It was there. It was him.

Thump, thump, thump intoned the ka\na, louder and more deafening, and he put his hands to his non-ears but could still hear the boy's mocking laughter coupled with Perelli's diatribe.

"You had it coming, Sikes!" Perelli was shouting. "I warned you about them! *I warned you! I—*"

Thump *Thump* THUMP **THUMP**

Thump!

Sikes sat up so fast that he slammed his head against the headboard of his bed.

He sat there for a moment, stunned. His apartment was in darkness. He sat up, reflexively running his fingers through his hair before it occurred to him that he should be surprised that it was there.

There was, of course, no rooftop dance. No human Cathy. No little boy. No Perelli . . . well, at least not on the roof at that moment. No . . .

No chance.

He drew his knees up to his chin and sat there in the darkness, trying to erase the memory of the boy's laughter, until the sun rose over the horizon.

"Morning, George."

George, seated at the kitchen table, idly dunked a tea bag into the steaming mug. The children had not come downstairs yet and, based on their history, probably would not do so until thirty seconds or less before they had to depart. Some mornings he felt that if he blinked, he might miss them altogether.

He glanced over his shoulder at the greeting. Susan, dressed for work, was standing there. She was pulling on the tips of her fingers, which was always a good indication that she felt guilty about something. If George had been of a mind to notice, it might have tipped him off to her mood and altered the nature of the subsequent conversation. But he wasn't remotely in the mood to be observant, and so he turned back to his tea without giving her another glance as he said stiffly, "How was your evening?"

She crossed the kitchen and started to make breakfast for herself. "Fine. How was yours?"

"Fine." He paused. "You came in late."

"You were asleep. I didn't want to wake you."

"Actually, I was awake . . . thinking . . ."

Before he could continue, he heard the expected sound of pounding feet. Buck and Emily tore into the kitchen like twin tornadoes. Buck tossed down a jelly weasel doughnut while Emily yanked open the refrigerator and pulled out the lunch that Buck had prepared for her the night before.

George was extremely proud of the way that Buck had assumed responsibilities around the house: taking care of Vessna, preparing lunches. It was the sort of nurturing characteristics one expected in a Tenctonese male. And if Buck ever slowed down enough for George to tell him so, then he would let him know.

As it was, Buck was shouting, "We're late! Come on!"

"What'd you pack me for lunch," she asked.

"What I always pack you," he said impatiently. "Peat butter and jellyfish sandwich."

In unison the hustling Francisco children called out, "Bye Mom, bye Dad," and out they went.

George found it nothing short of amazing. Yesterday Emily had been angry about something that had seemed to have—at least at the time—tremendous importance to her. Yet now, off she was going without any sort of resentment. The length of time that children held grudges was miraculously short.

Unlike their parents.

Time to end this, he realized sadly. Time to do what you decided last night.

"George," Susan was saying, "I've been thinking, too . . ."

"Before you say anything," George interrupted her, "I've decided . . . since it means so much to you—"

"George—"

"Please," he said firmly, putting up a hand to indicate that he really wanted to say what he had to say. She stopped, prepared to listen to him, but looking very uncomfortable. But he knew that his next words would end that discomfort. "I've decided not to father Albert and May's child."

"Oh!" She sounded genuinely surprised. And then, more softly, she said "Oh," in a tone that George could not quite decipher. She lowered her head.

"That's what you want, isn't it?" he asked.

"Yes." Her voice was barely above a whisper.

"Good."

Usually when George made a decision, he felt good about it. Wrestling with a problem was always the difficult part; once it was done, then it was done, and there was no point dwelling on it.

Not this time, though.

There had been times in George's life where he knew that he had made the wrong decision. But always they had seemed for the right reasons. This time he felt as if he'd made the wrong decision for the wrong reason: Namely to satisfy some emotional dynamic in Susan that had just blossomed to life and that he didn't like at all.

But he was her husband, and her happiness above all was important.

Very tentatively, he touched her temple. Then he went out, leaving behind a triumphant Susan.

Except that if he had seen Susan's face, he would have noticed that it was not the face of a woman who looked remotely triumphant.

"So what do you think's going to happen with Mom and Dad?"

Buck shrugged as they approached the junior high school that Emily attended. "I don't know. They'll work it out, I guess. They always do."

At that moment, Emily's friend Jill came running

up to them. Buck really wasn't particularly wild about her, since she seemed to have this knee-jerk compulsion to flirt with him every time she saw him. He kept waiting for her to outgrow it.

"Emily, Emily, look at my face!" Jill was saying excitedly.

Emily gasped. "You're wearing lipstick! And eye shadow!"

Jill, obviously feeling very much the grown woman, turned to Buck. "Hi, Buck," she said with every ounce of female sizzle at her command.

Buck rolled his eyes. He had the feeling that if he suddenly grabbed her and kissed her as hard as he could, she'd probably run screaming in the other direction and that would be the end of it. That would be a way to solve this nonsense, but it would also probably cost Emily her best friend. And besides, they'd probably try to have Buck thrown in jail for good measure. Wasn't worth it. He'd just have to tolerate it as best he could.

"You look so old!" Emily was gushing.

Jill paused dramatically. "And . . ."

She raised the hem of her skirt to draw her leg to Emily's notice. Emily squealed, "Nylons!"

"What about you?" said Jill excitedly. "Did you? Huh?"

"Yeah!" said Emily.

She had been wearing a large, bulky sweatshirt. But now she peeled it off, much to Buck's astonishment. Underneath the sweatshirt, she was wearing a backless, potniki-revealing sweater.

"Oh, God," said Jill in awe. "That is so mo'bo."

"You can't wear that!" said Buck in alarm.

"Who are you?" said Emily disdainfully. "Jesse Helms? Besides, Mom bought it for me."

"For you to wear on your sar\nat day!" said Buck.

"That's not for a long time yet. Now you're too young!"

"I am not!" said Emily, angrily stomping her foot. "And if you tell Mom and Dad, I'll kill you!"

She grabbed Jill by the hand. "Come on!" she said, and they dashed towards the school building. As they ran, a teenage Newcomer boy happened past. He took one look at the potniki on Emily's back and made a loud seductive clicking noise, which was the Tenctonese equivalent of a wolf whistle.

Buck put an unfriendly hand on the teen's shoulder and said simply, "That's my sister."

The boy looked from Buck to Emily and back again. "She's ugly," he said.

"Thank you," replied Buck.

The teenager moved off, but Buck watched Emily take off with increasing trepidation.

This little maneuver of hers did not bode well at all.

CHAPTER 21

SIKES, BLEARY-EYED AND not particularly well-rested, bumped into George as he was entering the precinct headquarters. "Oh . . . morning, George."

George studied him. "Are you quite all right, Matt?"

"Fine. I'm fine. Just not my best night, that's all. You?"

"Oh, quite well, thank you." He paused. "I thought you would be interested to know that I have decided that the key to the long-term health of my relationship with Susan—in this instance—is summed up in that Earth saying about Rome."

"You mean, when in Rome, do as the Romans do?"

George nodded. "Yes. I've decided not to father Albert and May's child."

Sikes stared at him, amazed.

"What's the matter, Matt?"

"Well, it's just that . . . Jeez, George, I can't ever

remember you taking my advice over New-comer . . . I dunno . . . policy."

"I'm adaptable. That's how we manage to survive, after all, isn't it. We're so adaptable." George was only partly successful in keeping the sadness out of his voice as he turned and walked into the station. Matt followed just behind him.

As they entered, Matt said, "Y'know, George, just so you don't get the wrong idea, I think your heart . . . hearts . . . were in the right place on this. And I got this feeling that, if you and yours hadn't come to Earth and gotten influenced by humans, then Susan would've probably felt different about the whole thing."

"Ifs and ands are pointless, Matt. If we hadn't come here, I'd never have become a police officer and met you. And you have been . . . very important to me, Matt. Earth has had its positives and negatives, and it's true enough in life that you have to take the good and the bad together. Trying to separate one from the other is a waste of energy. You accept the entire package or you don't."

Slowly, Matt said, "There's a lot in what you say there, George. About a lot of things."

Francisco looked at him curiously, but Sikes didn't seem inclined to continue the conversation in that direction. Instead he said, "What are you going to tell Albert?"

"The truth," said George. "Susan's against it, and I have to respect her feelings."

As they entered the squad room, George looked around for Albert, but didn't see him. He did, however, spot May by her sandwich cart. Unfortunately, she saw him as well, and waved happily.

George managed a weak wave back. Fortunately, May then became involved in selling a sandwich, and George and Sikes were able to move toward their desks without George having to talk to May and, in all likelihood, give her the bad news.

On the way they stopped by Zepeda's desk. "Beatrice, have you seen Albert?"

She chucked a thumb in the direction of the holding cells. "He's with the big guy."

George nodded, figuring that he should have known that. As he headed off in that direction, Sikes asked, "Any luck on that Opsil thing?"

She shook her head. "Still working."

This puzzled Sikes. Zepeda was the best when it came to this kind of thing. If it was taking her this long, then it must be buried pretty deep in somebody's system.

He turned to ask George for his opinion, but the Newcomer had already gone on ahead. Matt tossed off a salute to Zepeda and hurried off after George, but then was interrupted when the phone on his desk rang. In a way, he decided, maybe that was better. George and Albert would probably benefit from privacy when George had to give him the bad news.

"Sikes," he said, picking up the phone.

"Matt, this is Cathy . . ."

For a moment the picture of her as a human, with that thick auburn hair, flared across his memory. Then he extinguished the flare. "Yeah, Cathy."

"Matt, something's happened that I thought you'd want to know."

"Got a feeling it's not good."

George stopped several feet away from Albert, who was standing and staring at the imprisoned giant as if he were in a trance. The giant was as listless as he had ever been.

George cleared his throat. He couldn't put this off any longer. "Albert . . ."

"They shouldn't move him," said Albert, not taking his eyes off the giant.

"What?"

"He's supposed to go to county jail today. But he's sick." He pointed. "Look."

Indeed, Albert seemed to have a point. Upon closer inspection, the giant had gone beyond listlessness. His face was ashen, and when George listened carefully, he could hear a raspiness in the giant's breathing. Even his eyes were starting to glaze over.

"He does look ill," agreed George. "I'll speak to Captain Grazer." Then he steeled himself once again. "Albert, I need to talk to you."

"He can't live without the baby."

This was becoming somewhat frustrating. Every time George managed to get up the nerve to broach the subject, Albert made it clear that he wasn't paying the least bit of attention. Trying not to sound frustrated, George said, "How do you know these things?"

"I just do," Albert said with a shrug.

There was a long pause, and then Albert said, "Is something wrong, George?"

This was it. He was going to have to face Albert's disappointment, and try to cushion it as best he could. "Albert . . ."

"Hey, George!"

This interruption from a new source was almost enough to make George punch the wall. Matt had come in, bustling with urgency, and before George could ask him to come back in a few minutes, Sikes said, "Cathy just called. The baby's real sick. They've taken her to the hospital."

Stunned, George said, "Let's go."

But as he was about to, Albert said to him, "George, was there something you wanted to talk to me about?"

"Oh. Right. Albert. Uhm . . ." He looked into the young janitor's eyes and then said, "I want you to keep an eye on the giant for us. Do exactly what you have been doing. Monitor him constantly. You're now an . . . unofficial part of the investigative team. Can you do that for me, Albert?"

Albert nodded, looking very serious. "You can count on me, George. You too, Sergeant Sikes."

"Thanks, Albert. I knew we could. C'mon, George."

They headed out, and as they did so, Sikes said in a low sarcastic voice, "That's the way to handle these things, George. Honest and direct."

"Buzz on, Matt."

"Off, George. Buzz off."

"That, too."

When Sikes had been very little, his mother had taken him to a local production of *Peter Pan*. The thing that he remembered most distinctly about it was the part where Tinkerbell—represented, as she so often was, by a small spotlight—was dying. She was depicted by a light that became smaller and smaller in diameter and then began to flicker. And you just knew that when the light was gone altogether, so too was Tinkerbell's life.

Now, standing next to the infant's bed in the hospital's pediatric ward, Sikes was experiencing the same feeling.

The child, who had seemed to radiate light before, now looked as if some technician somewhere were rendering her dimmer and dimmer. A liquid crystal monitor above gave her life readings, but Sikes did not even pretend to understand it. All he knew was that he wanted to burst into applause in some desperate attempt to keep the infant going.

Of course, that would not have helped in the

slightest. But as Cathy finished examining the child (for the third time within the last half hour) and turned to face the police officers, Sikes got the distinct feeling that clapping would have been as useful as anything else medical science was going to be able to provide.

"She's failing," said Cathy, trying to sound as businesslike as she could. It was clear to Sikes that all her attempts at professional distancing were not particularly successful. It was as if Cathy were living and dying with each labored breath the infant took. "Respiratory and cardiac rates are up. Blood pressure is down. Bi-tozeg function is almost nonexistent."

Although he suspected he already knew the answer, George still said, "Why?"

"I don't know," said Cathy a bit desperately. "Her physiologic status is an unknown. She's very difficult to evaluate." She pointed to the monitor as if George or Matt could make any sense of it. "Look at her arterial oxygen saturation. It's normal for a Newcomer, but it would be fatal to a human."

George and Sikes looked at each other. "The giant is sick, too," George told Cathy while watching Matt. Matt simply nodded in agreement. "Albert thinks they need one another."

"Albert's no doctor," said Cathy more sharply than she would have liked. She stopped and composed herself, rubbing the bridge of her nose in a manner that indicated she hadn't been getting a lot of sleep lately. "Then again, I am. And I certainly don't have any scientific explanation, much less an unscientific answer. Maybe he's right."

At that moment, a nurse walked in and asked, "Excuse me, are you gentlemen Detectives Sikes or Francisco."

"I'm Sikes or Francisco," said Matt.

"You have a call," she said, chucking a finger at her desk.

"I'll take it," George volunteered, and immediately headed out to the desk.

Matt and Cathy stood there, shuffling their feet a moment in discomfort. "What are you going to do for her?" he asked finally.

"Try to fashion some sort of life support," said Cathy. "We'll do the best we can. But it doesn't look good."

"Maybe we should try bringing them together . . ."

Cathy shook her head. "I have strict orders against it."

"But if you could explain the situation . . ."

"We don't have a situation, Matt," she said patiently. "We have Albert's hunch. That's it. If I can uncover a medical reason, that will be a different story."

"I see."

The silence fell between them again. Sikes desperately tried to come up with something he could say that would bridge the gap between them. "Cathy—" he started.

George came back in, not giving Matt a chance to proceed, which wasn't that cataclysmic, since Matt really hadn't a clue as to what to say anyway. "That was Zepeda," said George. "She traced Opsil. It was a classified government operation run through the Bureau of Newcomer Affairs. There's a man at the federal building we can talk to."

"Let's do it," said Matt. "Cathy, it might be that the baby's only hope is finding a medical reason to bring her and the giant together. Otherwise . . ."

He didn't finish the sentence. Really . . . there was nothing he could say.

CHAPTER 22

FAR FROM THE concerns of hospitals, giants, and police officers, Emily Francisco and her friend Jill were sprawled on the grass in a park, doing their homework. Jill, blowing bubbles with her gum, had been staring at the same paragraph in her American history text for the last fifteen minutes. Finally, she rolled over onto her back, her arms spread wide.

"Manifest destiny," she moaned. "I hate manifest destiny."

Emily was lying flat on her back, having finished the text twenty minutes previously. Her chin propped in her hands, she said, "The Indians didn't like it either."

Suddenly Jill sat bolt upright. "Oh, shoot! I gotta go! I promised my dad I'd clean the aquarium!" Not that, under ordinary circumstances, she'd really give a damn about remembering to clean the aquarium or not. But when it came to excuses for ditching homework, Jill was a master. She started gathering her materials together and asked, "You wanna come over?"

Emily shook her head. "I'm gonna get a little more UV before the sun goes down." She lowered her head and rested it on its side.

Jill shoved her books into her backpack, heedlessly crushing two important notices for her parents. "'Kay. See you tomorrow."

"Bye."

Emily closed her eyes as Jill ran off. The sun was warm on her face. She listened to the gentle noises of kids calling to each other in the distance, tossing a Frisbee around. There was a rustling of the trees as the wind passed through them, and a bird took off—she could hear the flapping of its wings.

Then she heard footsteps coming in her direction. She waited for them to veer off, but they didn't. Instead they stopped not too far from her. She looked up, opening her eyes and squinting.

A Newcomer teenager boy was standing directly in front of her, backlit by the sun so that he had a sort of aura about him. He was eyeing her appreciatively, and with a guilty inner thrill, she realized that he was regarding her potniki. "Hi," he said. His voice was low and confident.

"Hi," she replied.

"My name's Dirk," he said. "Dirk Knight."

"Emily Francisco."

He squinted at her. "You go to Marshall High?"

A little warning bell went off in the back of her head, informing her that maybe this was more than a casual question. It might be that he was trying to get a feeling for her age because . . .

Nah. He just wanted to know if he was talking to some dorky junior high school kid or not.

"Uh-huh," she lied.

"I've never seen you."

"I just transferred," she said easily. That was the wonderful thing about lying. Once you've done it, it becomes that much easier with every passing moment.

He nodded in the general direction of some other Newcomer teens who were in the distance. "I'm with some friends. We're looking for lichens. There's some really good rock moss in the trees over there," and he pointed in the direction of the trees. "You hungry?"

"Yeah," she said as eagerly as if she hadn't eaten in two days, instead of, in fact, having snacked up less than a half hour ago.

She stood and they started toward the trees. He looked at her with what appeared to Emily to be mild suspicion. "How old are you?"

Coyly she said, "How old do I look?"

He shrugged, unsure. "'Bout fifteen."

She was thrilled beyond belief. Fifteen! That was practically grown-up! Jill had to trowel makeup on her face and wear nylons to look older, and here Emily seemed fifteen just from her stylishly low-cut sweater. Not to mention, of course, the very mature way in which she presented herself.

"Good guess," she said cheerfully.

She went with him, walking side by side and chatting amiably as they walked through the trees and into a clearing surrounded by tall pines. Emily paused as she entered, and the first buzzing of being uncomfortable started to trill.

There were several Newcomer couples seated on blankets. They were engaged in activities that were not exactly conducive to scrounging around rocks. The earth term was *making out*. They were rubbing temple to temple, humming low and melodiously. One of the couples was even further along, with the girl fondling the inside of the boy's elbow. He looked as if he was about to pass out from the enjoyment.

Emily gulped.

"So much for the rock moss," said Dirk, not sounding particularly upset about it. "Y'know . . . my ankle's sore. Let's sit down."

He guided her over to a fallen log, now limping somewhat noticeably . . . which was odd, Emily realized, considering that he hadn't been limping at all up until that point. They sat and watching the young couples who were so involved in pleasuring each other that they were totally oblivious to the presence or existence of anyone except themselves.

"Looks like fun," Dirk observed.

Emily gulped even more loudly than before.

Dirk didn't seem the least bit deterred by her obvious nervousness. In fact, he seemed oblivious to it. From his backpack, he withdrew a rather grubby looking, single-serving milk carton and offered it to her.

She shook her head and waved it off. Dirk looked at her thoughtfully for a moment, then downed some of the sour milk himself. He licked his lips, moving his tongue very slowly and in a manner that would have been suggestive to Emily, had she been savvy enough to know what he was suggesting. "Y'know, Emily, I really like that sweater."

"Thanks." Before she would have been thrilled for an older boy to say something like that. Now, though, it made her feel creepy. Reflexively she crossed her arms.

"You cold?" he asked, upon seeing the movement. He slipped his arm around her back, and partly by accident—but mostly intentionally—let his fingers drift over her potniki as if to warm them. She gasped quietly.

"No . . . I'm okay," she said, her voice partly strangled.

"Yeah," said Dirk appreciatively, "you sure are." He continued to rub her back, and said, "Why don't you have a little sour milk. It does a body good."

Emily wanted to stand up. She wanted to run. But she couldn't get her legs to support her. "I . . . better get home."

"You just got here," he protested. He moved in to nuzzle her temple. Her eyelids fluttered, her body was starting to turn to warm Jell-O—and then her eyes snapped open, her brain screaming a kick-start warning to the rest of her that this was going too far, way too far.

"I gotta go," she said, trying to get up off the log.

"No, you don't . . ."

"My dad might get worried . . ." and then, underscoring the significance of this, she said in a mildly threatening voice, ". . . and he's a policeman."

Dirk didn't seem remotely interested in anything except her temple and her spots. "Really . . . ?"

He pulled her close and started to hum.

Her legs had no strength in them at all, as if they weren't remotely interested in getting her out of this. But she still had her upper body weight, and the moment he started to hum it was all she needed to send her into a full-blown panic. She lurched backwards, so fast that Dirk wasn't able to get clear. With a yell, they both tumbled back off the log.

"Hey!" shouted Dirk, lying comically on his back.

But comical or no, Emily wasn't laughing. She was, however, on her feet, her traitorous legs suddenly flaring back to life. "I lied!" she shouted. "I'm only twelve years old! I don't go to high school . . . I go to junior high! I'm a kid! And I don't want to do this!"

And with that, she turned and bolted, leaving Dirk lying on the ground, his head spinning.

"Should've started with rubbing her foot," he muttered.

CHAPTER 23

THE OFFICE IN the federal building had once been teeming with workers. But the cutbacks in federal budgets had winnowed the staff down further and further, with money being routed away from Newcomer projects and into programs that were oriented to the needs of human beings. There were enough lobby groups and enough influential people who were still stridently anti-Newcomer, that it prompted any politician to think long and hard before approving money for anything earmarked for Newcomers.

When Sikes and Francisco entered, they made their way around desks, chairs, and filing cabinets that were gathering dust. The thick dust on one desk had a vile anti-Newcomer slogan traced in it and Sikes, in the lead, casually wiped it clean before George spotted it.

There didn't seem to be any signs of life. Overhead a fluorescent bulb hummed, and another was flickering. Sikes had the sneaking suspicion that if a light blew in this joint, no one ever came to repair it. The point at which this office would be shut down for good was the point at which the last of the bulbs went out and one couldn't see anything anymore.

Presuming that there was anyone left.

"Anybody here!?" Sikes called out for what seemed the twentieth time.

And this time, he was rewarded with a response. "Yeah! Down here!"

Sikes and George maneuvered their way through the files and found, in a distant corner, a desk. There was a diminutive man seated there who kind of looked like Yoda, except for obvious differences such as skin color and lack of pointed ears. On his desk was a nameplate that read simply Mr. Brown.

He had absolutely nothing on his desk. No papers. No books. Zip. A computer screen with the glowing word Ready on it, and who knew for how long it had been sitting there ready. The keyboard had dust on it, so that was a clue right off the bat.

He simply sat there with his hands folded. Sikes wondered what in hell could possibly inspire this guy to get up in the morning and come to work. It sure wasn't the hustle and bustle of the workplace.

"I'm Detective Sikes. This is Sergeant Francisco."

"We need information on a program called Opsil," said George.

Brown wrinkled his brow, which surprised Sikes. He didn't think it could possibly get any more wrinkled than it already was.

"Opsil . . . that was Operation Silence," said Brown after a moment's thought. "Jeez, that must've been . . . four, five years ago. We had a bunch of Newcomer programs back then." He pointed to different areas around the room. "AquaNuke. Bioprobe. NewTech. We had this one guy," he said wistfully, "who was from DOD. Thought Newcomers could jam enemy radar with mind waves. There was money back then," he added with a sigh.

Desperately trying not to lose patience with the man's reminiscences, Sikes said, "What can you tell us about Opsil?"

Mr. Brown turned to his computer and started typing in some letters. Typing might actually have been too generous a description. He'd study the keyboard, his finger skimming along it until he found a letter, and then he'd enter it. Then he'd repeat the process to find the next letter, and the next after that. Sikes resisted the impulse to yank the keyboard away and entered the damned thing himself.

"Okay," said Brown, seemingly three days later. And then he gripped the monitor and swiveled it so that it was not facing Sikes and Francisco. Upon seeing their puzzled expressions, he said, sounding a bit apologetic, "Some of it's still classified."

He then took what felt like an additional week running his finger over the keyboard. His lips moved quietly as he read. "There's not much here," he said finally, "but hey, if you want, I can give you an address."

"That would be great," said Sikes.

"Tell you what . . . just so it's easy to read, I'll type it up for you."

"No!" shouted George and Matt.

The desert facility was as desolate a place as Sikes and Francisco had ever seen. Matt tried to imagine that the place could ever have been the source of any real serious government activity. It seemed dead now.

Tumbleweeds blew across the grounds as Matt and George got out of the car. Matt, who was used to the hustle and bustle of the city, always felt a bit disconcerted upon coming out to barren sites like this. The silence was, indeed, deafening.

He sniffed the air. "Y'know . . . it smells like there was a fire somewhat around here recently. Yeah, look." He pointed to the side of the building, and there was some scoring on the brick face.

George, for his part, was standing in the driveway and looking down. "These tire tracks," he said slowly, "look relatively fresh."

"For a dead place, it's been pretty lively around here."

They walked to the guard shack, and Sikes pulled a faded note off the door. "In case of trouble . . ." he started to read, and then looked over to George, whose attention was still focused mostly on the tire tracks. "Guard left his home number. I guess he doesn't have to punch a time clock," he said, sarcastically.

George nodded absently, and then turned his attention to the building. "Let's take a look," he said.

The door was hanging almost off the hinges, and George pushed it aside. They entered and the smell of burnt air was even more pungent in their nostrils.

But if there had been a fire, it seemed largely to have been confined to one area. The shafts of light from high broken windows filtered down onto areas that seemed largely untouched by any sort of disaster. The place was dark and discomforting, and Sikes started to have the feeling—not exactly rational, he knew, but he had it nonetheless—that he was in a place where great evil had been present. The fact that it was now gone did nothing to make him feel any better.

Then he heard George start to choke.

He spun, thinking that someone was attacking his partner. But George was looking off to the side, his superior vision picking out something before Sikes's eyes had fully adjusted to the dimness. George pointed wordlessly.

Now Matt saw them, too. Rows of huge jars, filled with formaldehyde. And from each jar the eyes of dead monsters stared at them.

No. Not just monsters. Newcomers. They were clearly Newcomers, but distorted and deformed, every one of them.

"Oh, my God . . ." whispered Sikes.

Sikes was simply appalled, but George looked as if he'd just come face-to-face with his worst nightmare. He sagged and would have fallen had Sikes not put out an arm and caught him. "I'm all right," whispered George, looking even more ashen in the non-existent light. Obviously he was steeling himself to deal with the horrors they had discovered. "I'm all right," he said again.

"What . . . is this place?"

"Chorboke," said George, speaking the name with loathing, contempt, and barely contained fear. "His experiments."

"Let's get out of here."

"No," said George firmly.

Now bringing himself to standing, he started forward again. Sikes followed him reluctantly as they made their way deeper into the building.

The images of those dead Newcomer freaks had seared themselves irrevocably into Matt's mind. And as long as he was in the building, Sikes couldn't shake the irrational fear that the little bastards would suddenly come back to life, break out of the jars, and seek revenge on the nearest life-form around.

Sikes had seen too many horror movies.

Then again, considering the horrors he had just witnessed, it seemed that movie people couldn't come close to the atrocities that existed in real life.

"Look," said George.

Matt was almost afraid to. After what he'd seen thus far, he wasn't sure that he could handle . . .

A crib.

In front of them was a baby's crib. Overturned nearby was a steel-framed bed that looked to be at least eight feet long.

"Call me crazy," said Sikes, "but I don't think this is a coincidence."

"This is where the fire started," said George, picking through the remains of burnt bedding. "No more than a few days old."

"Hey, George . . . what does this mean?"

Sikes was tapping some Tenctonese writing on the wall. George walked over to it, and the sharp intake of breath when he read it was enough to tip Matt off that it wasn't Tenctonese for "For a good time, call Zelda at . . ."

"What's it say?" said Sikes.

George looked at him as if he'd seen a ghost.

"Chorboke is coming," he said quietly.

CHAPTER 24

THE FIRST THING that George and Matt noticed as they pulled into the driveway of the small, isolated ramshackle house was the large construction truck that was parked outside. The sign on the side read Ariel's Pools and Hot Tubs. Dust blew around the tires of Matt's car as they rolled to a stop.

The sounds of digging filled the air as they got out, and Matt gestured to George that he was going around back. George nodded and followed as they made their way to the back of the house.

A Bobcat bulldozer was digging dirt out of a marked-off area. Standing there surveying the work with obvious pride was a middle-aged man wearing beat-up jeans and a polo shirt tight across the middle.

"Emmet Cutter?" Sikes shouted to him over the din of the bulldozer.

Cutter turned and looked at him cautiously. Strangers coming up out of the blue in this deserted part of the world was a rather rare occurrence. "Yeah?"

Sikes flashed his shield. "Police. You're the security guard at that desert facility?" He pointed in the general direction of the building they'd left several miles behind them.

Emmet bobbed his head in a manner that struck Sikes as being a somewhat nervous one. "I'm on my way back there. I just came home for a minute. There, uh," he cleared his throat, "there isn't any problem, is there?"

"Who was living at that facility?" George asked.

"No one," said Cutter a bit too quickly. "It's just a storage facility. Buncha things in jars." He shuddered, and that at least seemed genuine. "I don't like to go in. Gimme the creeps."

"We found a very large bed and a crib in there."

Emmet shook his head so violently it looked like it might topple off his shoulders. "I don't know nothin' about it."

Sikes had had quite enough. He put his arm around Emmet's shoulders. The guard stiffened faster than a warped board. "Come here, Emmet," said Sikes with false joviality. He walked toward the pit, pulling the reluctant guard along. "Nice to have a pool out here in the desert. Can't be cheap." He scratched at his chin. "I'd say, what, about seventy . . . eighty thou? Hmmm?"

"Well . . . uh . . ."

Sikes didn't wait for the answer because he knew it would be a lie. "Not easy on a security guard's salary." He smiled into Cutter's face, and then the smile turned nasty. "You know, Emmet, the government gets very nasty when an employee gets caught taking bribes. *Very* nasty. They like the heads of folks like that on silver platters, y'know? And they don't have nice luxurious pools in Alcatraz, Emmet. Not at all."

Emmet swallowed.

"But us," continued Sikes, "we're not with the government. And we don't want your head. We just want information. So here's the deal. You tell us what we wanna know, and we'll forget all about your swimming pool."

Cutter looked into Sikes's face to try and see if he was telling the truth . . . and then came to the realization that, ultimately, it didn't matter. He simply had to *hope* that Sikes was telling the truth, because the rest of it was out of his hands. "Okay," he said, beaten. "There was this real big Newcomer and this baby . . . we called 'em Bonnie and Clyde."

George pulled out police photos of the giant and infant, and handed them to the guard. It was a somewhat unnecessary gesture, because he was sure already of what the guard would say. And sure enough, the guard glanced at the photos and said, "Yeah. That's them. It was weird . . . the giant couldn't do anything unless he was holding her. Couldn't even talk. And the baby, well . . . it was like she did the thinking for him."

"Who are they?" demanded George. "How did they get there."

Emmet shook his head. "Somethin' to do with an experiment. Everything in there was some kind of Newcomer experiment."

George looked to Matt. "Chorboke's experiments."

"I don't know," said Emmet. "I just started there six months ago. The program was pretty much shut down. Bonnie and Clyde were the only things still alive."

"What happened to them?" asked George.

Emmet started to speak, and then he stopped.

"Now . . . you gave me your word about the pool . . ."

Sikes grabbed him by the shirt front. "You're gonna be *part* of that pool, buddy! Now what happened to them?!"

"A Newcomer came around!" Emmet cried out. "Said he wanted Bonnie and Clyde! Said he'd pay me a lot of money if I faked death certificates for 'em!"

"And you did," Sikes said.

Emmet nodded with the air of a man who had discovered his weaknesses, and his price . . . and wasn't happy about it. "He took 'em about a week ago."

"The Newcomer was Chorboke, wasn't he?" said George, not able to keep the loathing from his voice.

"I didn't know his name," said Emmet. "The man didn't say, and I didn't ask." He paused, and then said miserably, "I did the wrong thing. I know I did. I . . . I feel like dirt."

"Oh, really?" said Sikes. "Well, you're in luck, Emmet."

And with a quick move, he slugged Cutter in the jaw. Cutter tumbled back and landed facedown in the bottom of the partially dug pit.

"You feel like dirt?" called Sikes. "Now you have all you can eat."

Cutter lay unmoving, unconscious. The operator of the bulldozer was sitting atop his machine in astonishment. He turned to look at Sikes.

"Take a lunch break," Sikes told him. And then he and George left without another word.

CHAPTER 25

SUSAN LOOKED OVER the storyboards and nodded with approval.

Molly, buoyed by what seemed to be the initial support from her boss, kept the storyboards moving. "You see I redrew the entire NuGuy deodorant campaign. Is this more what you're looking for?"

Susan smiled. "Clean . . . pine trees . . . oh, that white terry cloth robe is a nice touch." She handed the sketches back. "Nice job."

Molly was positively beaming. "Thanks."

Susan glanced at her watch, and now she was starting to feel some genuine concern. "Have you seen Jessica?"

"She didn't come in today," said Molly, shaking her head. "Didn't call in sick . . . nothing . . ."

Then she caught a movement from the corner of her eye. "Oh! There she is."

Jessica walked in, and she looked so miserable that if someone had been lying in the room in a deep coma, that person would have woken up and said, "Wow, who died?"

Her eyes were puffy and red-rimmed from crying. She had made some effort to disguise her appearance with makeup, but it was like putting Band-Aids on a sucking chest wound.

Molly and Susan exchanged glances, and Molly immediately said, a bit too loudly, "See ya." She got out of the room as fast as she could. She nodded to Jessica as she left, but Jessica just stood there like a zombie.

Susan went over to her. "Jessica . . . are you all right?"

She put her hand out, but Jessica moved quickly as if she were loath to be touched. "I'm fine, baby," she said in a tone that probably, to her, seemed to have much of her usual zip. But it was only her imagination. "Kissy kissy," she added forlornly as she sat down at her desk and started to set up her T square.

"What happened?" said Susan, amazed at the change that had come over the normally boisterous woman.

"Oh, honey, nothing," Jessica said dismissively. "I was about ready to throw him out of the house anyway."

"Who?"

"Who else? Frank. He left me." Her voice was a flat monotone. Then, in a pathetic attempt to change the subject, she said, "Lordy day, I've got a lot to catch up on."

Susan was stunned. "Your husband left you?" Jessica nodded. "How could that happen? I mean . . . you know so much about men . . . I mean . . ."

Jessica laughed, but it was not the kind of laughter to which Susan was accustomed from her. There was a self-deprecating tone to it. "Oh, I'm an expert." She swiveled her chair around to face Susan. "You know what Frank said? He said I could keep the house—everything—just as long as he never . . ."

Her voice caught. If anyone could ever choke on something as insubstantial as a word, then Jessica was about to manage it. She swallowed hard and forced out, ". . . never saw my face again."

In a whisper, Susan said, "Oh . . . Jessica . . ."

"No, no." She slapped the desk firmly. "It's time for a change. Shoot, I've been married to Frank since I was eighteen. It's about time I got out there and played the field, wouldn't you say?"

Susan was so accustomed to agreeing with everything that Jessica said, and learning from her vast experience with married life in specific and men in general, that she found herself saying automatically, "I guess . . ."

"Sure it is, baby . . ."

And then Jessica cracked.

The tears started to roll down her cheeks, smearing her makeup for what had to be the fourth time that day. "Ohh, damn. I promised myself I wouldn't do this." Her voice was trembling and sounded high-pitched, almost like a child's.

Susan handed her a tissue. "Here . . ."

Jessica wiped her eyes, and when she spoke it wasn't to Susan but to herself. "Why didn't I see it coming . . . ?"

Susan put her arms around Jessica, comforting her. Jessica completely unraveled, her shoulders heaving, her body racked with sobs. She buried her head in Susan's shoulder and kept saying, "Why didn't I see it coming . . . ?"

But Susan had no answer. Jessica was the one who had always had all the answers. Instead, all Susan had was questions of her own.

And she was coming up with answers that she didn't like one bit.

CHAPTER 26

"HAVE YOU GOT an answer yet, Cathy?"

Cathy made a quick gesture to Albert to indicate that he should be quiet. Albert immediately obeyed.

She was in the holding cell with the giant. Just outside the cell were two cops with tranq guns, just in case. But it was clear to all that they were not going to be needed. Clearly the giant did not have the strength to tie his shoes, much less make a break for freedom.

Cathy had a stethoscope to the giant's chest, moving across it meticulously. She showed a brief moment of being startled, but then she nodded as if she'd discovered something that she should have anticipated. She removed the stethoscope then and placed it in her bag.

As she did so, Albert noticed the arrival of George and Matt. "Cathy," he said cautiously, not wanting to disturb her once more. But when he saw that she looked up at him in an expectant fashion, he continued, "George and Detective Sikes are back."

"Thank you, Albert."

She got up and went to the cell door. One of the cops unlocked the door and let her out, all the time watching the giant warily. But it seemed as if leaving the cell door wide open with a red carpet unrolled in front of it would still not have gotten a rise out of the behemoth. He didn't even blink when the door slammed shut again.

"How is he?" asked Sikes.

She shook her head. Sikes had seen that look in TV shows and movies a hundred times. It was the look the doctor gave when informing family or friends that a patient was dead or dying.

They returned to the squad room. All that way, Cathy walked a bit apart from Matt. Her body language said it all. She wasn't sure how to deal with what was between them, and so opted to try and keep as much distance between them as possible until it was sorted out. Matt couldn't blame her. At the same time, it hurt tremendously.

"I ran a blood test on our infant," she said, once they were settled in. "It revealed an alkaline phophotase level of an adult."

"Alkaline what?" asked Sikes.

"It's an indicator of bone activity—of growth," Cathy told him. "It's naturally much lower in full-grown adults. I then x-rayed her femur. The calcium layers, much like rings on a tree, confirmed her age."

"So what is she?" he asked. "Six months? Nine?"

"She's twenty-five."

Sikes looked surprised. "You're telling me that kid is twenty-five months? That's the most underdeveloped two-year-old I've ever—"

Cathy leaned forward, resting her knuckles on his desk. "Matt, you're not reading me. She's twenty-five *years old.*"

Sikes and George looked at each other in shock.

"Cathy, are you sure? I mean, there's no margin for error?"

She shook her head. "None."

"Twenty-five?" said George, astounded. "That . . . that means she must have been born on the ship."

"She can't be a hybrid!" said Sikes. "Grazer is gonna be ecstatic. He can call another one of his beloved news conferences and announce it was a false alarm. That'll shut the Purists up, at least until they find something else to . . ."

"There's more," said Cathy, interrupting. "I ran a cell comp on her and the giant. They're twins. Identical twins."

"You mean fraternal."

Cathy rapped on his desk with impatience. "Dammit, Matt, if I meant fraternal I would have said fraternal. Stop challenging me."

"I'm sorry!" he said in exasperation. "I don't mean to . . . but . . . but, I mean, what are you saying? They can't be twins! I mean, okay, I don't mean to keep acting like I disagree, but I mean . . . look at them! What's identical?"

"I'll tell you one thing," said Cathy firmly. "I just examined the giant. He also has only one heart."

Matt, who had been fiddling with a pencil, tossed it down onto the desk. It bounced away and under his chair. He paid no attention to it. "Somebody want to tell me what's going on here?"

And George, very quietly, said, "I think I know." He wasn't looking at Cathy and Sikes, but rather seemed to be staring inward. "The infant . . . the giant . . . they're one. They're two halves of one creature."

"Right. Sure. Happens all the time," said Sikes.

George ignored the sarcasm. "They're incomplete without each other. The security guard said it. The giant can't do anything without the baby . . . the baby does the thinking for him. We saw that, remember? He couldn't talk until the baby was in his arms. Then what did he say? 'I'm fine.' Singular."

Even Cathy looked doubtful. "Still . . ."

"They came from Chorboke's lab! You know the kind of experiments he performed!"

If Sikes needed any proof that George wasn't exaggerating Chorboke's reputation, he got it when he saw Cathy's expression. She looked as if someone had just kicked her in the throat. "Chorboke," she whispered.

"Yeah," said Sikes. "We saw some of his handiwork."

"You said it yourself, Cathy. They're genetically identical. What if Chorboke was able to separate one being into two—the mental and the physical . . ."

Cathy was mulling it over. The introduction of Chorboke into the equation made anything possible. "And now they're both sick . . . they're both dying . . ."

"Because they're apart," affirmed George. "They need each other. They *are* each other."

"This is nuts," said Sikes. "This is really nuts. But . . . I'll tell you. We better get them together. Cathy, this has got to be more than enough in terms of medical reasons to bring the giant and baby together, right?"

"I would think so," said Cathy. "A human doctor might not fully understand, but if I run it by our Newcomer head of medicine—"

"Yeah, let's do that," said Sikes. "And if he still gives us problems, well, I can be a pretty persuasive guy. Because otherwise, the giant and the baby don't have a prayer."

* * *

As Sikes, Cathy, and George hurtled toward the hospital, with Sikes driving in his typically berserk fashion, two Newcomer doctors were heading down the hospital corridor. They looked brisk and no-nonsense. They walked up to the nurse's desk, and one of them stepped forward and said, "Hello, I'm Dr. Miller. This," and he nodded toward his companion, "is Dr. Stein. We're from Cedars Sinai pediatrics. We're consulting on the hybrid baby."

The nurse pointed down the hallway. "Room twenty-three," she said. "Check with the guard outside the door."

"Thank you," said Miller.

As they started down the hallway, the nurse called after them, "I sure hope you can help her. She's the sweetest little thing."

Miller tossed off a salute. "We'll do our best," he said confidently.

The two doctors walked with authority up to the guard. It was Newcomer police officer Sandy Beach, who was holding a clipboard resting against his belt buckle. He looked at them carefully as Miller pointed to himself and his companion and said, "Dr. Miller. Dr. Stein."

Sandy checked over his clipboard and frowned. "Miller . . . Stein . . . No, I'm sorry, you're not here—"

But a second later, Sandy Beach wasn't there either. The two bullets fired from the silencer-equipped gun that "Miller" was holding had more than done their job. They struck him dead center of both his hearts, killing him instantly. He started to sag to the floor, and "Miller" and "Stein" caught him by either arm before he could sink so much as a foot. They dragged his body into the room, with "Miller" —who, a day or so earlier, had been wearing a guard uniform with the name River on it—taking a last quick look over his shoulder to make sure no one had seen.

And then they set to work.

Outside the hospital, Sikes's car pulled up to the restricted parking area, where a guard stood in a booth. Between Matt and George waving their badges and Cathy waving her medical ID, they wound up getting a space so close to the main entrance that they were practically parked in the lobby. They ran in, took the elevator up to the pediatrics floor, and headed down the hallway.

Immediately Sikes knew that something was up. "There's supposed to be someone on guard there," he said, when he saw no one standing in front of the baby's room.

"He was here earlier," said Cathy. She turned to the nurse on duty. "Did the guard leave?"

"No," said the nurse, looking puzzled. "But you know . . . I don't think I saw him since those two Newcomer doctors came by . . ."

George and Matt looked at each other, and then pulled their guns and ran ahead, with Sikes gesturing to Cathy that she should hang back.

They darted inside the room.

The walls had been spray-painted with Purist symbols and the slogan, "2-4-6-8, SLAGS AND HUMANS WILL NOT MATE." Cathy gasped upon seeing it. Sikes and Matt, meantime, spotted Officer Beach lying on the floor, eyes open wide but looking at nothing.

George crouched down next to him, shaking his head and passing his hand over Sandy's eyes, closing the lids. Sikes heard George murmur something in Tenctonese, probably some benediction for the dead. Personally, Sikes felt like a creep. No "Son of a Beach" jokes for the fallen officer. No children for his new wife. Just a knock at the door when two officers came to inform her that her husband wouldn't be coming home. "Bastards," he said.

He crossed quickly to the crib, trying to tell himself that the best thing he could do for Sandy now was get the bastards who had done this. "She's gone," said Sikes.

Cathy was looking around. "The Purists did this . . ."

Sikes didn't even bother to look. "Yeah, you kinda get that idea. But I have my doubts. How about you, George?"

"The nurse said that two Newcomers were the last ones in here. Newcomers obviously wouldn't be Purists."

"But they could have sneaked in here afterward without the nurse seeing them," Cathy pointed out.

"True," said George. "But the Purists simply would have killed the baby. Not taken her."

That point seemed fairly incontrovertible. "Then who?" demanded Cathy. "Why?"

"Chorboke," said George firmly. "For some reason, he wanted them."

"We gotta find out who this Chorboke is," said Sikes. "And where he is."

"The baby's in critical condition," Cathy said, checking the last notations that had been made on the baby's chart. "You don't have much time."

"No," said George with a deep, burning anger, looking down at Sandy's body. "It's Chorboke who doesn't have much time."

Mr. Brown, he of the deep, sunken corner of the federal building, looked up in surprise as George Francisco and Matt Sikes seemed to simply materialize in front of his desk. He opened his mouth to say something by way of greeting, but without preamble George said, "Chorboke was involved in Opsil. What human name was he given?"

Brown blinked owlishly. "I can't tell you that," he said with the air of someone who was surprised that such a topic would even be broached. He sounded almost scolding.

Sikes slammed a palm on his desk. "Somebody's gonna die if we don't find him!"

"That information is still classified," said Brown serenely.

Sikes leaned forward. "How would you like me to pull your stomach out through your mouth?"

"Violence won't accomplish anything, Sergeant."

"Yes it will. It'll make me feel a hell of a lot better. Why is the government protecting him? Answer me!" His voice was getting extremely loud.

"It's part of the deal," sighed Brown. "You want something from somebody, you make a deal. You guys do it all the time." He actually smiled, as if that explanation was so simple that it solved everything.

"Chorboke is a monster!" George said, furious. "What could you want from him?!"

Brown snorted. "Monster. Such a word, *monster*. The man's a genius! He knew more about genetics than anyone on earth! You don't waste a mind like that simply because of negative labels."

George lost it.

He grabbed Brown out of his seat and held him high in the air. Brown's arms and legs writhed madly. "A 'genius'?" George spat out. "Do you know how many people this genius tortured and murdered?!"

"He's done some great things for this planet! Lemme go!" howled Brown. "This is police brutality!"

"You'll need a witness to make that charge stick," Sikes informed him. "I don't see anybody else around, do you?"

George tightened his grip. "What great things? Did he make some chemical weapons? Nerve gas, perhaps?"

"I was diabetic!" Brown squealed, his voice rising an octave. "If it hadn't been for Chorboke, there wouldn't be a cure!"

There was a dead silence.

George threw Brown down. He landed in his wheeled chair, and it shot back and smacked into a wall, rattling Brown's teeth.

"Thanks for your help, pal," Sikes called over his shoulder as they strode out.

"Diabetes . . . Hadrian Tivoli," said Sikes as they headed for the car.

"Chorboke," said George. "And we may have found out too late. By the time we find the child and bring her back—"

"Then we don't take the time, George. We take the giant with us."

"Grazer will never permit it."

"Not a problem," said Sikes. "We'll use finesse."

Captain Grazer, walking down a corridor, was surprised to see Albert coming from the other direction, wheeling a large laundry cart. He stepped in his path and Albert stopped, looking up at him politely. "Yes, Captain?"

"Albert, what is this?" He scanned the top of the cart.

"Laundry, sir. We're sending these vests out to be cleaned."

"Bullet-proof vests?" said Grazer incredulously.

"Yes, sir. Dry-cleaned, sir."

"Why?"

"Order came down, sir. I was cleaning up in your office when the call came from the chief, sir. Something about trying to improve the look of the force. Actually, he said it was supposed to have been done a week ago and wanted to know if you'd taken care of it."

"I don't remember getting a memo about that," said Grazer nervously.

"To be honest, sir, he seemed rather upset that you weren't there to tell him personally. Something about 'endless lunches.'"

Grazer swallowed.

"I'm . . ." Alfred looked embarrassed. "I'm afraid I lied, sir. I told him that you'd already told me to take care of it. I didn't want to risk him getting more upset with you, sir. He told me that if you already were on top of it, there was no need to call him back. In fact, he sounded kind of pleased that you'd already done it. But if you want, you can call him back and clarify that—"

"No! No, Albert. That's . . . that's fine," said Grazer. He patted Albert on the back. "Good work."

"Thank you, sir."

Albert kept on pushing, and then the captain called, "Albert!"

"Yes, sir?"

He pointed a finger and smiled. "I owe you one." He walked away, relieved. Between this and being able to announce that the baby was not a hybrid, he was going to be completely square with the chief.

Moments later, Albert had pushed the cart into the alleyway. He glanced right and left, and then said, "Okay."

Sikes and George clambered out from under the vests, shoving them aside. And then they hauled out the giant, whom they had practically had to bend in half in order to get him to fit. But he had put up no

257

resistance whatsoever. Quickly, they crammed him into Sikes's car.

"Albert, you're a champ," said Sikes.

"I didn't like lying," Albert admitted. "But . . . it was to help the giant. It was a good cause. And you know, now that I've tried lying, I've found I've got a talent for it."

"Good for you," said Sikes. "You'll find that'll serve you well in married life."

CHAPTER 27

TWO SECURITY GUARDS in the front entranceway of Dual Pharmaceuticals looked up in surprise as two uniformed police officers charged in. Their surprise turned to shock when two men in street clothes, one of them a Newcomer, came in on the heels of the two uniformed cops; and shock became pure numb amazement when directly behind the two men in street clothes lumbered in a giant Newcomer who was looking around the lobby as if he were in a sort of haze.

"Police!" snapped Matt Sikes. "We have a warrant to search these facilities."

One of the guards grabbed for a phone, but George —with deathly calm—merely yanked the phone off the wall. He handed the unit to the guard without a word.

"Keep an eye on these two," Sikes told the uniforms. They nodded briskly.

Both of the uniformed cops were Newcomers.

Both of them had been friends of Sandy Beach. And both of them, when asked by George and Matt if they wouldn't mind not noticing that a giant Newcomer was accompanying them on this bust, had simply replied, "What giant Newcomer?"

Sikes turned to the giant. He had no idea if the big guy could understand him or not. But he said, "Let's go find her." He grabbed the giant by one arm, George took him by the other, and they headed upstairs.

They got in the elevator and Sikes punched all the buttons. The elevator started up as the giant stood there listlessly. The car stopped on the second floor, and there was no reaction from the giant. Nor on the third.

[*"She's somewhere here"*] said George intensely. [*"You have to find her."*]

No reaction on the fourth. And on the fifth . . .

The giant looked up. It was more instinctive than anything else, as if he had not consciously realized that he was reacting to something.

It was enough for Sikes and Matt. They pushed him out onto the fifth floor.

Before them stretched a corridor with doors lining either side. They were labeled simply "Laboratory A," "Laboratory B," and so on.

They started down the hallway, using the giant as something akin to a Tenctonese divining rod . . . waiting for him to react in some way that would tell them that the infant was nearby.

"Where is she?" Sikes demanded of the mute giant. "Where is she?"

The giant's eyes remained glazed, his face expressionless.

[*"You can do it"*] George urged him.

They stopped in front of one lab door after the other. "Come on, pal," Sikes said nervously. For all he knew they were on the wrong floor. "You getting any vibes?"

And then, in front of the eighth door, the giant suddenly raised his head. But he wasn't looking at the door they were facing. Instead he seemed to be focused farther down the corridor. He started off at a lumbering run, clumsy but distance-consuming because of the length of his legs.

"He senses her," said George with certainty.

Sikes was in no position to argue. They ran after him as fast as they could.

They caught up with him, because he had come to a halt in front of a large sealed door marked "No Admittance." He shoved against it, moaning pitifully.

"Let's give him a hand," said Sikes.

They threw their weight against the door. With a wrenching crack, the frame gave way and the door flew open.

It was the interior of a lab. At the far end was a crib, and Hudson River and Bic Penn, both in guard uniforms, looked up in surprise as George shouted, "Police!"

River was standing in front of the crib, Penn behind it. River immediately went for his gun, and he was a damned quick draw. He actually got the weapon clear of its holster, and then George fired. The blast blew River back, sending him crashing into a wall.

And now Penn was in the clear.

But he was holding the baby . . . and a gun to the baby's head.

"Back up!" he shrieked. "Back up and get out or I'll kill her! I swear I will!"

Sikes and George froze.

But the giant did not. He did not fully understand the impact of what Penn was saying. All he knew was that the baby was there and was threatened, and he was going to get her no matter what.

He charged forward, heedless of anything else.

Penn was startled, not expecting it, and as he saw the giant bearing down on him he did the natural thing—he swung his gun up and fired at the giant. But it was a hurried shot, and a nerve-racking one, considering the behemoth that was charging him. The bullet struck the giant a glancing blow on the arm, and the giant roared.

At the exact same instant, the baby shrieked in matching pain. She twisted so violently that Penn lost his grip and the baby tumbled out of his arms.

Seeing the baby falling, the giant hurled himself forward in a desperate lunge. He caught the infant in his outstretched arms just as she reached the ground.

Penn brought his gun around and was about to fire point-blank. He was not going to miss.

Neither were Sikes and Francisco. They fired together and Penn was blown completely off his feet, his gun falling out of his hand. Penn crashed backward over an examining table and lay still.

The giant was oblivious to everything that had happened. He held the infant against his chest tenderly. Then he half turned and angled her toward the detectives, so that they basked in the glow of her angelic face.

"Thank you," said the giant, the voice of the infant passing through the mouth of the titan.

It was at that moment, having a few seconds to breathe, that Sikes and Francisco slowly became aware of their surroundings.

Eerie geometric shadows crisscrossed the room. There were shelves lining the walls, and each of those shelves had large jars in rows, carefully labeled with dates and notations. They were connected to what appeared to be some sort of giant circulatory feeding system through a common umbilicallike cord.

And in each of the jars, floating in embryonic fluid was . . .

"What is this?" demanded Sikes. "Those things in the jars . . . I remember . . . Vessna was . . ."

"Newcomer pods," George said coldly. "Yes. He's creating in vitro life."

"That's correct," came a passionless voice.

Tivoli had entered, looking utterly self-possessed. Sikes didn't like it. He seemed entirely too self-confident for someone who should be concerned about going down big time.

"Chorboke," said George in a cold fury.

"You," said the Newcomer once known as Chorboke, "have no right to be in here."

The giant was whimpering. He clutched the infant tightly to himself and backed away.

"You're under arrest, Doc," Sikes informed him.

Tivoli laughed. "On what charges?"

"It should be for the murder of thousands!" George could barely contain himself.

Trying to keep George on the beam, Sikes said firmly, "The charge is kidnapping."

"Kidnapping?" Now Tivoli looked extremely amused. "How can I kidnap something that belongs to me?"

He looked for a long moment at the giant and infant. Although the giant looked as fearful as before, the infant was regarding him with gentle, even thoughtful eyes.

"It's my child," said Tivoli. "I created it." And he indicated the jars. "Just like these."

"What is all this?" demanded George.

Tivoli spoke with genuine pride, walking in a small circle and waving. "I'm advancing our species.

263

Past you. Past me." He pointed to the giant. "I came close with that—close to making a purely mental being. A being free of the baser needs of the body. Free to learn, to explore, to create . . ."

The giant stepped forward now, emboldened by the lack of fear in the infant. As the infant's gaze locked with Tivoli's, the giant said proudly, "The body is partner to the mind. It is its vehicle . . . its instrument."

"The body is corrupt," said Tivoli disdainfully. "IT is a prison to the mind."

This is insane. He needs a sex class, Sikes thought giddily.

"We cannot be separated," said the giant firmly. "We are meant to be one."

Tivoli sighed, long and deep. Indicating the giant, he said sadly, "This was a failure. I'll study it. I'll learn from my mistakes."

"If you succeed, you will only create monsters," said the giant.

But George shook his head. "He won't be creating anything."

And Tivoli played his trump card. "The government won't allow you to prosecute me. We have a deal. You're wasting your time."

And the giant's voice changed. For just a brief moment, it seemed as if two voices were speaking as one, blended in seamless harmony. "This will not happen," the giant cried out, outraged by the sheer cold brutality of the being standing in front of them.

The giant swung a huge arm. Surprised, Tivoli ducked away, and a bottle of ether was caught in the sweep and knocked off the table onto the floor.

"Stop!" shouted Sikes. "Hold it!"

Tivoli stumbled back, and his foot hit the gun that the now-deceased Penn had dropped. He grabbed it up and ducked for cover behind a table.

"Get down!" shouted George, charging toward the giant and knocking him aside.

George needn't have worried. Genius, scientist, cold-hearted bastard, all these things Tivoli was. But a marksman he was not. The shot went high and blew one of the overhead lamps free of its moorings, sending it crashing to the floor . . .

Where the sparks hit the ether.

A ball of flame erupted from the flammable liquid. The giant staggered back with a roar as a wall of fire immediately leaped into existence, blocking Tivoli from the door.

Sikes grabbed a fire extinguisher off the wall and tried to turn it on the blaze. But the flame had already reached another bottle of ether, fueling itself. The flame roared higher.

Tivoli backed up, trying to angle his way around to an exit. But the new blast of heat drove him back, and he crashed into one of the shelves with specimens on it. The bottles crashed all around him, shelving collapsing on top of that. He was completely pinned by his specimens. It was as if the Newcomer pods were holding him there, waiting for the flames to get to him.

The fire extinguishers were doing no good whatsoever against the flame. With every passing second it was finding new and even more flammable liquids upon which to feed.

Sikes tossed aside the extinguisher. George was grabbing the giant, dragging him away and outside of the lab. And then they heard screams and had a brief glimpse of a body aflame, writhing about in agony, surrounded by unborn Newcomer pods.

George had heard screams like that before. They were the types of screams that had come from the laboratories where Chorboke performed his atrocities.

And as Sikes, George, and the giant ran from the lab, ran to safety outside of the building, George reflected on the consistency of it all. Chorboke's final laboratory had screams coming from it, just as was always the case.

But these screams were Chorboke's . . . all Chorboke's. . . .

CHAPTER 28

GEORGE AND THE giant leaned against Sikes's car. A building crawling with firemen was the only kind of place that a seven-foot-tall Newcomer cradling an infant could go pretty much unnoticed. George watched the two creatures in fascination. Then he looked up as Sikes walked over to them.

"The lab was completely destroyed," said Sikes.

He looked at the serene, beautiful face of the infant who once again used the giant as her vessel of communication.

"What will you do with me now?"

"It's not up to us," George said to the infant. "There'll be a trial."

"Will I be separated again?" asked the giant nervously.

Sikes didn't know what to say. He gestured helplessly. "Look . . . we just bring you in. Other people make that decision."

There was a long silence. The infant studied the

two of them, her expression impassive and gentle as always.

"I'm not afraid to die," said the giant with quiet conviction. "But please, don't let them separate me again."

Sikes turned to George. Neither of them needed to tell each other of the pity they were feeling for the pathetic creature. It was written on their faces, and the giant and the infant saw it there as well.

"I know a place you can take me," the giant said softly.

Sikes rolled his eyes. "That'd be a serious breach of regulations, wouldn't it, George."

"Yes," said George sadly. "I'm afraid it would."

"And considering that, it seems there's only one thing we can do."

They were in the middle of nowhere.

The desert stretched endlessly in all directions. The giant turned the infant so that she could survey the barren landscape.

"Yes," said the giant. He actually seemed to be smiling. "This is a very good place."

"If you came back with us," said Sikes, "there's a chance . . . maybe everything would turn out okay."

But he knew the answer before the giant even spoke. The infant turned her gaze upon him, and the giant said, "It's better this way. Thank you." Then he turned to George and said [*"Thank you."*]

Slowly, George reached out and touched the temple of the infant. [*"Farewell"*] he said.

Sikes did the same. "Yeah," he said.

A smile seemed to play across the infant's lips, and then the giant said, "Good-bye."

He held the infant close, shielding her from the sun as best he could, and he started out across the desert.

Sikes and George watched the creature go.

"It doesn't have a chance," said Sikes.

And George slowly shook his head. "It never did."

They stood there, waiting—by unspoken agreement—until the giant could no longer be seen. It took a very long time until finally, enveloped by shimmering heat waves, the giant finally disappeared behind a sand dune.

And they never saw it again.

CHAPTER 29

JACK PERELLI, WEARING a white terry cloth robe, answered the pounding at the front door of his apartment. To his surprise, Matt Sikes was standing there.

"Matt!" said Perelli. "Long time no see." He studied him. "You look like hell. You want a drink of water or—"

"No," said Sikes firmly. "I just got something I got to say to you."

"Well . . . sure." Perelli stepped back. "Come on in."

"No, I can say it from here. First, I gotta tell you . . . you saved my ass at the clinic the other day. So I thank you for that."

"You were there? Well, glad I could be of—"

"And you taught me a lot of stuff. You shaped a lot of my opinions about . . . about everything."

"Matt, what's bothering you?"

"What's bothering me," said Matt hotly, "is that you're an asshole. That's what's bothering me."

"I see."

"When the Newcomers first came here, there you were, day after day after day, saying that they were filth. That they were going to ruin humanity. That they didn't know about human love or emotion. And you said . . . you said that any human who was willing to accept them or get close to them was a traitor to the whole damned human race." Matt's voice was getting louder and louder. "And I hung on every word you said, Jack. Every damned word. And it poisoned me for ages. Well I met a Newcomer woman, Jack, and I love her, and I'm tired of pretending I don't. Tired of being afraid of so many stupid things. And I work with a Newcomer. And—"

"Jack? Is something wrong?"

It was a female voice, coming from the area of the bedroom.

Sikes blinked. The voice sounded familiar.

Moments later, a female form also wearing a bathrobe emerged from the bedroom area.

Matt's jaw fell to somewhere around his ankles.

"Well," she said, folding her arms. "Matt."

"Vi . . . Vivian," stammered Sikes. "Vivian Webster."

Jack looked from her back to him. "You know each other?"

The Newcomer sex counselor smiled. "Oh yes. Matt's in my Human/Newcomer sex class. Or at least he was. Or is he still?" Her voice sounded musical and very amused.

"Yes. I . . . I am," he said. "Uh . . . how long have you and Vivian . . ."

"About a year," said Perelli. "That's why I was at

271

the sex clinic the other night. I was coming by to pick her up anyway."

"Oh. Uh . . . Jack, I thought you . . ."

"Hated Newcomers?" He shrugged. "I did. But people change, Matt. They realize they're wrong sometimes if they let themselves realize that they're never too old to learn. You can, too, teach an old dog new tricks. May take 'im longer to learn, but he can learn 'em."

"I guess so," said Matt.

"We all done here?"

"Yes, sir."

"Gonna be at my retirement dinner next month?"

"Yes, sir."

"Good. Bring your Newcomer girlfriend. Love to meet her."

"Yes, sir."

"Oh, and Matt . . ."

"Yes, sir?"

"You're an asshole." And he slammed the door in Matt's face.

"Yes, sir," said Matt to the door.

George entered his house, looking downtrodden and wasted. He flopped down in his favorite chair and just sat there, staring at the wall.

Emily came in. She regarded him silently for a moment and then, to his surprise, went over to him and hugged him tightly before heading upstairs. He wondered what that was about. He would, in fact, never find out. Nor would he really have wanted to know.

Susan walked in, and she was carrying a robe wrapped in dry-cleaner's plastic.

"I had this cleaned for you," she said.

He took the garment and stared at it. "My ceremonial robe. Why?" he asked in genuine confusion.

"You'll need it . . . when you father Albert and May's child."

He stared at her. "Susan . . ." he whispered.

"Forgive me, George." She looked skyward, clearly embarrassed. "You were right. I acted so . . . human . . ."

He set the robe down and took her in his arms.

"I love you," he told her.

CHAPTER 30

VIVIAN WEBSTER STOOD at a podium set up inside the sex clinic with a pile of diplomas in front of her. She smiled out at her students, dressed in their best clothes, all standing to one side of the room. Family and friends were on the other.

"I'm very proud of these students here tonight. They've worked very hard the past three months. They've persevered during a very difficult time for them and for this city."

Matt took Cathy's hand and gripped it tightly. Across the way, George had an arm around Susan. Next to them stood Albert, his hand resting lightly on the swollen belly of his wife.

"Because of love and with love," continued Vivian, "they have pushed aside the prejudice. They have pushed aside the ignorance. They have pushed aside the fear. In accepting the mystery and beauty of their partners, these graduates have discovered the mystery and beauty in themselves. Congratulations."

Friends and family began to applaud as Vivian started handing out the diplomas.

"Sharon and Noel Parking," she called out. "Debbie Degner and Colonel Mustard. Cathy Frankel and Matthew Sikes. Sharon Wessner and Buddy Holly . . ."

The names had all been called, the congratulations made. The winks, the grins. All of it once would have embarrassed the hell out of Matt Sikes.

Now, though, it was of no consequence to him. In fact, he thought it was great.

Matt and Cathy approached the front door of their apartment building. They stood there a moment, hands clasped, and smiled at each other.

"Shall we?" he said.

They started up the front stoop, and then a passing car suddenly slowed down and started honking. They stopped and turned.

A smiling white-haired man poked his head out the driver's side window.

"Cathy Frankel!" he called out. "Cathy, isn't it? From the pottery class! Hi, how y'doin'?"

"Hi, Joe!" she said. "This is a pleasant surprise!"

Sikes stood there, gaping.

"Joe," Cathy continued, "this is M—" And then she stopped. "Oh, wait. No. He said he wouldn't want to be introduced to you because he wouldn't know what to say."

"Oh, okay. Well . . . I gotta go. Take care." And he drove off.

Sikes managed to get his mouth moving. "Th— that was Joe DiMaggio!"

"Yes, I know," she said. "I told you I knew him."

"Yeah, but . . . I thought when you said it that Joe DiMaggio was a Newcomer!"

"Oh, no. Actually, I think he used to advertise coffee makers, or something like that."

"That was *Joltin Joe!* Quick! Get him back here!" Sikes started to run off the stoop. "I'd love to get his autograph! To talk to him! To—"

And then he saw the way she was staring at him. And he grinned sheepishly.

"I guess it can wait," he said.

"Good," she said. "Because I can't."

Sikes, bare-chested, stood next to his bed. Cathy, in a slip, was standing next to him, embracing. Temple to temple, they nuzzled one another. Sikes hummed softly, unable to imagine that three months ago, he was self-conscious about it. After a moment, Cathy gave him a long, human kiss.

They broke apart, staring into one another's eyes, their passion growing. Sikes slid the straps of her slip off her shoulders. Her slip fell noiselessly to the floor. She stood nude before him, her back spots fully revealed and arching down in a beautiful, glorious curve.

Cathy's hands moved across Matt's muscular back, caressing it. He pulled her onto the bed. They kissed again, rolling over in each other's arms.

She nuzzled his chest, her kisses traveling downward across his belly. She unsnapped his jeans and Sikes arched his back, pulling Cathy back up to kiss her. His lips moved down her cheek, onto her neck. Cathy turned, offering her spots to him.

Sikes began to hum, Cathy joining in, and the noise continued as he worked his way down her back.

She arched against him, turned and reached for him.
He paused, gazing at her.

"You are so beautiful," he murmured.

"No," she said softly. "We are."

And they came together . . .

. . . body and soul.

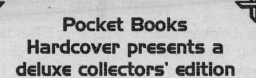

STAR TREK®
"WHERE NO ONE HAS GONE BEFORE"™
A History in Pictures

Text by J. M. Dillard
With an introduction by
William Shatner

**Available at
a bookstore
near you**

POCKET
BOOKS

1008-02

HERE IT IS!

The definitive reference book for STAR TREK® fans. This massive encyclopedia is the first book ever to bring together all three incarnations of this incredible television and feature film phenomenon: the original STAR TREK series, STAR TREK:THE NEXT GENERATION®, and STAR TREK:DEEP SPACE NINE®. Pocket Books is proud to present the one book that captures every fact, figure, and detail of the awesome STAR TREK saga:

THE
STAR TREK®
ENCYCLOPEDIA

A Reference Guide To The Future

Michael Okuda, Denise Okuda, and Denise Mirek

POCKET
B O O K S

Available from Pocket Books Trade and *limited* Hardcover editions

933-02